To a Widow with Children

Lionel G. García

Houston, Texas
1994

This book is made possible through support from the National Endowment for the Arts (a federal agency), the Lila Wallace-Reader's Digest fund and the Andrew W. Mellow Foundation.

Arte Público Press
University of Houston
Houston, Texas 77204-2090

Cover Design by Annette Rose-Shapiro

García, Lionel G.
    To a widow with children / Lionel G. García.
        p.   cm.
    ISBN 1-55885-069-4 : $9.50
    1. Man-woman relationships—Texas—Fiction. 2. City and town life—Texas—Fiction. 3. Mexican Americans—California—Fiction. I. Title.
PS3557.A71115T6 1994
813'.54—dc20   93-36397
                                                              CIP

The paper used in this publication meets the requirements of the American National Standard for Permanence of Paper for Printed Library Materials Z39.48-1984. ∞

To my mother, Marillita Saenz
3/16/11—9/19/92

To a Widow with Children

Prologue

In the 1800s an old limestone road that led from Corpus Christi west to Laredo crossed a similar road running from San Antonio south to the Rio Grande Valley of Texas. This crossroad was and still is the heart of south Texas, an area of choking dust that became part of Texas through war but forever remained Mexican. It is inhabited by people steeped in a mixture of Catholicism, mysticism and witchcraft, living among plants with thorns, wild animals with fangs, livestock and a land that produces only enough to keep hopes from evaporating like the sweat that is required to work it.

In 1867, a tall and lean French priest, Father Claude Jaillet arrived at Corpus Christi by boat. The Bishop, surprised to see him, took one look at Father Jaillet and saw him to be extremely fit to endure the trials at the edge of civilization. He took Father Jaillet's trunk for safe-keeping, turned him around and led him to the Corpus Christi-Laredo stagecoach that would drop him off at a small community at the crossroads that had been named San Diego.

He arrived at San Diego at night only to find that the Indians had invaded the town and killed forty of its inhabitants. He slept under a tree for the first time in his life and shivered at the thought that he might be killed by Indians or eaten by what he thought were wolves. Later, he was to learn about coyotes.

In the morning, glad to be alive, he said mass for the forty dead. He tried to speak with the survivors but no one knew English and he knew no Spanish.

At first he lived from shack to shack, eating the most meager diet of pomegranates, prickly pear pies, jack-rabbit, rattlesnake, armadillo and a soft Mexican bread called panocha.

With the help of the men, he was able to build the first church and rectory of the town, a twelve by eight primitive building in which he placed a mesquite crucifix full of thorns. He had the women weave the stations of the cross from mesquite beans.

When he had learned the language and his fear of the area subsided to the point that he would venture on his own beyond San Diego, he began to hold masses on the farms and ranches surrounding the little town and once he accepted the people and their customs he began to think of ways to raise money to build a more substantial church. He did what most priests would have done. He raffled his horse.

He was able to raise a few dollars and, with some money of his own—his inheritance from his mother—he went to Corpus Christi and brought back a tremendous load of timbers. Soon he had his church.

A year after his arrival, a yellow fever epidemic struck all of south Texas, killing almost half the population.

When he stopped to think of the absurdity of his new life, he sat down and began to write down his thoughts. He published a chapbook in 1880 and titled it "Catholicity in Texas."

The years went by like the nightly flickers of the fire-flies that he so admired. Later, he became so hardened by the land and the people that he took to converting Indians.

In 1900 he received two surprise visits. The first was the railroad, a single track that would connect Laredo and Mexico to Corpus Christi. The second surprise was in the form of a person: Father Peter Bard, a short, ruddy Englishman that spoke no Spanish.

Three years later a northern spur was added at San Diego. This connected the Corpus Christi train to San Antonio.

In his early sixties, Father Jaillet was called to the bishopric in Corpus Christi, given his trunk, and was placed on a boat to return home. In France, no one believed his stories and he was sent to an old priest's home for his own protection. Moreover, no one ever had the heart to tell him why the Bishop at Corpus Christi had been surprised to see him. He should have gotten off the boat at Tampico, Mexico, along with a company of French soldiers.

Father Peter Bard stayed, learned the language and the customs and became Father Pedro. He developed a love for raffles, raffling everything that he could find, and in a few years was able to convince Don Antonio Garibay, the richest landowner, to give him enough livestock to raffle so that he could build a larger church. Don Antonio Garibay let him have cattle, sheep, mules, horses and chickens. Father Pedro was able to raffle off all of the livestock in one year, except the chickens. He raised enough money to build a church that by all standards was too large for the community. Father Pedro kept the chickens in his yard and from there came the well-known roosters whose crowing resounded through the whole town.

Father Pedro died on March 4, 1920, the day that Father Fernando de la Vega arrived to find no one at the depot and the town deserted. After the train had left him on the platform, he thought that perhaps the Bishop had made a mistake, that the town no longer existed. He did not know that all the people were at the funeral.

Father Fernando was a Spaniard, born in Guipuzcoa in the northeast of Spain. He was short and thin and had dark eyes with heavy lids. He settled down and was loved by all. He gained weight on prickly pear pie, pomegranates, armadillos, rattle-snakes, jack rabbits and panochas. As he grew fatter, his name changed from Father Fernandito to Father Fernandón. After adding still more weight, he was

9

lovingly called Father Non.

He learned from the people what Father Jaillet and Father Bard had learned before him: the wonders of life are time, distance and fate—when one is born, where one is to live and when one is to die. He took up the love of raffles as though he had been sired by both Father Bard and Father Jaillet. He also developed a fondness for things magnetic. The only thing he did not inherit was Father Bard's love of roosters.

Chapter One

Once again Father Non complained about the old rooster to himself, sleepily pulling off the covers as he heard the rooster crow the morning in. He dangled his feet off the side of the bed and rubbed his magnetic ring, feeling the strength that it gave him.

"How much longer can he last?" he asked himself as he went to the window. Father Non's gaze moved slowly upward and there, on top of the hen house, was the rooster. He was quiet now, moving his small bald head from side to side, thinking of how he could outdo himself.

Father Non thought of how long the rooster had been bothering him, how many times he had tried unsuccessfully to raffle him off. He exhaled slightly the last of the night air and hissed, "The scoundrel . . . no telling what he'll do next." As if to respond, the rooster flapped his wings against his frail body, feeling the sharp pain from the gout in his kidneys. He continued flapping, not wanting the younger rooster, whom he spied hiding under the bushes, to know of his poor health. He took in an excessive amount of air, much more than his lungs and air sacs could comfortably hold, filled up to his gizzard and let out a crow packed with so much force that it rebounded like a fist of noise through the church yard, bounced off the church and then against the rectory, freeing itself to the front yard, crossed

11

the wrought-iron fence, went through the street to the center of the little dusty town, rebounded against the drug-store and bounced across the street to the Post Office, resonating and spreading like circles of ripples to the out-skirts of town to the depot where Lupito, the telegrapher, had already met the trains from Corpus Christi to San Antonio and Laredo. From there it echoed to the little houses beyond, where the townspeople lived and from where, exhausted, the noise tried to gather itself and failed and died on the ground like a spent bird that had finished with its message.

Father Non stood silently amazed, as though he had not only heard the sound but had actually seen it. Exhausted from such a great effort, the rooster climbed down slowly, foot over bumble foot, and proceeded, in his goutish way, to try to chase the oldest of the hens, simply a show for Father Non. Even the old hen had too much speed and evasiveness for him. She looked back and Father Non thought he could see a measure of disgust carved into her beak.

Pedro, the sacristan, was on his knees cleaning out the hen house when he heard Father Non's bedroom window slide open. He looked up through the chicken wire and saw Father Non taking in large breaths of fresh air. "I love the smell of a raffle," he heard Father Non say. Then sensing that there was someone in his presence, Father Non said, "Can anyone hear me?"

Pedro adjusted his hat to the back of his head and said, "It's me, Pedro . . . Father Non."

"Fool," Father Non said and closed the window.

Pedro waited for the inevitable. Father Non reopened the window and yelled out, "Pedro, be sure the hen house is clean for the turkey. Extra clean, I might add. No foolish-ness."

Pedro lowered his head automatically, as though he were receiving a dose of Father Non's mixed blessings and he said, "Yes, Father. It's clean."

"I will inspect it," Father Non shouted from the second floor. And knowing how badly Pedro could clean, he said,

12

"I'm warning you."

Pedro crawled out of the hen house and, dusting himself off, replied, "It's clean." He was, of course, lying.

"Well, it better be," Father Non warned him again and slammed the window shut. He could not find any reason for keeping the sacristan, but yet, like an old habit, he had never been able to get rid of him.

Out in the street, Father Non heard the sounds of the milkman, Celestino. He heard the jingling of the milk bottles inside the milk boxes on each side of Celestino's horse, Relincho. He heard Relincho clear his nostrils.

⽊

María, the young widow, had prayed her morning rosary and then cooled her forehead with mentholated alcohol while the children gathered in Cota's and Frances' room, rolling cigarettes, lighting up, taking heavy drags. Cota, twelve years old and the oldest of the children, sat on her thin bedding. Her given name was Eloisa, which is what her mother called her. Everyone else called her Cota. They were passing around the postcard of San Antonio which they had found that afternoon at the town garbage dump.

"They've done it again. Only one family would throw away a picture like that one," Cota said in her self-assured way, flipping the postcard to Matías. "Look at the address."

"We already have," said Juan, the eleven-year-old doubter in the family. "How many times do we have to?"

"Juan Garibay," said Matías, reading from the postcard. He was nine years old and the youngest of the children. Matías held the card in his hands, studying it. He was referring to Juan Garibay, son of Antonio Garibay who had donated the livestock for Father Bard's raffle that built the church.

"To be so rich, like Juan Garibay and his children . . . To be able to go to places like that," Cota dreamed out loud, filling her little head with fantasies. She sucked on her cigarette and let out the smoke in a rush of air that sounded like a wistful sigh.

"Can we go some day?" asked Frances, ten, the youngest of the girls.

"Sure," Juan replied, "and we can go to the moon too."

This was not the first postcard they had found at the dump. And this was not the first dream they had had of visiting a city. Before, when they found another postcard addressed to Juan Garibay and his family from Corpus Christi, they had looked at the photograph of the ocean until it was imprinted into their memory. They showed the card to their mother, María, and she told them the story again of having gone as a child to spend the night in Corpus Christi, of seeing the beaches and the ocean, a body of water so immense that it seemed to suspend the sun and the moon at its horizon for hours on end; of the deafening noise of the relentless waves, the wind so powerful that one had to lean into the sea in order not to be blown away and that the beach was covered with little crawling animals that carried their own shells.

One year, the children found several postcards from Laredo. They studied with interest the bridge across the Rio Grande River separating Mexico from Texas, the people crossing back and forth into Mexico and Texas, some of them carrying rifles into Mexico to fight in the revolution. They inspected a scene of downtown Laredo and they imagined gold and silver could be found on the streets. They did not realize that the glimmer over the town was the oppressive heat which was so intense in the summer that the birds left the city and migrated to the mountains.

Another time, Matías was digging in the dump and found correspondence to Juan Garibay and his family and inside the envelope were photographs of Brownsville, another city by the Mexican border where they believed gold and silver could be found in the streets. Judging from the photographs, flowers grew the size of plates and fiestas lasted for months and children could be seen dancing in costumes in the streets.

Each year their curiosity grew and even Juan, the skeptic, became eager to go and find out what was in those cities.

At night, after supper, they were so eager to get into Cota's and Frances' room to smoke and view their photographs that they quit helping María with the dishes. María did not complain. Instead, she smiled as she cleared the table and said, "Go dream your dreams in photographs. That's more important than doing the dishes."

Juan and Matías decided one night that they wanted to go to San Antonio so badly that they vowed to ride underneath the floor of the box-cars to get there.

So one morning, while Cota and Frances distracted Lupito, the telegrapher, Juan and Matías climbed under one of the box-cars and hid. But as soon as the train began to move they started tugging at each other and they fell under the train at the north spur, not fifty yards from the depot. They lay still until the train passed over them and then ran across the right-of-way, crawled under the barbed wire fence into Juan Garibay's pasture among the sheep and kept running into the thorns of the heavy brush as Lupito tried to chase them down. They hid all day at the edge of town in the brush by Juan Garibay's pasture.

At first it was only Lupito whom they had evaded, but later in the morning Sheriff Manuel was driving by the depot on his way to see Don Pedrito, the faith-healer, about his unexplained anger and he saw Lupito running parallel to the fence row looking for something. Curious as to what was going on, Sheriff Manuel stopped the car, got out and walked over to Lupito. Lupito told him that María's children were in trouble again.

Father Non noticed the unusual scene also as he was driving his old car to visit Juan and Carolina Garibay and the Garibay children. Father Non felt the jolt of the car when the tires passed over the tracks. As the car jumped, he looked to his right and there, running alongside the fence on the edge of the grass and mesquite, were Lupito and Sheriff Manuel. He drove over to the depot, parked, got out and walked slowly to where Lupito and the sheriff had stopped to rest.

"What is it?" Father Non asked before he even got to them. "A snake?"

"No, worse," Sheriff Manuel replied. "It's María's two boys, Juan and Matías. They're hiding in the grass. They tried to ride the train to San Antonio and fell off at the curve."

Lupito adjusted his collar and said, "They were underneath. They could have gotten killed. María would die if that happened."

"I would appreciate it if María is not told of this," Father Non said. "Poor woman. She has suffered enough."

"I can't keep it from her," Sheriff Manuel insisted, feeling a need to worry María. He didn't particularly like the children or María, although his wife, Inez, would hire María to clean house.

The next morning, Sheriff Manuel came to talk to María about Juan and Matías, and at the same time he brought up the incident of the oranges: the children had been seen stealing sour oranges at the courthouse orchard.

"They are up to no good, María," the children could hear him say as he sat at the table in the kitchen. They were outside, listening under the kitchen window. "Ever since Gonzalo was killed last year, it's been impossible for you to keep up with them. They are in need of a father's influence."

"My children are the best children in town," María replied. She counted her children on her fingers for the sheriff, going over the good qualities of each child: "Cota, the smartest girl in school, an actress. That's what she is, an actress. Juan, not so good in math, but one day an accomplished musician. You ought to hear him play the comb."

"I have . . . at the courthouse when they were asking for money," the sheriff informed her, not impressed with Juan's talent.

The children waited in anticipation of their mother's

words. "Well," María continued, "Frances, already interested in sewing . . ."

"That's not enough," Sheriff Manuel said.

"Matías, the smartest boy in school. Excellent in
math . . ."

"A year in an orphanage would do them good. Scare
them," Sheriff Manuel said, noticing that María had not
even offered him a sip of coffee.

"For taking some sour oranges?" they heard María
reply.

"And riding under the train, and . . . well, many other
things."

"You're insane, Manuel," she said. "Where did you get
this orphanage idea? How did you think it up?"

"It came to me in a dream," Sheriff Manuel replied.

María, incensed with the sheriff's answer, said, "You're
making fun of me and I don't like it. You're talking about
taking away my most precious possessions and you're making fun of me."

The sheriff leaned back in his chair, wondering what
María was so mad about. "I'm not making fun, María," he
said. "I have thought about it until I dreamed it. An
orphanage. That's what I think."

María realized that the sheriff had indeed dreamed
about an orphanage. She said, "I know that they are not
perfect, like Juan Garibay's children, but . . ."

They heard the sheriff push his chair back and interrupt. "An orphanage, María. That's the answer."

The children heard a heavy thump on the table as
though their mother had stuck a knife into it for emphasis.
They heard the shifting of footsteps. When Sheriff Manuel
hurried out of the house, they scrambled underneath to see
him descend the ditch, come up at the other side, get in his
car and quickly drive off.

⋇

It was in the summer after school was out, that the children loved to dig in the town dump. Even some of the old codgers who did not work, who stood around town all day long, took time off from their daily routine to go watch them as the children, under Matías' expert instructions, would build tunnels and breathing tubes leading to caves deep into the recesses of the old trash. Here they would hide from the other children, especially Juan Garibay's children, who were always so neatly dressed and always wanted to crawl into the holes with them. But they would run Juan Garibay's children off so that they could enjoy a cigarette in peace in the coolness of the excavation. Likewise, Father Non came to visit the children and marveled at their ingenuity. It was on one of these visits, while examining objects the children had found deep in the recesses of the dump, that Father Non realized that not only had he a love for his magnetic ring, his lariat and his mouth harp, but that he also felt more than a passing interest in the archeology of the town. That new found interest, he thought to himself, would be developed during the month of rain that washed through the little town once a year.

One morning, while rummaging through the dump, María's children came across an old bicycle that someone had thrown away. All it needed was tires, a seat, handle bars and a chain. After a few days they decided to go back to the dump to see if the bicycle was still there, and if it was, to bring it home. When they brought the bicycle, María took a good look at it and started to insist that they take it back, but then she relented and allowed them to keep it.

That night, as she finished her rosary, she realized that she had overreacted with the children, that the death of her husband, and her worrying about the children had made her say things that she was sorry for later. The next morning, feeling remorse, María walked out into the yard and looked over what the children were doing with the bicycle. She studied the bicycle closely as the children watched, hoping to gain her approval. At first she offered a suggestion on how to make a set of handlebars out of wood, but after a few days of showing them how, she realized that it was useless, and she took over the job of remaking the bicycle herself.

The bicycle began to take shape with a broom handle for handlebars and a seat made from a wooden box. María then bought, at the limit of her resources, two tires and tubes and a chain from Don Chema, the tailor.

In two weeks, the bicycle was ridable, and Juan and Matías would go for a ride through town, Juan pumping and Matías sitting inside the box, causing great laughter among the old codgers, Don Porfirio the druggist, Don Lupe the mayor, Don Napoleón the postmaster, and anyone else who happened to be in town. Cota rode the bicycle, taking Frances along on the handlebars. That caused great laughter also as little Cota, barely able to reach the pedals, pumped furiously, trying to keep the bicycle from falling over on its side, with Frances screaming for her life all the time.

One morning while taking what they called their pleasure ride through town, Juan and Matías saw a sign at Don Chema's window asking for anyone who owned a bicycle to apply for the job of delivering and collecting laundry and dry cleaning. They stopped, showed the tailor the bicycle, and the tailor immediately recognized it as the old delivery bicycle he had thrown away at the dump. He was impressed at what had been done with the two-wheeler. Of course, Juan and Matías did not mention the part their mother had played in rebuilding the it. They took all the credit for the work. The tailor, thinking that Juan and Matías had become two industrious boys at last, hired them to begin deliveries on the next day.

When they got home, Cota and Frances were playing out in the yard, waiting for the bicycle. Matías and Juan informed them that they had found a job to end all jobs, because it would pay them enough to get to San Antonio by train.

But this was not to be. The job lasted only one trip. As usual, Juan was pedaling as fast as he could trying to scare

Matías. He was standing as he pedaled, not able to sit on the box, since that was where the tailor had strapped the clean laundry. Matías, who was sitting on the handlebars, was screaming at Juan to slow down. With one hand, Matías steadied himself on the handlebars; with the other, he held the dry cleaning as high as he could to keep the clothes from getting tangled up in the spokes of the back wheel. To get even with Juan, Matías started to wave the clothes from side to side, obstructing Juan's view of the road. So Juan never saw the large hole in the road. He ran right into it and the bicycle pitched forward, the box with the clean laundry banging hard against Juan's boney rear-end. With the force of that blow, the packaged laundry exploded off the box and the clean clothes fell, tangling in the spokes of the rear wheel. At the same time the rear wheel came down and hit the ground, and the bicycle bucked forward again like a wild mechanical animal and threw Matías off the handlebars. The dry cleaning that he carried high in the air made a loop over his head and came down in front of him and wrapped itself around the spokes of the front wheel. Both wheels were now locked, the spokes stuffed with clothing. Juan shot forward as though he had been kicked from behind, and as he did, he finished pushing Matías over the handlebars, across the wheel tangled with clothes. Juan landed on top of Matías, and the broken bicycle, not much farther behind, landed on top of both of them.

On his way again to see Don Pedrito, the faith healer, Sheriff Manuel saw Juan and Matías on the bicycle carrying the laundry, poking each other back and forth. He stopped his car to see how far Juan and Matías would go before they had an accident. As he saw the two small boys run into the hole and topple from the bicycle, he thought again about the orphanage. Sheriff Manuel started his car and drove to where Matías and Juan lay on their backs moaning, each blaming the other. He picked up the arguing pair and took them, the bicycle and the clothes to Doctor Benigno. The doctor, preoccupied with still another mistress and his newly arrived electric machine, took a very quick look at the two boys, asked them a few questions and informed the sheriff that there was nothing wrong with them. "María's children are indestructible," he informed Sheriff Manuel as he led them to the door and began to lock up for the day. "Just like their deceased father. It would take a train to kill them."

"They're full of mischief," the sheriff replied, offering his diagnosis, hoping that Dr. Benigno would agree.

He did. "That too," the doctor said as he turned the lock on the door and looked wistfully to his right at the blooming mimosa that a month of rainfall had kept him from enjoying.

"What do you think of an orphanage for María's children, then?" the sheriff asked.

The doctor pulled on the door to make sure it was locked. He rattled the door handle three times as was his compulsion. He walked off toward his car and the sheriff and Juan and Matías heard him say: "There is not an orphanage built that can hold Gonzalo and María's children."

The sheriff drove Juan and Matías home and they unloaded the bicycle in pieces, as María fretted over what the sheriff was telling her. "They will kill me some day," she complained to the sheriff.

The sheriff adjusted his khakis. "I believe you," he said. "I keep telling you, but you don't listen. These boys have about as much sense as that old mule Gonzalo used to have."

"Less," María agreed. Sheriff Manuel's comparison had made her think of the month of rain. She said, "Less than the mule when she drowned."

The sheriff, not one to argue about Juan and Matías, scratched his head and said, "You may be right." The fact that María had so far agreed with him made him bold, as though he thought that she would agree to further punish the children. "I tell you, María," he said, reminding her, "that the best place for them is in an orphanage."

He had miscalculated María's feelings. "Not my children," María replied very emphatically, leaving no room for discussion. She added, "No."

"In time you'll see," Sheriff Manuel said, "And regardless of what happened, María, you're going to have to mend the clothes before you can take them back to the tailor."

"I know," María said.

"Remember what I told you about the children," he warned as he pointed his large finger at María.

"Please don't point at me," María said to him, taking his finger and shoving it out of the way. "I don't like it."

⋇

Without money and no hope of getting any, the children's interest in San Antonio was slowly dying. Cota could see it in everyone's face as they met during the day in the shed or in the caves to smoke. They were beginning to talk less of the pictures on the postcards and more about Father Non's raffle. María could tell that they were giving up.

"Remember your dreams," María said one noon as the children began to eat their lunch slowly, without an appetite.

Afterwards, the children went back to the shed. Sitting on her father's old saddle on the floor, Cota sighed in resignation as she took a deep draw from the little cigarette. She exhaled freely and the smoke came out of her mouth and nose making her look like a small dragon. She looked around the room. "I don't know what else to do," she sighed. She held on to the saddle horn and rocked herself slowly to the beat of her frustration.

Juan raised his hand for permission to talk, and Cota looked at him and nodded. "What if we fix the bicycle, and then, when we fix it . . . well then, we sell it?" he asked. He looked around and then blushed.

Cota looked at him and shook her head for a long time and said, "How can you be so dumb? Who in his right mind is going to buy that piece of junk?"

"Cota is right," Frances agreed. "Nobody is going to buy that piece of junk."

Matías took the opportunity to rub it in. "See what I mean? See how dumb Juan is? Who in his right mind is going to buy that bicycle?"

"Hey!" Juan yelled angrily when he stood up and threw his cigarette at Matías. The cigarette hit Matías on top of the head and exploded into hundreds of burning cinders. They saw small fires erupting from Matías' hair, Matías beating the top of his head to put the fires out. Cota and Frances jumped up to help him, both slapping his head. When the fires were out, Juan saw the angry look on his brother's face. Matías ran at him, but Juan fled out the door before Matías could get to him. He slammed the door and put the weight of his body against it. "It was just . . ." he strained as he put all his weight on the door, "just an idea," he finally shouted from the outside as he kept on leaning against the frail door.

Matías was trying to push his way out of the shed, battering the door with his feet. "I'm going to kill you!" he shouted.

"No you won't," Juan said, laughing.

At supper, when María asked why Matías' hair looked and smelled odd, Cota told her it was the new style in school.

"All the boys are doing it to their hair," she replied.

"Everybody, except Juan," Matías said grimly. "He's going to wear it differently."

"Now, Juan," María said, "don't you be doing that. One in the family is enough."

"I promise," Juan answered, seriously.

"He may, Mamá," Cota said.

"Heaven forbid," María sighed and she ran her hands through Matías' scorched hair and smelled her hands and made a face. "This smells burned," she said, perplexed, as though she had not expected that particular smell.

"That's exactly what he did, Mamá," Cota informed her. "Matías burned his hair. That's the new style."

"Heaven help us," María said, resigning herself to the times. She walked to the little sewing room, her refuge. At the door she stopped and, without looking back, she asked, "I ask you, God, what is the world coming to?"

That same night, when everyone was asleep, Matías got up, went to the shed, brought back the fleecing shears and, as Juan slept soundly, cut off most of Juan's hair.

In the morning María saw Juan as he approached the table; she dropped her coffee, shattering the cup and saucer. "My God in heaven!" she cried out. "What new style is this?"

Chapter Two

Cota drew on her cigarette. She slowly let out the smoke. She looked first at Frances and then at Juan and then she rested her gaze on Matías. She smiled and said, "I've been thinking and thinking. This is what I think." Cota looked up to the rafters and exhaled. "The only way to get money is to sell a quilt before we make it. Take the money. Buy everything. Then make a quilt."

"That's a good idea," Frances agreed.

"Who's going to draw it for us?" Juan asked.

Cota blew the last of the smoke up to the rafters and said, without hesitating, "Matías."

In the next days as he smoked in the shed, Matías designed a geometric pattern so complicated and extensive by using only a string and a pencil. The first day after he was through, without consulting with their mother, the children walked to Juan Garibay's farm to show the pattern to Carolina, his wife. When they arrived, Carolina was by herself. Carolina informed them that her children were at the garbage dump playing. "I wish they wouldn't go there," Carolina complained nervously. "It's so filthy. All that garbage and junk."

"No it's not, Mrs. Garibay. It's real clean. We go there all the time," Juan replied.

"I know," Carolina said. "The children tell me. I wish

you children wouldn't go there, either. Isn't it dangerous?"

Wishing to change the subject, Cota said, "When we sell this quilt we'll make enough money to take our Mamá to San Antonio."

Carolina was as taken with the children's thoughtfulness as she was impressed and confounded by the pattern on the quilt. She immediately wanted it for her eldest son, Antonio's, birthday. The thought came to Carolina without any hint from María's children. "With this quilt," she reasoned, like any parent figuring out how to help her child, "he can even learn his mathematics. He's not so good at that, you know."

This was an opening that Cota could not resist. "I guarantee," Cota said, hitching up her little skirt, "that Antonio will study the quilt, study the diagrams designed by Matías and he will do better in school. That's what the quilt was designed for, wasn't it?" she asked, looking back at her brothers and sister.

Matías, Juan and Frances, standing behind Cota, nodded at the same time, as though someone was pulling their heads with a single string.

Cota was not one to stop at one example. She knew from school that Anna, the Garibay's eldest daughter, was not so bright. So she continued, trying to impress Carolina. "And Anna could use it too. She needs the work in math."

"That's true," Carolina replied, thinking further of the possibilities.

"And Petra," Cota kept on, knowing how poorly the other daughter was also doing in mathematics. "And even little Gabriel," she concluded. She also knew how poorly Gabriel was doing in school.

Cota had struck a chord, and she and the rest of the children knew it. They watched Carolina rubbing her hands to ease the pain of arthritis. In her mind's eye she saw Mr. Rodríguez, the school principal, presenting all her children with the annual school award for mathematics.

Cota looked at Carolina and wondered if she needed more convincing. Cota decided to add, "We guarantee that anything Antonio is making a C in he will make a B. If he's making a B, he will make an A. If he's making an A . . . well, God only knows what's after that."

Carolina had been distracted with her own dream. She woke up suddenly at the sound of Cota's pitch. "An A?" Carolina asked, having caught the last of the conversation.

"Yes, an A," Matías replied from behind.

"Look at Juan," Cota said, pointing her thumb behind her at Juan. "Last year he barely passed. This year, with the help of a similar quilt, he is at the top of his class."

Carolina looked curiously at Juan and asked, "What happened to Juan's hair? And Matías?"

"Oh nothing," Cota replied, waving the boys away, "that's the new style in school." She was slightly irritated that the conversation had taken a different direction and that Carolina was one of those people who have a hard time concentrating on a single topic.

"They look odd," Carolina said, putting her fingers up to hide the expression of her mouth.

"Oh, Juan? That's because now he's so smart," Cota replied. "He's at the top of his class."

Matías could not resist. He shouted, "In fighting!"

"Don't pay attention to Matías," Cota remarked to Carolina. "That's just his way of playing."

But behind her back, as Cota spoke, Juan pushed Matías off the porch and jumped on him and began pummeling him with both fists. Carolina, seeing this, drew her hand to her mouth once more, but this time to stifle a gentle scream. "Oh . . . Oh!," she said softly as Cota looked around to see what was going on.

"They're only playing," Cota informed her as she watched with disgust Matías and Juan rolling on the dirt, hitting each other.

"Playing?" Carolina remarked. "They are fighting!"

"No, they're not," Cota insisted, on her way down the steps to stop the fight.

"Don't tell me they aren't fighting," Carolina complained as she held the door open and watched Matías and

Juan flailing away at each other.

By now Cota had become so disgusted with her brothers that she joined in the fight, and trying to be even-handed, was hitting Juan one time and Matías another. Frances was going around and around the three, trying to hit everyone she could. Carolina was yelling for all of them to stop.

"Get out of here," Carolina cried out, helpless to stop the fight. She kept wringing her hands. "I never have allowed my children to fight. If only Mr. Garibay were here right now to stop this," she said as she stepped inside, leaving the children to fight it out in front of the house.

They returned home disappointed and went into the girls' room to smoke. Cota rolled her cigarette, lit it and began to think. The others rolled their cigarettes in silence as they waited for Cota to finish her thoughts. Presently, Matías called out to her. Cota awoke from her trance at the sound of her name and leaned forward, the thin cigarette dangling from her mouth. She picked up the old baseball bat that was leaning against the corner of her room, and she stared at each one of them as she rotated the bat; then she said, "I've been thinking. I know what our problem is."

"What's that?" Matías asked, impatiently. "What is it?"

Juan said, "Tell him, Cota . . . tell him so he can shut up. If not, he'll be asking all the time. You know how he is."

Cota walked over to Juan and Matías, waved the bat, hitched up her skirt and said, "I want us to promise that we'll never fight again. That's what holds us back all the time. That's our problem."

Frances got up and took the sack of tobacco from Cota's pocket and began to roll her cigarette. "Cota's right. We fight too much," she said.

Cota had a hard time convincing both Juan and Matías, but in the end she won. Juan and Matías shook hands, agreed verbally to a pact that Cota thought up quickly, while the feeling of trust was present. Then Cota passed a piece of paper around and everyone signed it. There was to be no fighting by anyone. "We're going to be like Juan Garibay's children," Cota said, blowing smoke toward the rafters.

"Does this mean we're not going to sell the quilt?" Frances asked innocently.

"Not on your life," Cota replied.

Chapter Three

Father Non sat at his desk and felt the pastoral ring on his right hand. The gold band symbolizing his marriage to the church had worn thin. He thought of the ring as an old wife who had gone through too much of life's pain with him, who had seen him vulnerable and exposed during his most painful moments. He could not find an atom of pleasure in it. When he gazed at the ring as one would an old and ugly wife, all he could remember, even the good times, was sad.

He looked out the window at Pedro who was taking refuge in his favorite place at this time of day. Pedro stood leaning on his hoe by the church wall where the weeds were few but the shade was refreshing. Father Non yelled at the man through the window. "Come here," he shouted at his grounds-keeper and sacristan.

Taken by surprise as he wistfully thought of María, Pedro looked around to see who had seen him taking his break and was now shouting at him. He drew the handkerchief from his back pocket and wiped his brow as if he had been perspiring.

"Over here, you imbecile," Father Non shouted. "Over here at the window. Don't you recognize my voice after all these years?" He could see Pedro grinning and exposing the long solitary upper tooth in his gums. "Don't grin at me. And hide that tooth! Come here immediately," Father Non said, disgusted with the repugnant sight of Pedro's tooth.

Pedro began to walk toward the window and Father Non said, "Hurry up, man. Drop the hoe. Hurry up."

Pedro dropped the hoe and came at a trot. "Of what service could I be to the good father?"

"What were you doing? Just standing there?" Father Non asked.

"Just standing there, good father."

"You were thinking of María again, weren't you?" Father Non said. "Don't lie to me. I've heard you talking to yourself."

Pedro sighed heavily, letting all emotions loose. "Yes, I'm afraid so."

"You, Pedro," Father Non said, "ugly and poor. Old too. How can you even dare to be in love with María, the most beautiful woman in town?"

"I don't know why, good father," Pedro replied. "It's the way I feel . . . If only I could talk about it to her. Every time I visit her, I can't speak."

"I forbid you to talk to me about María. Do you understand?" Father Non said, studying his sacristan through the window screen. "You must be crazy."

Pedro leaned into the window and whispered finishing Father Non's statement, "For her."

"Don't talk to me about María. . . . Do you remember what today is, Pedro?" Father Non asked him in an irritated voice.

"Today?" Pedro asked and placed his hand on his chin, as if he had to go into deep contemplation. He knew this would further irritate Father Non. "Let's see . . . today? Let's see . . . today? Today?"

"The turkey, imbecile," Father Non said, gritting his teeth. "The turkey."

Pedro grinned. "I knew that, good father. Today I go and get the turkey from Juan Garibay."

Father Non forced a smile in defeat. "You'll be the death of me some day, Pedro. I believe you can exasperate me more than anyone I know. I believe I've ground down my teeth half an inch since you've come here. I really don't know why I've kept you employed for all these years."

"Probably because no one else will have the job . . . as little as it pays and all the praying one has to listen to," Pedro replied without thinking. Then he realized what he had said and waited for the verbal lashing. He raised his eyes and in his own defense and said, "It's not an easy job, Father, being constantly bombarded every time I get near the church. When it's not the rosary, well . . . why, it's the novena. When it's not the novena, it's the Stations of the Cross. It's always something. Somebody is always wanting something from God. There are some days when I wish that I had taken up another profession—something other than sacristan."

"Be glad you have a job, as ignorant as you are," Father Non scolded him. "Be appreciative of what the Lord sends your way. I picked you up off the streets. I know you don't want to think about it. Remember that all you ever did was drink and gamble?"

Pedro looked wistfully through the window and into the room and looked at the image of Father Non filtered through the screen. His thoughts shifted to the glory of those days. "Those were good times, Father Non," he said, wetting his tooth with his tongue.

"No they weren't," Father Non corrected him. "You just thought they were good."

Pedro started to disagree with the good father, but he knew that to do so would only bring on a stream of insults and advice. Instead, he bit his lower lip with his solitary tooth, projecting it out of his mouth like a turtle tail. "As you say, good Father," he answered, as he made a sucking sound with his mouth.

"Pedro," Father Non said, looking at Pedro and briefly feeling empathy for his sacristan, "how many times have I told you that he who was born to be a flower-pot will never leave the porch?"

"Many times," Pedro replied, not recognizing that Father Non had meant this to be an analogy for Pedro's life.

Father Non said, "You'll never leave the porch. As ignorant as you are. Now, go on and check the hen house
again."

"I already have," Pedro replied and giggled, like a fool,
covering up his mouth and its tooth with his hand.

⊁

The following day, a Saturday when the small town
always came to life with the influx of surrounding farmers
and ranchers, the talk was that someone had seen Pedro
running past the back of the stores, carrying a turkey
inside a burlap sack from Juan Garibay's farm to the rectory. They had followed Pedro and had seen him lock the
turkey in the hen house behind the rectory, after which he
covered the sides of the hen house with burlap to keep the
object of this year's raffle a secret.

Father Non had stood on the front porch anxiously
waiting as he caught sight of Pedro running toward the rectory. Father Non saw Gumercindo,one of the old codgers,
following slightly behind Pedro. "Damn it," Father Non
grumbled under his breath. "I so wanted to surprise the
town. Every year I try, but I never succeed."

That same morning, the children were playing in the
front yard when they noticed Martina open the front door
across the street, go to the edge of the porch and look in
both directions to make sure that there was no one in the
ditch. She walked carefully down the stairs, and when she
came to the ditch, she slowly lowered herself at an angle
and climbed out at the other side. She crossed the street,
crossed the ditch on the other side, and made her way
toward the children. She adjusted her bonnet and said,
"Children, is María home?"

"No," Cota replied, as they stopped their play. "She
won't be back until late, Martina. She's cleaning houses."

Martina looked toward the house to make sure Cota
was not lying. Not seeing any sign of María she turned to
them and said, "Tell María that Father Non is raffling a

turkey this year. The whole town knows. Father Non has failed again—to the point where he has taken off the burlap from the hen house. Ha! Poor Father Non. A juicy turkey. Tell María, if she doesn't know already." She stopped when her mind distracted her. Unconsciously her mind had picked up something unusual. "And why aren't you children fighting?" she asked.

"We don't fight anymore," Frances was proud to inform her.

"Yes," Martina scolded them, "now that you've almost worried your poor mother to the grave. . . . Now, you stop."

"We don't have any fun anymore," Matías said, picking up a rock and throwing it into the ditch.

Martina adjusted the peak on her bonnet to hide her face from the sun. "It's strange not to hear all those ugly sounds," she said. "What happened to your hair?" she asked Juan, but left without waiting for an answer because she knew she would not be told the truth. When she walked by Matías, she noticed his hair for the first time and she rubbed it between her fingers. "It's burned," she whispered to herself, smelling her fingers, as she went down into the ditch.

By the time Martina crossed both ditches and the road and entered her house, the children were running toward town and the rectory. When they got there, Pedro was sitting at the door of the small hen house, guarding the turkey and thinking of María. The sound of the children running toward him disturbed his thoughts. He awoke and pulled his hat forward as the children stopped in front of him.

"How are you orphans doing?" asked Pedro, goading the children. And then he came up with something that he knew always worked to get the children angry. "And how's that beautiful mother of yours?" He stood up and hitched up his wide khaki pants. They could see the perspiration at the belt line as he undid his belt and then tightened it. He patted his large belly. "There are a lot of beers in this belly," he reflected, as he noticed that they had been staring at him. "But," he continued as he sat down on his stool again and took off his hat to wipe his brow, "if the right woman came along, I'd give up drinking and carousing in no time. . . . Tell your mother that, children. Tell her that I'm going to be just like your dead father, Gonzalo. I'm going to learn to be a carpenter. A painter. A plumber. A sheep shearer. Tell her that."

Cota stared at Pedro and spat on the ground. "Sure," she said, "but why don't you tell her yourself? . . . One Tooth."

Pedro smiled to himself, showing off his tooth, ignoring the insult. He re-creased his old dirty hat and placed it at an angle on top of his head. He leaned forward and rested his elbows on his lap. He smiled and winked at them and said, "I'm a man of honor. I don't believe in speaking of such things directly. I may send her a love letter. . . . Tell her that." He leaned back and laughed at what he had said. "That's right," he joked. "I'll send María a letter. That's what I'm going to do."

"You don't even know how to write," Frances sneered.

"I don't have to know," Pedro replied and cocked one eye toward them, trying to intimidate. "I know people who write letters. Don Porfirio. Don Bruno. Genoveva Marín. They're not cheap. But when it comes to your mother, nothing is too expensive for her."

Juan took one step toward Pedro. Pedro could see the anger in his eyes. "You'd better not show up at our house," Juan warned him.

Pedro laughed his mocking laugh.

Matías began to check the ground, looking for something to throw at Pedro.

"Wait . . . wait . . . wait," Pedro said, raising both his hands as though he had given up. "I'm playing with you. Don't you understand? I see you didn't learn your lesson when I locked all four of you in the hen house the other day."

"You'll never do that again," Juan said. He heard Matías scratching the dirt behind him, and he turned and saw Matías digging out a rock.

"We hate you, Pedro!" Frances cried out in anger.

"You'll never trick us again, One Tooth," Cota muttered out at him. "We'll fix you one of these days."

"Yes," Frances said, "we'll fix you one of these days. And you're going to be in a lot of trouble. One Tooth."

Pedro rocked on his stool and absorbed all the insults and threats. Confident that the worst of that conversation had passed over, he lowered his voice and said, "I know how you youngsters feel about your father . . . him dying and all that so recently. But you've got to accept that your mother has natural urges that only a man can fulfill."

"If you come near our mother, you'll regret it," Cota warned him, raising her hand as if to hit him.

Pedro lowered his head between his knees and began to laugh silently, his body shaking. From this position he raised his hands to signify a truce. "Wait. Wait. Wait a minute, all of you. I'm only kidding," he said. "You children would have made your father proud . . . the way you take up for your mother . . . it's very good. Shows character."

Cota said, "You better not talk about our mother that way again or we're going to tell Father Non."

Hearing the threat, Pedro got up hastily and cleaned the seat of his large pants and took the stool and folded it. "No. No. No," he pleaded. "No cause to do that. I was just playing with you. Don't you children know when someone is playing with you? Didn't your father ever tease you? What kind of father was he not to tease his children?"

Matías walked out in front of Pedro and stood defiantly. "Our father is dead," Matías told him. He had dug the rock out of the dirt and held it in his hand.

"I know that," Pedro replied, eyeing the rock. He took out his handkerchief and wiped his brow, killing time. "Who do you children think dug the grave? Huh? Me. Me. Me," he cried out, pointing his thumb at his chest. "I cried when I was digging your father's grave. But then again, I cry for everyone. That's what makes this job so hard."

Cota stared at Pedro without blinking. Gradually Pedro's attitude changed, and she sensed that the man seemed ashamed of all that he had said. She decided to temporarily forgive him, knowing how ignorant he was. "Anyway, we came to see the turkey," Cota said to him.

"Oh, the turkey," Pedro answered, subdued. "Well, there he is," he said and moved out of the way so that they could better see inside the hen house.

"All the town has been here ahead of you. Not one bad comment. He's so precious that Father Non has told me that I am here to guard him with my life until after the raffle winner is announced," Pedro explained. "What a beautiful Christmas dinner someone is going to have with this fat one. He reminds me of one of the ladies who comes to rosary every night. The one that comes with your mother all the time," he added. "What's her name?"

Cota said, "You're hateful, Pedro. You know that? You know the lady's name. Martina."

"Martina. Martina. Martina. How could I forget," Pedro said, snickering like a little boy.

"Can we go in to touch the turkey?" Juan asked, and Pedro thought about it for a moment.

"No. No. Father Non would kill me if anything happened to him. You can pet him from the outside," he said while he took his hat off and placed it on top of the hen house. Then he went inside to catch the turkey for the children. "Notice how nice I'm being with you," Pedro said. In a crouch, his arms extended, he tried to corner the turkey. All the while the turkey ran from side to side, flapping its immense wings, beating Pedro with them. Pedro protected his face with his arms from the onslaught of the wings and pushed forward. When the turkey was subdued in a corner, Pedro wrapped his arms around its body and picked the bird up and brought it over for the children to touch. "Tell your mother how nice I am," he said, grinning through the chicken wire, stroking the turkey's head. The turkey, afraid of being held, and sensing a chance to inflict harm on the person holding him so tight, cocked his head and struck Pedro on the side of his head with its enormous beak. Pedro fell to the ground holding his head, moaning, gasping in pain.

"I'm dead," the children heard him groan as he lay on his back, the turkey standing on his chest.

The children could not control their laughter. They were jumping up and down. Matías threw his rock in the air and Cota said, "Thank God that he made you ignorant and with a thick head. Nothing can kill you."

"Nothing can kill you . . . not hitting you on the head," Frances said.

On the way home Juan started to imitate Pedro's voice, something that he had learned to do very well. Then he began to laugh while searching inside his shirt for something. And when Cota asked him what he was doing, Juan pulled out Pedro's hat from inside his shirt. He had stolen it.

"When did you do that?" Cota asked him, full of admiration.

"When he put his hat on top of the chicken coop," Juan said. "He forgot he took it off."

"Let me have it," Cota said, extending her hand to Juan. Juan gave her the hat. Cota placed it on the railroad track, and they waited there to watch as the evening train returning from San Antonio shredded it to pieces of dirty perspired felt.

Father Non had called out to Pedro to ring the bell for the rosary, and not hearing a reply, went to the hen house to check out his sacristan. He found him passed out inside, the turkey lying on top of his chest.

"You left the door untied. Thank God the turkey did not escape," Father Non said as he helped Pedro crawl out of the hen house. "This is God's warning."

"Oh, my head," said Pedro.

⋈

Sheriff Manuel had not quite finished dressing for his nightly rounds. He took money out of his pocket and paid María for cleaning the house. He watched María put on her shawl, as Inez, his wife, stood around and smiled. He and Inez escorted María to the door and let her out, noticing that nightfall had come. María started to say goodnight to him, but she sensed the discomfort that he felt when she was around. Standing at the porch, María shook Inez's hand and Inez grabbed her and hugged her. Then María said, "Goodnight."

Inez held her around the waist and walked her down the steps and then turned to her and said, "I'll see you in two days?" Sheriff Manuel had already gone back inside.

María nodded and said, "Two days . . . If God wills it."

Sheriff Manuel went back to the bedroom and looked for his cuff links that were miniature stirrups. He could not find them in their usual place. He went down, drawer by drawer on his side of the chiffonier. Next, he searched for them in his wife's side, starting at the top drawer, working his way down. When he reached the third drawer, where Inez kept her underclothes, he rummaged about, moving the delicate clothes around. He felt something at the bottom, a hard metal object. He pushed the underclothes away from the object. Then he saw something puzzling: an old plumber's wrench.

He took it out and studied it. When he knew of nothing more to do, he smelled it and said to himself, "This smells like a plumber." And then he tasted it and said, "This tastes of tears." He placed the wrench back in the drawer and went to sit on the edge of the bed. After spending a while in thought, putting his fears into focus, he rubbed the back of his head and said, "At least now I know what I've been trying to forget." What he was referring to, of course, was Inez's infidelity. He would have to go see Don Pedrito, the faith healer, to tell him he had found the basis for his discontent. Now he could explain his hatred of María and her children.

※

While Sheriff Manuel contemplated the renewal of his anger, Benjamín Argumedo, soldier of fortune, discredited colonel of the Mexican Revolution, pushed his thin body flush against the lip of the river bank, trying to hide from the lights coming from the border guards. He heard their voices directly above him. He cringed when he heard the growl of the guard dogs, remembering the wild dogs which once had made him plead for his life in the bull-ring in Durango where the *federales* had taken him to die. He remained fixed in place against the river bank. The dogs intensified their growl, and then one of them began to bark in a high pitch. Benjamín Argumedo stopped breathing. The guards above him lit their cigarettes and continued their watch, pulling their dogs along.

When he saw that he could move again, Argumedo, using his foot, pushed his suitcase down the river bank. He heard the thump as it hit the ground below. There was still his bicycle to walk down. He took several deep breaths and felt his way in the darkness. He heard the distant growl of the dogs, and men running at the edge of the river bank. Benjamín Argumedo heard rifle shots, the guards shouting at someone to stop. Someone else was trying to escape. He ran to the river and jumped in, bicycle and all, and landed in mud. He had never been on the Rio Grande before. "This is shallow," he said, picking himself up and wading across with his bicycle.

On the other side, with the voices carrying over the water, he heard the guards shouting that the revolution was dead. Argumedo had gotten out in time.

Chapter Four

Sheriff Manuel fidgeted all day about the wrench. Finally after supper, he rushed once more to see Don Pedrito, the faith healer.

Don Pedrito had long since diagnosed the cause of Sheriff Manuel's unexplained anger. Employing simple acts of deduction, Don Pedrito had narrowed it down not to one episode, but to one man: Gonzalo, María's dead husband. When Sheriff Manuel heard what Don Pedrito had to say, he took in a large breath of air and exhaled it with a tremendous sigh, so full of worries and cares that Don Pedrito felt there was no room left for them both in the shack.

"Gonzalo," Sheriff Manuel repeated. "María's husband. That explains the wrench. Now I know why I hate her and her children."

"It was a primordial response," Don Pedrito explained, flaunting his vocabulary and knowledge of animal nature. "Without knowing why, you felt anger. It's all very simple, if one can think like a dog."

"I've never been able to think like a dog," Sheriff Manuel replied, in what seemed to be a complaint.

"It comes with time," Don Pedrito reassured him.

"What do I do for a remedy?" Sheriff Manuel inquired.

"Well," Don Pedrito replied while stroking the stubble on his chin, "can you forget?"

Sheriff Manuel, without giving it a thought, answered, "No."

For once, Don Pedrito felt sorry for Sheriff Manuel. He said, "Then I'm afraid you are ready for the Capsule of Oblivion."

Don Pedrito stood up and went behind the curtain that separated his laboratory from the rest of the room. In a short while he parted the curtain and came out holding a vial in his hands. Sheriff Manuel could see the blueness of the capsules inside.

He recognized them from the night at Genoveva Marín's when her boarder had committed suicide.

"Remember," Don Pedrito cautioned him, giving him the capsules, "that the last man to try this committed suicide at Genoveva Marín's boarding room."

"I remember it well," the sheriff replied, taking the vial and looking at it. "I remembered that night the moment I saw the capsules."

"Do you want oblivion?" Don Pedrito asked him.

"Oblivion is what I crave," the sheriff replied, slipping the vial into his shirt pocket.

"But not forgiveness?" Don Pedrito inquired, still trying to convince the sheriff.

"Never," Sheriff Manuel replied and struck the table with his fist.

"We will have trouble," concluded Don Pedrito.

⊁

After supper, María was sewing little pieces of cloth together as she sat at the table with the children, watching all of them do their homework. She was thinking how grateful she was to Mr. Rodríguez for not suspending the children from school for riding the train.

She could not help but smell the burned odor on their clothes. She sniffed the air, remembering just how good the smell of menthol could be.

She looked at Juan as he struggled with his math. "Put

your tongue in, Juan," she said very lovingly, trying not to discourage the boy. "You don't do mathematics with your tongue."

Matías scratched his little head and read out loud: "There is no greatest whole number. Whole numbers go on without end. Did you know that, Mamá?"

"Where in the world did you learn that?" María asked in amazement.

"Here in the book," Matías said, showing her the page.

María looked at it, stared at the figures and equations and said, "Where did you get this book? This is not the one for your grade."

Matías took the book back and said, "Oh, no. Mr. Rodríguez lends me these books. They are too hard for the other children. Look," he continued, showing María the examples from the next page, "numbers are whole and are infinite."

"I don't believe it," María replied. "Numbers are numbers. Numbers end. If not, one would remain counting and never go to sleep. Anyway, I thought you were studying magnets and iron filings. I thought that was why you always collected the filings from around the railroad track."

"I already know about magnets," Matías said, turning the page of his mathematics book slowly.

"He's just showing off," Cota said, deep in study, as she curled her hair with her finger unconsciously.

"He thinks he's real smart," Frances volunteered. She was cutting out a pattern for a skirt.

"Aren't you through cutting that pattern?" María asked Frances.

Frances shook her head.

"I'm glad you don't sew for a living," María informed her.

María sighed so softly that she would not have disturbed a butterfly. "I don't know what I'm doing sewing by hand when I have the sewing machine. Sometimes I think I do crazy things. But, I guess I love to be here with you children. Strange, isn't it? If I didn't have a sewing machine, I'd be begging God for one."

At first, the sounds on the porch sounded like someone

had raked a chair across the floor. María asked Juan to stop making the disturbing noise. Juan, deep in thought, confused by his mathematics, barely answered, not giving any indication he knew what his mother had asked.

María heard the sound again. She looked at Juan and realized that he was not moving, that there must be someone on the porch. Then she heard the unmistakable sound of a heavy knock.

"Who could that be?" María asked. "Are you children expecting anyone? Juan Garibay's children?"

"Oh, Mamá," Cota answered, "you know those children never have anything to do with us."

"You ought to be friends with them," María said. She got up, walked to the door, and opened it and saw Pedro.

"Good evening, María," he said, taking off an old hat, embarrassed by it.

"Pedro?" María asked. "Is that you?"

"Yes, me," Pedro admitted.

"Why aren't you guarding the turkey?" she asked.

Pedro kneaded his old hat. "Look at me," he said, quickly ignoring the question. "I'm ashamed of my hat. God only knows what happened to my good one. I had it one moment, and then it was gone. Those are strange things that happen, aren't they María? One day one is here. One day one is gone. Gone. Like my hat."

"I'm sure you didn't come to tell me that," María said rather curtly. She had not wanted to see anyone but the children tonight. Then she realized that she had hurt Pedro's feelings and she said, "I'm sorry, Pedro. I'm sure I interrupted you."

Pedro cleared his throat after he had felt the embarrassing rush of blood to his face. He always had a hard time getting started with María. If only, he thought, he could say the things to María that he felt in his heart. "I've come to tell you," he stammered, "that . . . that . . ." It was too much for him to say the words. Instead he said, " . . . that Father Non is raffling a turkey for Christmas. One of Juan Garibay's turkeys. The old man himself donated the turkey."

44

"We already know about the turkey, Pedro," María said. "You're bringing me old news."

"Well, I just wanted to be sure that you knew. I know how hard you work. You're not around the town like some busybody women." He paused and cleared his throat. "May I come in?" he managed to say in a weak whisper.

"Don't let him in, Mamá," Cota cried out from the door in the hallway. "He's real mean. He talks filthy."

"Don't let him in, Mamá," Frances said.

Matías and Juan came into the hallway. Matías said, "He talks dirty, Mamá."

"He does," Juan said. "I wanted to hit him."

Pedro lowered his head and started to snicker, his body jerking up and down. He covered his mouth to hide his tooth. "The children, María . . ." he said, forcing himself to keep on snickering. He pointed to the children with his hat, "You know how seriously they take everything. They've never been kidded. I can tell."

"You children go into your room," María ordered. She turned around and she could see them going into Cota's room. "This is my house and I say who can come in and who can't. Excuse them, Pedro," she said to him. "Sometimes they run all over me. And sometimes I have to put my foot down."

Pedro was looking past María's shoulder as the children disappeared into the room. He felt uncomfortable for having caused María to get after the children. "I'm sorry," he said.

"Don't be. Come in," María said, holding the door open for him.

Through the cup of coffee Pedro talked nervously, going around the subject, hiding his tooth, covering it with his hand one moment and his hat the next, talking about the turkey, how he had brought it over from Juan Garibay's farm, how Gumercindo, the old codger, had seen him running behind the deserted stores, the turkey slung over his shoulder, how Gumercindo had followed him to the rectory, to the hen house and watched everything as he unsacked the turkey and covered the hen house with burlap to hide this year's raffle prize. "All was for nothing," Pedro said, gaining more confidence now that María was sitting across from him and the children were safely away in their rooms. "The secret was out as always. Father Non has not been able to keep the raffle prize a secret for all the years I've worked for him. First there was the mule, remember? Then the hawk. And then, if I remember correctly, was the goat that had triplets every year. Everyone wanted her. Then the parrot. Remember the parrot? Then the donkey. My God, he could bray. Then the peacock that went bald. Remember? That one no one wanted. I remember we didn't sell any tickets for that one. . . . Ahemmm," he cleared his throat, realizing that he had talked too much.

"Father Non has had his problems," María agreed.

"María?" Pedro said, softly, more resolute. He had finally decided to strike.

"Yes?" María answered.

Pedro looked down at his cup and swirled the coffee in it a few times. He licked his tooth and lost what little bravery he had gained and said, "Nothing. I must be leaving."

"Goodnight then," María said, getting up from the table. She sensed that Pedro was trying to say something else. She was not sure, but she suspected that Pedro's visits were more than wanting a cup of coffee. She was relieved that he had lost his nerve.

". . . Before the children run me off," Pedro joked, and he picked up his hat and left.

⟩⟨

Cota sat in her bed surrounded by Frances, Juan and Matías. They had exhausted themselves in describing their hatred for Pedro. Juan had imitated him until the children could not laugh anymore. Then to make his brother and sisters start laughing again, he had started to imitate the turkey.

"I could just pull that tooth out and make him eat it,"

Cota finally said and they all laughed.

"And me," little Matías volunteered, "I would like to put a magnet in his brain and put him on the railroad track and let him get stuck there and let the train run over him." He took out his magnets from his pocket and examined them, choosing the biggest one and showing it around. "This one!" he cried out, laughing.

This excited Juan. "Yes," he cried out, flailing away at an invisible Pedro with both hands, "just like we did with his hat. Crunch him with the train."

"I just hate his guts," Frances mentioned in passing. "That's all."

"And Mamá let him in," Cota reminded them. "I can't believe her."

The children thought about what Cota had said. None of them could believe that their mother would be interested in "Fat. Old. Ignorant Pedro," as Matías had put it. They grew quiet for a while, passing the pouch of tobacco around. When they had lit up, Matías asked the group, "So what are we going to do?"

"To fix Pedro?" Juan asked.

"No," Matías replied. "Forget about Pedro. I've been thinking again about the postcard. What are we going to do to get to San Antonio?"

"I've been thinking about San Antonio again, too," Cota said as Frances handed her the tobacco pouch. " And I've been thinking of something else, too."

"I knew you were, Cota," Frances said." I could tell. You've been real quiet."

"About what?" Matías asked Cota.

"Leave her alone, Matías," Frances complained.

"Everybody listen," Cota said, raising her hand for silence. "What does Father Non do every year to earn money for the church?"

"He has a raffle," Juan replied, promptly.

"A raffle," Cota repeated. "Just think about it. You get your money right away. We need to raffle something."

"But we don't have anything to raffle," Frances objected.

Cota replied, "You don't need to have anything before you start to raffle something. You can get that later . . . after you have the money. That's what's so good about a raffle."

"Is that honest?" Frances asked.

"Sure it's honest," Cota told her. "What if Father Non sold tickets to the raffle before he got the turkey? Is that honest?"

"He did it," Juan said. "Father Non has sold some raffle tickets before he had the turkey in the hen house. We saw him do it in the sacristy. Right, Matías?"

Matías took a long drag on his thin cigarette. "We saw it," Matías concurred. "He sold some to Antonio and Gabriel Garibay."

"They would be the first to buy . . ." Frances complained, not being able to hide her dislike for the Garibay children.

"That settles that," Cota interrupted Frances. "We will hold our own raffle."

"What will we raffle?" Frances wanted to know.

"Easy," Cota stated, as she poured the tobacco into the folded paper in her little hand, "we raffle a quilt. We'll use Matías' drawing. The one Carolina Garibay liked so much. Show the drawing to everybody. Sell the tickets. Get the money. Then make the quilt. Then we can go to San Antonio."

"What if we get caught?" Matías asked.

"What if nothing, Matías," Cota scolded him. "You're always thinking too far ahead . . . anyone got a match?"

H

Later that night, Lupito, the telegrapher, was reading *The Secrets of Love*, a book that he kept hidden in the rafters above the commode. He heard the urgent whistle of the train from Laredo to Corpus Christi. It was carrying a passenger: Benjamín Argumedo.

Benjamín Argumedo was a small delicate man whose

looks did not mirror the ferocity with which he fought in battle. He was dressed in an old woolen suit and a broad checkered tie. He carried a cardboard suitcase. On his head he wore a black flat hat with a fringe around the brim. When he got off the train, he walked not toward Lupito and the depot but to the back of the train where he tapped on the door of a freight car. Lupito saw him wait patiently for someone inside to open the door. A loading board slid out slowly until it touched the ground. Benjamín Argumedo rested his suitcase on the platform and walked up the incline and disappeared inside. He walked out guiding the most beautiful red bicycle Lupito had ever seen. Carefully, Argumedo brought the bicycle down until he had it on the platform. He kicked the bicycle stand and stood it up on its own and stepped back and admired it.

Lupito had seen many things at the depot, but this was the strangest of sights. He turned first to see the last lights on the caboose as the train receded into the night, and then he turned to the mysterious man who had arrived. Not knowing what else to do, he waved at Benjamín Argumedo who was still standing by his bicycle. Benjamín Argumedo waved back. Lupito removed his cap, scratched his head and remembered that the oddest thing he had seen up to now had been one night when Juan Garibay and his family had returned from San Antonio, where Juan Garibay's sister and her husband lived. That time, Garibay had gone to the back of the train just as the stranger had done. He had knocked on the freight, car and had gone in and come out shortly thereafter being dragged by two of the largest and smelliest billy goats he had ever seen.

"Billy goats," Lupito murmured out loud, deep into his thoughts of that night.

"No," Benjamín Argumedo replied, starting to walk his bicycle toward Lupito, "it's just a bicycle."

Benjamín Argumedo walked to where Lupito was standing, his hand outstretched. "Benjamín Argumedo is my name," he said, sensing Lupito's discomfort. "I can see that you are not used to anyone getting off the train here."

Lupito remained intrigued and silent. He shyly put out his hand for Argumedo to shake.

"I could tell that I disrupted your routine," Argumedo kept on. "You haven't moved since I arrived. You did not ask for the receipt for my ticket from the conductor. You forgot the water for the train. The engineer had to do it himself."

"I forgot the ticket," Lupito replied, slightly embarrassed. "The engineer . . . sometimes he does the water himself. But you're right. I am confused."

"No one gets off here?" Argumedo surmised from the look on Lupito's face.

"No," Lupito answered simply.

"Never?" Argumedo inquired, fascinated with the thought.

"Well," Lupito replied, "only when someone leaves, then they return. But strangers? I only see them through the windows of the train as they go by."

"Do you ever wonder who they are?" Argumedo asked.

"Yes," Lupito replied, "all the time."

"That shows that you are a thoughtful person. And your name?" Argumedo asked.

"Lupito García," Lupito replied. Then he realized that he had forgotten the stranger's name. "And yours was?" he asked.

"Argumedo," came the reply. "Just remember that it starts like an argument. Benjamín Argumedo. From everywhere in revolutionary Mexico."

Lupito, not knowing what to reply, said, "I'm from here. But they say that the revolution is bad."

"That's true," Argumedo replied. "I've come to escape the revolution. This looked like a good place to stop."

"It is a good place. But then, I've never been anywhere to be able to compare," Lupito admitted, reminding himself of the solitary life he had led for thirty-five years.

"One day you will go with the winds, Lupito," Argumedo informed him. "Wait and see. When you fall in love. You see me? I've come with the winds." Argumedo laughed, taking a flask from his back pocket and drinking from it. "Fate," he added while he offered Lupito the flask. But Lupito, ever faithful to his job, refused.

"Later on, perhaps," Argumedo told him, taking another huge swallow.

"My job and my mother won't let me," Lupito explained.

"Your mother is a widow, then?" Argumedo said.

Lupito almost smiled when he heard the statement, fascinated that Argumedo could know so much about him. "Yes," he replied, "but how did you guess?"

"Putting things together," Argumedo explained. "Now, let me guess some more. You worshiped your father. You love your mother but . . . you have never been in love."

"That is exactly right," Lupito answered, amazed that Argumedo could continue to deduce so much about him.

"And now, my good Lupito," Argumedo asked, "enough of this. I already feel like I know you. Where is a good place for a man to stay? I'm tired from all the traveling."

Lupito said, "There is only one place. Genoveva Marín has a room to rent. She is the only one who will put up a man. She has a neutral reputation."

Argumedo took another drink and said, "Well, Lupito, to Genoveva Marín's I will go . . . if you will point the way."

At that moment, they saw Sheriff Manuel driving by. He was on his way home to confront Inez with her infidelity.

⋊

Inez refused to admit anything. And when Sheriff Manuel produced the wrench from the drawer with the underclothes, Inez told him that the wrench belonged to her father, Antonio, the plumber. Inez's answer made Sheriff Manuel less sure of his accusation. He had not thought about Inez's father when he had found the wrench. Nevertheless, after several exchanges, he was not convinced that Inez was telling the truth. Besides, Don Pedrito was a master on human affairs. He insisted on her infidelity. A ferocious argument erupted and Inez took her possessions and moved to the opposite side of the house. Later she moved what furniture she had brought into the marriage and stacked it down the middle of the house, forming a barrier between her and her husband.

Chapter Five

Two blocks from the main street and in the center of town, Argumedo, following Lupito's perfect map, found Genoveva Marín's house. From the road, straddling his bicycle, he studied the house. It was a long, old wooden building that he could tell had been elegant at one time but now was in need of scrubbing and a new coat of paint. In the moonlight, he could see the front yard overgrown with weeds that reached above a man's head. Only now and then, among the weeds bathed in moonlight, could he see the Queen Anne's lace swaying. It had once grown to such profusion that every casket in town had been adorned with its white sprays. Now all Argumedo could see were the white tiny flowers clustered in large braces as they bent toward him in the breeze, fighting their last among the overpowering weeds.

Benjamín Argumedo peered through the window at the lighted sitting room and saw Genoveva Marín in her favorite chair by the lamp. Her half-rim glasses were down to the tip of her nose. She was reading a book. Argumedo noticed that she was thin and that she combed her hair back into a bun in the manner of the women of Chihuahua. She was dried and shriveled by the alternation of the winds and the heat and the dust and the yearly month of rain. Her fingers curled around the pages, ready to turn them over as soon as she was through. Her outward bearing carried with it an integrity that surprised him for an instant, and then he felt the genuineness of her spirit. He liked her as a friend from that moment on. He went to the door and gave the door bell a twist. He could hear the stirrings inside as the old lady moved about, looking for something to cover her head. "I'm coming," he could hear her say. "Just be patient. I'm coming. I wonder . . . who could it be at this hour? Who is it?"

Argumedo adjusted his hat with the fringes on the brim, as if the lady were standing in front of him. He tilted it slightly to his right, a gesture of chivalry never before seen in the little town. Genoveva Marín opened the wooden door. She leaned toward the screen door and peered outside. It irritated her that she could not distinguish Argumedo in the darkness. She was a woman who always wanted to be in control. "Who is it? Make yourself known," she demanded.

"Argumedo," he said, trying to be as soft as he possibly could, not wanting to offend Genoveva Marín or disturb the neighborhood dogs. "Benjamín Argumedo," he corrected himself, being more proper.

Genoveva Marín, very alert for being in her eighties, opened the screen door, the lamp cradled in her hands. "Argumedo?" she asked, frowning in disapproval. "What kind of a name is that? From Michoacan?"

"My God-given name, from wherever," Argumedo replied. "Benjamín Argumedo, at your service, madam."

Genoveva stepped outside and raised the lantern to illuminate Argumedo's face. She could see the hat and the fringes on the brim. "What kind of hat is that?" she asked. "It's covering your face."

"Asturian," Argumedo replied, smiling broadly. It amused him to see Genoveva walk around him, examining his hat in detail. "It's the fashion in Mexico," he said.

"Pray tell. Let me see the rest of you," she said as she lowered the lantern to inspect his clothes which were very dirty and wrinkled and ordinary in quality. "What else is in fashion in Mexico? Not the clothes, I would hope."

"No," Argumedo apologized, "the hat. That's all."

"Well? Did you come to show me your hat, or what?" Genoveva inquired.

"No . . . I've come for a room. Lupito . . . that is his name, isn't it?"

"At the depot?"

"Yes."

"That's his name. A little odd, isn't he?"

"Yes. One could say so," Argumedo answered.

"He's lived with his mother all his life," the old woman remarked. "The poor man has never known the love of anyone except his mother."

"Yes," Argumedo said, "I was able to surmise that."

Genoveva Marín continued, "You don't know that Lupito had difficulty being born. That is why his mother, Mercedes, loves him so much. Women love to suffer during childbirth. I was there. We could only find one testicle on that rascal. And he, in turn, loves his mother more than himself. But just wait for the first love of a genuine woman that hits him. Especially with his one testicle."

"He tells me you rent rooms to men. If that's true, I would like to rent a room from you."

Genoveva raised her lantern toward Argumedo's face. "The room may not be much, but I'm particular who I rent to. Turn around. Let me see you again."

Argumedo, the hero of many battles, the man who had walked through hails of bullets, turned around very patiently so that the old lady could examine him.

"He's short and thin," Genoveva said to herself aloud, taking off Argumedo's hat. "That's a good sign. I don't like tall heavy men. They are not only very clumsy, but their thighs rub together when they walk and these men perspire and smell by early afternoon. Assuming they didn't smell already in the morning. I can't stand the breathing of a heavy man around me. Do you bathe?"

"Twice a day." Argumedo turned to face Genoveva. "Ever since the war, I've become as clean as a drop of water."

"Ah yes, the war. I won't ask for which side you fought," Genoveva remarked.

"I can bathe once a day," Argumedo said. "If that pleases you."

"Once is enough. Clothes? How often do you change?"

"Every day since the war," Argumedo replied.

"Where are your clothes?"

"In my suitcase on the bicycle," Argumedo said.

"Bicycle?"

"Yes. Bicycle."

"I would expect a man like you to arrive in town with a horse."

"Not since the war," Argumedo said. "You don't have to feed a bicycle. A bicycle doesn't colic or founder as a horse does."

"And how long do you wish to stay . . . one day? A week?"

Argumedo pushed his thick black hair back and said, "For exactly how long I do not yet know. If good fortune—fate—has dropped me here, then it will be a long time. If misfortune has crept once more into my life, then I will be gone shortly, madam."

"I see. A resilient man," Genoveva Marín figured.

"Not so much resilient as practical," Argumedo replied.

Genoveva concluded that Argumedo was a man of his word. "You can stay in the back room by the garage," she said, returning Argumedo's hat. "I'll show it to you. You can come in and out through the garage. No need to be going through the house and bothering me. Just be careful with the car."

"As you wish, madam," Argumedo said as he followed Genoveva Marín along the side of the house, walking his bicycle next to him.

Genoveva stopped, turned around and said, "I don't know where you got it, but that bicycle is the most beautiful thing that has ever come to this town. Be sure and take good care of it."

"I can take care of the bicycle and myself," Argumedo informed her.

Genoveva sensed some of the aggression in Argumedo's words, a feeling, she felt sure, that still lingered in the men who had fought in the revolution. She was going to scold him, but thought better of it. Instead she said, "No one will steal it. You can be sure of that. It's just that you'll have a hard time with it here . . . the dust, the wind, the month of rain.   If you are not using it, you must keep it inside." She sniffed the air and said, "Just now the winds have changed and I smell whiskey on your breath."

"You are right," said Argumedo.

They walked quietly. Genoveva Marín led Argumedo through the garage and unlocked the door that led into the room.   Argumedo walked in behind Genoveva Marín. She went to the stand by the bed and lit the lantern.

Argumedo was surprised at the size of the room. It was spacious by his standards.

"This is your bed," Genoveva said to Argumedo, dusting off the bed-cover and fluffing up the pillow. "You can leave your bicycle in the garage with my car, or you can bring it in here. Whatever you wish."

Argumedo looked at the small bed against the wall and approved. He took the pillow and smelled it. "This smells like the revolution," he informed her.

"Gun powder. . . . The last man who lived here killed himself," Genoveva said.

"Why?"

Genoveva shrugged her shoulders as she went about straightening the room. She knew it had been love, but refused to say. "Here is the bath," she said as she opened the curtain at the door that led into the bathroom.   " W e have running water from the cistern. And here," she said walking over to the far wall, "is the closet, if you need it."

"Why did the man kill himself?" Argumedo persisted.

Genoveva shrugged her shoulders and said, "Love. Some say he came here to forget and couldn't. Others say it was the Capsule of Oblivion."

"I have heard of the Capsule of Oblivion," Argumedo said. "I have never seen it, though."

"It is bluer than blue," Genoveva replied.

"That is what I've been told," Argumedo said.

"It makes one turn blue," she said, "so that everyone knows when one is taking it."

"Did you know the man well?" Argumedo asked.

"No," Genoveva replied, standing at the door. She cracked the door and looked out. "What a beautiful moon," she said. Then, "He was a loner. A very private man. He seemed to keep everything to himself. It did him in."

"Poor man," Argumedo remarked.

"It was tragic," Genoveva murmured.

Argumedo was sitting on his bed. "I'll see you in the morning," he said.

Genoveva acted as though she were leaving, but then she turned back and closed the door. Argumedo thought that she had forgotten something. She was not through with him.

"And why are you in San Diego?" she wanted to know.

"Who knows?" Argumedo answered. "All I know is that I needed to get out of Mexico. The revolution is over. I needed to go as far as the train would take me."

"Well, Benjamín," Genoveva said, "no one knows what is to happen. It might be fate."

"It may be so," Argumedo remarked.

Chapter Six

After a breakfast of chorizo and eggs which stirred up heartburn even as he ate it, Benjamín Argumedo adjusted his shirt and coat, tucked his pants into his boots and pushed his hat down on his head while Genoveva admired his bicycle. Earlier in the morning he had decided to take a close look at San Diego. Genoveva had encouraged him to go. She looked up from the bicycle to him and said, "I hope you enjoyed the meal."

Argumedo suppressed his instinct to burp and said, "With that chorizo I will be busy digesting for a while."

"I always add more vinegar than normal," Genoveva explained, accepting what she took to be a compliment.

"It always seems to me," Argumedo replied, "that chorizo that causes indigestion as one eats it is always the best."

"Definitely," Genoveva agreed. "It is the Mexican way . . . to suffer even as one eats. And it also brings back the memories and sorrows of yesteryears when one repeats the same meal."

Argumedo took the bicycle by the handlebars and walked it to the street. "One meal like that one can last forever," he said, and he placed his cupped hand to his mouth to protect another burp.

Genoveva remarked that Argumedo made quite a sight,

at least for San Diego, wearing a black suit, black boots, a black hat with red fringes. "You're too much for this town," said she. "Of course, the men will all be jealous. But don't pay any attention to them."

"I won't," Argumedo replied as he ran by the side of the bicycle and then jumped on it. He turned around and waved at Genoveva.

Genoveva yelled, "Be careful." She bit her lip and said to herself, "Listen to me. Talking like a mother to her son."

At the first corner, Argumedo turned right. He pedaled toward the center of town, toward the old codgers who were already at their posts at the drugstore talking with Don Porfirio, the druggist, and at the post office waiting to see who had received mail for the day. The few who had been inside the post office came running out when they heard the commotion that the codgers made when they saw Argumedo on his bicycle. Argumedo waved at the old men as he flashed by. The old codgers had been caught by surprise and did not know what to make of Argumedo. They waved back. But as soon as he had passed, each group gathered around in a circle to discuss the bicyclist. Then the codgers who had gathered at the post office ran across the street to join the group at the drugstore. Don Porfirio came out of the pharmacy, twirled his moustache and asked, "What was that?"

No sooner had he gotten his moustache back in place, when Argumedo rode by again, waving happily at them. From the post office came Don Napoleón, the postmaster, crossing the street and hitching up his pants. "What is it?" he wanted someone to tell him.

Don Porfirio replied excitedly that it was some kind of man on a bicycle.

Gumercindo, the biggest rascal of the codgers, had seen and made comments about many things in his life, but this one was the first to leave him dumfounded. As the other codgers looked at him he could only say, "This man bears watching. If we can ever slow him down."

Argumedo was not satisfied with creating an uproar in

the center of town. He continued the length of every street in San Diego. He would start at the end of the street, cross town all the way to the other end, go over one block and come back on the adjacent street.

When he went by the rectory, he stopped long enough to introduce himself to Father Non, who was outside by the front gate looking for Pedro. Argumedo asked the priest to describe Pedro, and Argumedo was able, from the description, to tell Father Non that Pedro was to be found on his way to the center of town, where Argumedo had seen him.

"Ah. To the post office," Father Non remembered.

Argumedo stopped at the courthouse to meet Herminia, the tax collector's assistant, Don Bruno, the tax collector, and Sheriff Manuel.

He found Herminia and Don Bruno arguing over the value at which the post office and the drugstore were appraised. Doña Herminia claimed that the post office building was of less value than its appraisal, and Don Bruno disagreed saying the appraisal was correct. In turn, he contended that the appraisal of the drugstore was inflated, and Doña Herminia disagreed. Neither would give in. Finally, Argumedo realized that he had to interrupt the two. He asked them who owned the deserted barn at the edge of town.

"Who else?" replied Don Bruno. "Juan Garibay."

Argumedo walked down the courthouse hall to meet Sheriff Manuel. Sheriff Manuel had been surprised. He was in the restroom taking his Capsule of Oblivion when Argumedo burst in. The sheriff came out, shook hands with Argumedo and decided that he did not like Argumedo. The conversation was very short and not friendly. Argumedo was too much of a threat to Sheriff Manuel. To Argumedo, a man like Sheriff Manuel was very common and no threat at all.

The children were at recess under Mr. Rodríguez's watchful eye when Argumedo went by the schoolhouse. Mr. Rodríguez had to warn the children to stay in the school yard, so many wanted to follow behind Argumedo.

In less than one morning, Argumedo had seen all of the

town, had been to all the streets, had seen all the houses. When he was through, he stopped in front of the post office. Gumercindo stepped out of the crowd to ask who he was. Argumedo told them his name, and in the Mexican tradition, added that he was at everyone's service, for them to do with him as they pleased.

Don Porfirio took a good look at him and asked, "And the bicycle?"

"My transportation," Argumedo replied, "for now. Until I get a good horse." Then he added, "I'm a good farrier."

Benjamín Argumedo dusted himself off. He looked around at the crowd that he had attracted and wondered why not one of them was working. He cleared his throat of the dust. "You men should be at work," he announced, turning slowly in a circle to face the ring of men. "Haven't you men heard of work?" he asked them.

"What work would you have us do?" Don Napoleón, the postmaster, asked.

"Is there no work for you?" Argumedo asked.

"Oh, there's always work," one of codgers replied.

"Work never ends. We found that out a long time ago," the postmaster responded.

It was now Don Porfirio who said, "We work. You may not see it, but we work."

"What about the creek?" Argumedo inquired. "Why is it full of limbs and dead trees?"

The crowd laughed at Argumedo's words. It remained for Don Porfirio to say to the crowd, "This man has never experienced the month of rain."

Argumedo leaned forward on his bicycle toward Don Napoleón and asked him if he ever delivered the mail to people's houses?

Don Napoleón wondered at such an idea. He scoffed at the suggestion. He said, "Of course not. Who ever heard of such a thing?"

"It's done," Argumedo informed him. "It's being done right now. I've seen it with my own eyes."

Don Napoleón gave a hearty laugh, making his large

belly shake, and said, "Who ever heard of such a thing? Why, if I took the mail to the people, then what would they do? What excuse would they use to get out of the house?" He reflected for a moment, and before Argumedo could say anything, he said, "And I would have to hire someone else to do it. It's preposterous."

"It's the new age, sir," Argumedo informed him, "and we can't overlook it. It'll be here before you know it."

Argumedo looked Don Porfirio straight in the eye and asked him if he knew that there were drugs available so powerful that they cured infections?

Don Porfirio could hardly stand up from laughing. He wanted to know where Argumedo had heard of such a thing.

The crowd understood the futility of what Argumedo was recommending and began to disperse. Argumedo got on his bicycle and pedaled off, nearly running over Pedro, who had been in the crowd and was now on his way to the rectory.

Ж

Earlier, Lupito, reading the chapter on the different types of love, had seen Argumedo go by like a black flash. Lupito had waved and Argumedo had stopped to greet him, to show him the bicycle in daylight and to thank him for recommending Genoveva Marín's rooming house.

After Argumedo went on, the telegraph machine began to buzz in preparation for a message. It was a message from Laredo.

Lupito felt the instrument and noticed for the first time a strange tenderness in its rhythm, a different stroke. He wrote the words out, letter by letter, as they crackled out. When he was through and the silence engulfed the small room, he read and re-read the telegram. He blushed as he read it. He quickly folded it and put in his pocket. Then he looked out the window at Juan Garibay's sheep as they grazed placidly, the prairie grass higher than their heads. He took the telegram out one more time and re-read it, savoring it this time, as though he had not believed what he had read the first time. He purposely mouthed every word slowly. It read:

> HAVE ADMIRED YOUR TALENTS FOR SOME TIME.
> WOULD LIKE TO KNOW YOUR NAME. LOVE.

Chapter Seven

After Argumedo had left, Sheriff Manuel sat in his office in the courthouse thinking of how he was going to write the letter to Don Jaime, the district judge. He would not mention Gonzalo's affair with his wife, Inez. He knew the judge would not rule in his favor if the judge knew of the affair. He could tell Don Jaime of how María had no means of support except money that she got from cleaning an occasional house, that María had lost Gonzalo in the train accident. He would write that this was the same María who had sold the judge the beautiful quilt several years ago. He would remind Don Jaime of how they had waited outside the house for María to place the last stitch on the quilt, of how he had told Don Jaime then how terrible María's children were. Did he remember that the children fighting in the front yard among themselves had caused the judge almost to miss his train?

Sheriff Manuel felt a rush of excitement as he jotted down his thoughts. He would write that now that their father was dead they were worse, if that were possible. The children were always scheming to run away and leave San Diego for other exotic places, like Laredo and Corpus Christi and San Antonio. María simply could not control them. They spent most of their time living in the town garbage dump, smoking cigarettes. María's children ran around town causing all manner of problems for themselves and for the citizens. He would write that the children would entice Juan Garibay's children into the dump and then would scare them. He would make sure that the judge remembered how generous Juan Garibay was every election year. Finally, the recommendation: In his opinion, Sheriff Manuel would write, the children should be taken from María and placed in an orphanage for a year or two or maybe more until their mother could establish herself financially, get over Gonzalo's death . . . maybe until the children could grow up.

He was about to begin writing his letter when his anger for Gonzalo overwhelmed him. Gonzalo was gone. The family would pay for what the father had done. No one, not even those remotely involved that made a fool of him would escape his wrath. He broke the pencil in half and then the two halves into fourths. He tried to break the pencil into smaller pieces but couldn't. Instead he threw the pieces out the window.

Sheriff Manuel leaned forward on his desk and took a fresh pencil from the drawer and began to think. He was about to wet the tip of the pencil, when he heard noise from the center of town.

He got up, went to the window and could not see anything except the codgers milling about in front of the post office and the drug store. He heard laughter. Had the codgers discovered Inez's infidelity? The thought enraged him. He rushed to his desk, took out his pistol, ran to the car and took off for the center of town.

He found the codgers standing in a circle, waving their arms excitedly as they each tried to outdo the one another in describing how Benjamín Argumedo had looked earlier on his red bicycle. The sheriff, convinced that the old men were talking about him and his wife's adultery, slammed on the brakes and jumped out of the car, nearly choking in the dust that the car had stirred up. He coughed as he ran toward the men, shouting at them to stand still and be arrested. As he ran, he drew out his pistol and pointed it at them, making them all run, like a covey of birds, into the post office. "No one laughs at me anymore!" he shouted angrily, casting an angry eye at the scared old men that peered at him through the windows. He took a menacing step toward the building and fired one shot in the air. "That's just a warning to anyone who does plumbing," he shouted, replacing his pistol in the holster and getting back in his car.

Once back at the courthouse, Sheriff Manuel rushed through the hallway past the tax office. Herminia saw him and lowered her head into the large tax book. She had seen him drive away and then return, parking outside the tax office, slamming the car door, making the whole car shake. She had seen him run toward the courthouse. Now that he was in the hallway she did not want to confront him. The sheriff passed through without acknowledging either Herminia or Don Bruno. Don Bruno had busied himself in another tax book. Sheriff Manuel rushed into the office and on into the restroom. He looked frantically through his pockets and found his medicine, took out another one of Don Pedrito's Capsules of Oblivion and gulped it down with a glass of water. This calmed him down a bit. He took the pencil in his trembling hand once again and began to write the letter that he hoped would send the children to the orphanage.

⨉

On his way home, Benjamín Argumedo saw María for the first time. He was not paying attention to his route. He was thinking that he had not seen a farrier anywhere, and he had seen the perfect little barn at the edge of town where he could work. He needed to go meet Juan Garibay, who owned the barn. As a result of his meandering thoughts, he did not see María. He almost ran into her. He awoke from his revery barely in time to avoid knocking her down into the ditch. He skidded on his back tire on the dirt road and brought his bicycle to a stop.

María had been walking with her head down, worried about her children and where to get the money to support them. Her bonnet covered her head and most of her face. She saw the blur that was Argumedo, out of the corner of her eye, through the side of the bonnet, and she jumped toward the ditch. Luckily, she landed on firm ground by the edge of the ditch, balanced herself and was able to avoid falling in. At the same time, when Argumedo was trying to control his bicycle, she let out a small scream.

That event was the fateful prelude that two individuals as diverse as María and Argumedo could not have foretold. When Argumedo turned around, astride his bicycle, to see if he had somehow injured the lady in black, he saw her beautiful face beneath the bonnet. His heart stopped, and he felt faint and damp, and he immediately fell in love with her.

"Excuse me, ma'am," he stuttered out. "I didn't see you in the way."

María smoothed out her dress and said, "I'm not hurt. You stopped in time."

Argumedo loved her quiet voice. So flustered was he that he tipped his hat nervously several times and jumped on his bicycle and sped home to see Genoveva Marín, to ask her who this beautiful lady could be.

"You're describing only one person in town," Genoveva said to Argumedo. "That is the widow María. The one married to Gonzalo . . . who was recently killed by the train."

Chapter Eight

Sheriff Manuel wet the end of the pencil with his tongue while he re-read the letter to the judge. He was satisfied that he had included all the problems that María's children had caused in town. He looked up to the ceiling trying to think of how to end the letter when he heard the sounds of María's children in the hallway. He quickly put his letter away in the middle drawer, afraid that the children would see that it was addressed to the judge. He sneaked out of the office and into the hallway.

Sheriff Manuel could see Cota, Frances, Matías and Juan in the hallway. He saw the children go in the tax office and he could hear Cota's voice all through the hallway. He tiptoed quietly to hear what it was that they were saying. From across the hall he took a peek inside the tax office and saw the children standing in front of the counter, talking to Herminia. Behind Herminia was Don Bruno, the tax assessor.

"This is the quilt," Cota said, as she showed Matías' drawing to Herminia and Don Bruno.

"It's soooo beautiful!" Herminia cooed, like a dove. She squinted her bird-like eyes at Don Bruno, showing him the full face that had prevented her from ever getting married.

Don Bruno was all business, choosing not to look at Herminia.

"Isn't that beautiful?" Herminia kept on.

"Matías here made the drawing," Cota said, acting as if she was proud to be Matías' sister.

"It's unbelievable," Herminia continued in her praise. She was so curious about the quilt that she had not heard what Cota had said. "And who did it, did you say? You?"

"No," Cota repeated, "Matías."

"Just look at this, Don Bruno," Herminia said, showing Don Bruno the design of the nonexistent quilt. "My," she sighed, "wouldn't you love to have a quilt like that? Why, this quilt would never touch a bed."

Don Bruno cleared his throat heavily. "Don't exaggerate, Herminia," he said, barely scanning the design through his half-glasses and then plodding away toward his desk.

"It's true," Herminia replied. "I've seen quilts hanging on the walls of homes in San Antonio. These are pieces of art."

"What do you know about art?" Don Bruno snorted.

"I know more than you," Herminia replied. "I just told you that I saw quilts like these hanging on walls in San Antonio. Art pieces."

"Wasn't that when your mother sent you away to San Antonio? Right after you had problems with your mind?" Don Bruno said without any sensitivity. "In the condition that you were in at the time, how could you have noticed quilts hanging on the walls? Most likely, those were the visions of a crazy person."

Herminia ignored him for the time being. "I love San Antonio," Herminia said with a sigh and a wistfulness in her voice that made the children feel sorry for her. "But I never go anywhere now."

"You'll go again some day," Cota assured her, trying to make Herminia feel good about herself.

"We'll take you with us when we go," Frances said.

Don Bruno made a disparaging noise.

Matías, staring at Don Bruno, said out loud, "Herminia can go with us any time she wants."

"Always," said Juan, adding to Matías' sentence.

70

To a Widow with Children

Don Bruno lit his old cigar, puffed on it one time and laid it in the ashtray on his desk. He picked up some papers and studied them, now and then casting a glance at Herminia. When Herminia began to trace the intricacy of the quilt design, he interjected, "That is why you never got married. You are too argumentative with men!"

Herminia shuddered at Don Bruno's words. After composing herself, she said, "That's not true. I was just never a beauty . . . like María. I was always the mule." She turned to the children and said, "I was in school with your mother. She and I went for one year. In those days no one wanted to educate a woman. They wanted us for other things. But that's another matter."

Don Bruno picked up his cigar without looking at it, feeling for it by its heat, and he placed it gently in his mouth. The children watched as he sucked on it a few times, engulfing himself in his own smoke while studying the paper in his hand. "As plain as you are, you could have made someone a good wife," he said, talking through the cigar in his mouth.

Herminia took her eyes away from the quilt design and looked at Don Bruno for the longest time. Then she said, "Must we always have this conversation? Must you always hurt me when someone comes around?"

"You started it," Don Bruno replied, faking innocence, not taking his eyes off the paper, knowing that Herminia's stare would turn him to stone if he looked at her.

"You started it," Herminia shot back as she studied the design once more. "And Cota," she said, ignoring Don Bruno, "when is the raffle going to be?"

Cota stepped forward once again in front of Frances and Matías and Juan and said, "The day before the turkey."

"That's not too much time. That's only two weeks away," Herminia thought out loud.

"Yes," Cota sighed. "That's why we want to sell as many tickets as we can today."

Don Bruno rolled his cigar around in his mouth and said, "We already bought tickets for the turkey. How can you expect the people to buy more tickets for the quilt?"

"Leave them alone," Herminia told Don Bruno. "These children need the money. María needs the money."

"Well," Don Bruno gasped behind the cigar smoke, "if María sews the quilt it will be good. And you children," he said, pointing at them with his cigar, "you ought to do something nice for Herminia. Being that she's always so nice to you. Go tell Lupito that Herminia loves him." And then he began to laugh with so much force that he swallowed smoke and began to alternately cough and laugh and gag until his face turned blue and he began to wheeze.

The sheriff had heard enough. He walked back to his office and quietly closed the door, hoping that the children would not disturb him. He sat down and, feeling some pain for the first time from the Capsule of Oblivion, he held his stomach with his left hand. He took out the unfinished letter and began to write another complaint.

Ж

The next day, Benjamín Argumedo awoke once more to the fragrance of chorizo. He lay in bed, inhaling and exhaling the smell of red peppers and pork frying in its own fat. His dreams had been filled with the beautiful María. His first view of her would stay in his mind forever. It must have been the radiance of the sun that day, falling on the face half hidden under her black bonnet. Whatever it had been, that would be the vision that he would carry to his grave.

He could hear Genoveva Marín in the kitchen next door, moving pans around, making as much noise as a raccoon. He turned over and studied his red bicycle and noticed how dusty it had become in the short time he had been in town.

Later that morning, after he had dressed and eaten, next to the car resting on blocks he found a hoe and a rake in the garage. He began to clean up Genoveva Marín's garden, hoeing weeds and raking them over to one side, where he created a large pile and later set it on fire. By early afternoon, only the small amount of surviving Queen Anne's lace remained in the yard. By that time, a few old codgers had gathered at the front gate to see what was happening and why someone in this town was cleaning a yard.

Had Genoveva Marín looked out her window during that time, she would have seen Argumedo working in the yard. Instead, she had eaten her chorizo and gone from the kitchen to the bedroom and stayed there to look over the photographs that she kept of her husband, Máximo Pérez, buyer and seller of hides. He made a grand figure, standing by the hides that he bought and sold after the month of rain. When she was through, she arranged the photographs in chronological order, by months of rain. When she closed the picture album she remembered that her first words to her husband were similar to what she had asked Argumedo the night he had come to town: "How often do you bathe?"

When she went back into the kitchen for a glass of tea, she passed by the window and saw Argumedo tearing up her yard, piling up weeds, setting fire to large piles, exposing the long abandoned Queen Anne's lace. For some reason she felt sorry for the dispossessed man and came out with a glass of tea. Not being one to put up with fools, she ran the codgers off.

She handed Argumedo the tea and said, "What are you doing here, working so hard? I thought you had said that you were going to see Juan Garibay about the barn?"

"I'm on my way," Argumedo answered, "just as soon as I finish here."

Genoveva watched as Argumedo sipped from his glass. Finally she had to smile. "You remind me so much of my husband and his hides," she said.

)(

Lupito was at the telegraph machine working at a tremendous speed. He was answering the following telegram:

I LOVE YOUR TALENT. WITHOUT KNOWING WHO

YOU ARE I AM VERY ATTRACTED TO YOU. LOVE, A
SMITTEN ONE IN THE LAREDO OFFICE OF THE
TEXAS MEXICAN RAILROAD.

Lupito read the words that he had copied, smoldering
in continuous sighs. They caused his heart to flutter and
his lungs to expand and contract rapidly with the heaviness
of his thoughts. He went to the bathroom and sprinkled
water on his face to cool down his passion. He looked at
himself in the mirror. He supposed that the changes that
he saw were the price of love. He noticed the wrinkles in his
collar, the spots of goat cheese on the front of his shirt, his
hair a little bit too long. He was demanding less and less
starch in his shirt. The lace-like fringes of his fried eggs
bothered him less and less. He took his book from the
rafters and read from it.

Later, he put the book aside and he sat down and
wrote:

THE FIRST CHANCE I HAVE I WILL GO TO LAREDO
TO SEE YOU. I SEE WHAT I THINK TO BE YOU IN
FRONT OF ME EVERYWHERE I GO. COULD YOU
POSSIBLY SEND A PHOTOGRAPH TO REINFORCE
MY LOVE? LOVE, YOUR ADMIRER, LUPITO.

The children were on their way to see Father Non about
the church raffle, when they decided to stop at the depot to
deliver the message that Don Bruno had suggested. They
inadvertently awakened Lupito from his romantic reverie.

He asked them what they wanted.

"Just to tell you," Cota said, hesitating, "that . . ."

"That what?" Lupito asked impatiently. He was irritated that they had interrupted his dream.

Cota took a swallow of saliva and looked at Frances and
Matías and Juan, who were just as embarrassed, if that
were possible. In this case it was. They were not comfortable carrying messages for the lovelorn. "That Herminia
loves you," Cota blurted out.

Lupito tightened his mouth into a straight line to show his contempt. "I know," he said with a sourness that only his mother would tolerate.

"You don't care?" Frances asked.

Juan and Matías were standing over the telegraph machine, hoping to see Lupito use it.

"She's too ugly," Lupito informed them. "Much too ugly. Besides," he said as he blew on his fingers and polished his fingernails on his shirt, "I already have a girl."

"Like Mamá says," Cota told him, "don't despair. In this world there's always someone for someone."

"And where are you children going?" Lupito wanted to know. "And how come you children are so well behaved now? I've noticed that lately. It used to be that every time you'd run by here you'd cause some kind of trouble. Change the direction on the tracks. Try to make the train go in the wrong direction. How many times have I had to help back up the train and help head it in the right direction? You haven't tried to leave town under the train. What's going on? Have you children finally grown up?"

Cota looked at Frances and Matías and Juan, and then she turned to Lupito and said, "Lupito, you're right." She turned her nose up into the air and said, proudly, "We have finally grown up. Right?"

Matías pressed on the telegraph key and said, "Right. We are like new people. We study. We obey all laws."

Lupito pushed Matías away from the telegraph machine. "Don't be doing that, Matías," he said. "You're too young to know about the telegraph."

Juan pushed Matías back toward the telegraph machine and Lupito pushed Matías back to Juan. Matías was acting like a rag doll, happily allowing himself to be pushed back and forth.

"We're going to see Father Non," Frances said.

"To do what?" Lupito asked.

"To buy tickets for the turkey raffle," Cota said, "but first we need to show you what we are raffling the day before the turkey."

She reached into her pocket and gave Lupito the paper with the design of the quilt. Lupito opened it and inspected it and thought how wonderful it would be if he showed up in Laredo with this masterpiece.

"How much are the tickets?" he asked.

"For you," Cota lied, "it's only fifty cents."

Lupito saw the vision of his beloved in his mind's eye and he pulled out his money purse and took out dollar bills that had not seen the light of day for years, that not even his mother knew he carried for emergencies. Lupito bought five dollars worth of tickets, exactly what the sheriff had bought.

"This is going to be a source of happiness for me," Lupito said, looking at the drawing of the quilt and listening to the clackety-clack of a new love note coming through the telegraph machine. He put his hand up to his mouth and burped and said, "This has me so excited that I won't be able to digest the goat cheese."

"The design is all square roots," Matías instructed him.

"Ingenious," Lupito burped at him again.

Chapter Nine

Father Non looked out the window into the yard between the rectory and the church. Off to his left behind the row of pomegranates that bordered the sidewalk to the church, he saw Pedro hiding, trying to ease himself into a comfortable position on the ground. Father Non walked over to the window and shouted at him. Pedro jumped up as though someone had shot him. He adjusted his old hat and hurried toward the hen house as Father Non shouted at him again. The more Father Non shouted, the more Pedro lowered and tilted his head as though Father Non's words were blows raining on his head. Then the doorbell rang.

Father Non went to the hallway and looked out through the glass pane. He saw María's children standing all in a row by the door. He was always glad to have them visit. Never had they come with the same news, the same complaint. Their freshness invigorated him.

"And what do you children want?" he asked, smiling, as he opened the door to let them in.

Cota grinned and said, "Dear Father Non. We have come to buy raffle tickets for the turkey. If you have any more left. It's a surprise for Mamá."

Father Non opened the door wider to let the children in. He casually gazed toward town and managed to see Argumedo at the far end of the street on his way to the depot or to the Garibay farm. Which one he didn't know.

"So you want to buy tickets for the raffle?" he asked as he sat down. He unlocked the bottom drawer that held the cigar box with the raffle tickets.

"If you have any left," Cota said to him.

"For you lovely children, I have some left," Father Non replied. "Let's see. Let me look." He opened the box and took out a handful of raffle tickets. "How is María these days?" he asked, sorting through the roll of tickets.

"Oh, fine," said Cota, arranging her skirt as she sat on the chair in front of the desk. Frances, Matías and Juan were standing beside her, watching what the priest was doing.

Frances said, "She's doing real well."

Matías was desperate to ask his question. "Father Non," he blurted out, "is a raffle like gambling?"

At first, Father Non showed some displeasure with the question by the flush of his face. Then he remembered that these were the kind of questions that stimulated him during their visits. He smiled once more at them. "I do not consider a raffle a form of gambling, no," Father Non answered Matías, trying not to sound apologetic for his love of raffles. "A raffle," he explained, "is more of a pooling of money by a group and distributed to one of the members. It is not gambling in the true sense. It is like this new thing they call death insurance, except that the winner doesn't have to die in order to collect."

"Then, if you take a little part of something and not all of it, then it isn't gambling?" Cota asked her prepared question.

"Or stealing?" Matías added.

"Well," Father Non replied, rubbing his chin, "it's kind of confusing, but if you put it that way, I guess it's not. I guess it would be more like harvesting." He was intrigued with the idea. "A raffle is like harvesting. Of a slight part of money, of course, for the potential good of everyone." He continued to rub his chin and bent forward. "The question is fascinating. If one takes a small amount of something, then it is not gambling or stealing."

"It's not a sin," Matías said, already having made up his mind.

"No," Father Non replied, "I suppose it's not."

"We agree with you, Father," Cota said.

Father Non smiled, satisfied that someone had agreed with him. "I knew you would," he replied. "You know, I love your visits. You children are very nice. I have always said that."

Cota squirmed in the chair. "We take life as it comes, Father Non," she said to him, trying to impress Father Non with her mother's philosophy.

"Good for you," Father Non answered her. "It's the way María would like it."

"And how is the turkey?" Juan wanted to know.

Father Non ran his finger around his celluloid collar and said, "Fine. Doing exceedingly well." He unfurled the string of raffle tickets. "How many tickets do you children want?"

"One," Cota replied, and she looked around to her brothers and sister to see if they still remained in agreement. All the rest nodded their heads.

Father Non pulled off the ticket, cutting it in half at the perforations. He gave one half to Cota and placed the matching half in the cigar box.

Matías had another question for Father Non. He asked, "Is there some way of winning the turkey?"

"For our Mamá," Cota added.

"What do you mean? I'm confused," the priest replied.

Matías looked at Father Non intently and cocked his little head. "I mean . . . is there a way that we could be sure of winning?"

"Don't be dumb, Matías," Father Non responded. "That's an impossibility. That's why it's called a raffle. Everyone has an equal chance. In order for me to guarantee that you would win, I would have to cheat and you would have to cheat. In other words, children, you need me to cheat in order to win, and I'm not going to participate. Everyone has an equal chance." No sooner had the words come out of his mouth then he remembered the number of tickets that had been sold. "Except for Juan Garibay, of course," he said. "He has bought ten dollars worth. Enough to buy two turkeys. But he has all the money in the world."

※

Argumedo rode up to Juan Garibay's farm. From the road he could see Carolina, Juan Garibay's wife, hanging out the wash. The children were playing in the yard. They were waiting for him when he arrived. Before Argumedo could say anything, Carolina informed him that Juan Garibay was out of town. He had gone to buy another ram for his sheep.

Argumedo made the mistake of leaving the bicycle by itself. The children were so fascinated by it that they began to jump on it. Carolina scolded them and Argumedo had to apologize for leaving the temptation in front of the children's eyes. He would return the next day, Argumedo told Carolina. She said that Juan Garibay would be glad to talk to him regarding whatever matter he chose.

"The deserted barn," Argumedo revealed.

"Oh," Carolina answered, "that old thing."

He was glad to leave before the children caused any damage.

Argumedo returned to his work on Genoveva Marín's yard, and in the late afternoon he quit to prepare himself to go see María.

On his way, Argumedo thought that the sameness of his life, his endless wandering, was about to end. He rejoiced silently, grinning about his good fortune at last. His heart felt to him almost bursting with love for María, that love growing in geometric explosions. At the same time, he got a whiff of the lemon oil on his body, thinking then of what Genoveva Marín had said to him when he told her he was on his way to see María. As he had gotten on his bicycle, she had smelled the lemon on him, the oil that he had rubbed on himself directly from the peel. Genoveva had told him he smelled like an orchard in bloom. She had swooned in exaggeration and he had smiled. Then she had looked curiously at him and asked, "Isn't love wonderful?"

To a Widow with Children

Argumedo had looked down, in the direction of the front tire and had blushed under the hat with the fringes. Genoveva had apologized for having exposed his emotions and making him feel uncomfortable. "I've destroyed the mood," she had said, disgusted with herself. She had walked back toward the house. At the door she had stopped and asked him why he had not eaten the bread and butter or had the milk.

"The smell of lemon took my hunger away," Argumedo replied and took off quickly, before Genoveva could say anything else.

From the front porch Genoveva could see the disappearing figure of Benjamín Argumedo as he rode furiously on his bicycle, and then she walked to the edge of the large pile of weeds that Argumedo had set on fire, crossed her arms, and watched it consume itself.

$\maltese$

"You children should have heard the rosary for the turkey," María said as she pulled the needle and thread through the cloth. "Father Non was proud of the bird. Afterward, we all went to the hen house to see how big it is."

"We're going to win the turkey," Cota informed her mother.

"Heaven on earth," María said, flabbergasted. "How in the world are you going to do that?"

"We bought one ticket for the raffle," Frances said.

"One ticket? Where did you get the money?" María asked.

"From the bones we sold . . . from the dump, Mamá. Remember?" Cota replied, winking at her brothers and sister. "We sold them to Juan Garibay for fertilizer."

"From the bones from the dump we sold to Juan Garibay," the rest of them agreed.

María looked at them doubtfully, yet trying to remember. Finally, when her memory failed her, she gave her children the benefit of the doubt. "That was why you children smelled? Is that why? Because you had been to the dump to pick up animal bones? I guess I remember now." María held up the pieces of cloth that she was sewing together and inspected them against the light of the lantern. "I wish," she said, "that you children would not go to the dump anymore."

"We love it, Mamá," Cota replied.

"It's too dangerous. You never know what can happen," María said, passing the needle through the cloth.

"It's only dangerous when Juan Garibay's children try to go in and play with us," Frances said.

"They don't know what to do, Mamá," Matías complained. "They're just in the way. Always trying to look in to see what we're doing. Trying to find out our secrets."

"We'll never tell them our secrets," Juan said.

"You should share," María said. "They are such wonderful children."

"We'll never share, Mamá," Cota answered.

"Still," María continued, "it's dangerous . . . not only for you but for Juan Garibay's children."

"We wouldn't have to go to the dump or pick bones, Mamá," Cota replied, "if only you would make us a quilt to raffle.   That would be good."

"Raffle a quilt?" asked María. "Wherever did you get an idea like that?"

"Herminia," Matías lied.

"Herminia?" María repeated, trying to think of how Herminia would suggest that the children raffle a quilt.

"Yes, Mamá," Cota said. "She told us that she went to San Antonio one time a long time ago. And she saw a quilt that was so beautiful that it was hanging on the wall."

"A quilt that costs a lot of money," Matías said.

"They don't even use it on a bed, Mamá," Juan said.

María thought for a few seconds, inspected her handiwork, and then said, "I could never sew a quilt like that. Those are quilts sewed by professionals."

"Like you, Mamá," Cota encouraged her.

"Like me?" María answered, pointing at herself with

the needle.

"Yes, Mamá, like you," Cota replied.

"You could do it," Matías said. "We could all help."

"We've got two weeks, Mamá," Cota announced, feeding María this piece of information. In her innate timing, she had sensed that this was the moment to begin to unveil their plan.

"Two weeks?" María responded, in a state of confusion. "I don't know what you mean."

The knock on the door was timid, like the rapping of a small bird. The children heard it first and María looked up from her thoughts and wondered what the children were listening to. Then María heard what the children had heard, a small rap-rap, as delicate as a butterfly.

María arose and the children followed her into the hallway and to the screened front door.

"Who is it?" she asked, rather shortly.

"Pedrooooo," he cooed, like a dove, and then they could hear him stifle a foolish giggle.

"Oh, no!," shouted Cota.

The children all made faces and María put her finger to her mouth and whispered to them to be quiet.

"Pedro?" she asked through the door, aggravated again that Pedro had come to interrupt her time with the children, and at a time when she was about to find out what her children were doing with a raffle for a quilt.

"Yes. It's me," Pedro answered, full of hopeful love.

"Go away," Cota shouted from inside the house.

María looked sternly at Cota and said to her, "Leave the man alone. Don't be insulting your elders."

Cota and Matías and Juan and Frances made faces at Pedro through the door. María opened the door to see Pedro standing on the porch with a bunch of naked poppies in his hand. He extended the flowers without petals to María. Pedro smiled when María took the flowers and shyly said, "I've been playing 'She loves me. She loves me not.'"

María could not help but blush at the flowers. "Come in, Pedro," she found herself saying while holding the door

open for him. Beyond Pedro's head, the glow from Argumedo's fire could be seen. "I guess you would want a cup of coffee," she said in a tired voice.

Pedro answered, "Yes," as he walked on past her and
into the hallway. He was so steeped in love that he would
never have caught the inflection in María's voice that
revealed her weariness with his company. When he turned
around to face María, he tried with all his might to show
her how much he loved her by smiling as broadly as he
could and squinting his eyes until they appeared closed.

María, aggravated with him at first for disturbing her,
now had to suppress a laugh.

Argumedo was standing nearby in the darkness. He
had actually arrived before Pedro but he had hesitated
when he saw the beautiful picture through the window of
María and her family sitting at their modest table. He
observed them with great curiosity while they talked to
each other in such an animated way. The domestic scene
made him long for a family of his own.

In his awed state he had thought he could not interrupt
such a heart-warming scene. Instead, he leaned on his bicycle and enjoyed the sight of María sewing bright little
pieces of cloth and talking to her children. And he was able
to imagine himself sitting with them, one of the children
sitting on his lap.

He was enjoying the vision of his happiness when he
saw the shadow of a man approaching on the road. He hid
himself and his bicycle inside the ditch and watched as
Pedro got closer and closer, talking to himself, plucking the
petals from the poppies, saying "She loves me. She loves me
not." Argumedo saw Pedro go to the steps and up to the
porch and walk over and knock on the door. He felt devas-
tated. His beloved María had a suitor, the old and fat sacristan. How could this be possible?

Inside the house, María ordered the children to go to
their rooms and she invited Pedro into the kitchen. Pedro
took his hat off and rested it on a chair next to him. He
adjusted his pants, tucked in his shirt, cleaned his tooth

with his tongue and sat down.

He sniffed around until he became familiar with the room's scent. "It smells a lot like tobacco," he said.

"No," María replied, "it's the bones from the city dump."

Pedro disagreed, but he was not about to start an argument with his beloved. Instead, he wanted to show her how much he cared and he said, "You look preoccupied, María."

"Oh," María answered as she poured the coffee, "it's something the children said. It's just sticking to my mind, that's all."

"No trouble, I hope," Pedro replied.

"No . . . nothing like that."

"Because if it is trouble, you know you can count on me, María."

"Thank you, Pedro," María said as she sat down with the coffee.

"You know," Pedro began, stretching himself out on the chair, "if it's the children in trouble again . . ."

"Please," María stopped him, raising her hand, "I'm worried. Can we talk of something else?"

"Like what?"

"I saw the smoke from a fire in town today. It is still glowing tonight. What happened?"

Pedro said, "All I know is that the codgers said that the stranger—Argumedo, I believe his name is—had set fire to the weeds in Genoveva Marín's yard. All I know is that I saw the smoke. The codgers say that Argumedo is an idealist. Looks at everything and wants it to be better. Wants everybody to work. Even the codgers."

María looked out the window and saw the glow from Argumedo's fire. "Argumedo is the new man in town?"

Pedro let out air, scoffing at the mention of Argumedo's name. He did not want María to like the man, so he said, "I heard him talking nonsense at the post office. A braggart, María. You know you don't like braggarts. Father Non barely likes him," he said, not considering it a lie.

María remembered the encounter in the street and said, "I wouldn't know one way or another how to judge.

I've never met the gentleman, formally."

"Well, I hear he's hard to like," Pedro replied. "So far, no one likes him."

María chose to ignore Pedro's comments about Argumedo. She was not about to admit to Pedro or anyone else that she had felt a twinge of emotion when Argumedo had almost run her down with his bicycle. Tonight, though, she could not take her mind off the children and the quilt. Finally, in desperation, she said, "Where is Don Antonio and the siren?"

"I don't know. Why?" asked Pedro.

"I wondered," María said, "because no one has sounded the siren for Argumedo's fire."

"It's not worth bothering with, María," Pedro said, trying to make light of the fire. Then, in the silence that took over, he straightened out in his chair and cleared his throat. He had decided on his way that tonight he would declare his love. "María," he began, very seriously, "there is something that I feel I must tell you. Something that I have to tell you. Something that I . . . that I . . . Well . . ." he trailed off in embarrassment.

"Well what?" María asked, drinking her coffee, wishing that he would go away. She could hear the children in the girls' room.

"Well," Pedro groaned in agony, his courage having left him, "well . . . it's this way."

"What way?" María wanted to know.

"Ah . . . the way of the turkey."

"The turkey?"

"Yes." Pedro said reaching for his hat and getting up. "The turkey has to be protected at all costs. I'm afraid I've got to go. Father Non would kill me if he knew where I was."

Argumedo spied Pedro as Pedro came hurriedly out of María's house. He wondered what had happened for Pedro to be in such a rush. Pedro mumbled to himself as he went past Argumedo, not seeing Argumedo in the darkness. "I almost did it," Argumedo heard Pedro say. Argumedo waited for Pedro to go a short distance and then he jumped on his bicycle and caught up with him.

"Good evening," Argumedo called ahead to Pedro, not meaning to, but scaring the sacristan, just the same.

Argumedo's words, in the darkness, surprised Pedro. He looked back and then jumped toward the ditch, the only place he felt he could go. He lost his footing and then his balance, sliding feet first into the ditch. Upon hitting bottom, Pedro moaned and yelled, "Who in heaven above is that?"

"Argumedo," Benjamín Argumedo replied from the top of the ditch. "Benjamín Argumedo. And you are Pedro, the sacristan?"

"Yes, Pedro," he responded. "Father Non's sacristan."

"I must apologize, Pedro," Argumedo said. "I didn't mean to scare you. Let me give you a hand."

Tonight was the second time that Argumedo had gotten a good look at Pedro. The first time, Pedro was on his way to the post office. Now it had been through María's window. Argumedo could not believe that a woman as beautiful as María would have anything to do with Pedro.

Argumedo got off his bicycle and slid part-way down the ditch. He found Pedro in the darkness and helped him climb out.

"You look sick," Argumedo said, as he saw Pedro's face up close, this time by the light of the moon. Pedro was less attractive than what he had at first thought: large eyes that looked like dishes, a long forehead, a short fat nose, thick lips. He could not keep his eyes off Pedro's solitary fang.

"I'm all right, Argumedo, thank you," Pedro replied. "You could very easily kill a man. You know that? Coming up from behind like that . . . in a street with ditches like these and all."

"Pedro, I'm sorry," Argumedo apologized, still amazed that Pedro would be calling on María.

Pedro dusted himself off and spat out dust from around his tooth. He surveyed his hat in the moonlight, cleaned it against his thigh and put it back on his head. "Well, I thought I was dead for an instant. I thought that I would never get to the bottom of that ditch. All that rolling. My God!"

"All is forgiven?" said Argumedo. "I hope. Have a drink on me." And Argumedo took out his flask and offered it to Pedro.

Pedro took the flask, drank from it and made a face as he replaced the cap.

Argumedo's curiosity was getting the best of him. He did not want to waste any time before interrogating Pedro. "You're coming from where?" Argumedo asked Pedro, unscrewing the cap and taking a drink himself.

"María's," Pedro said as he started walking. He was feeling his head.

Argumedo walked next to him, holding on to his bicycle. "And María? Who is she?" Argumedo asked, trying to draw information from Pedro.

"María is my love," Pedro proclaimed, releasing his head and touching his heart with both hands.

Argumedo felt his own heart miss a beat, but even though it hurt him to the marrow of his soul, he continued. "You two are getting married, then?" he asked. He held his breath, waiting for the reply.

"Yes," he heard Pedro answer. To Pedro, who had expectations beyond his capabilities, it was not a lie. He sincerely believed that he could make it happen.

"When?" Argumedo wanted desperately to know.

"Very soon," Pedro answered. "Before summer and the month of rain."

Argumedo found it hard to believe that a woman as beautiful as María would want to marry not only an older man but an ugly and poor sacristan, as well. "How could you have enticed her to marry you?" he asked, strolling alongside his bicycle.

Pedro looked out to the shadows of the moonlight on the road. "Don't you think that I deserve a woman like María?" he asked. Then gazing at Argumedo suspiciously, he added, "Do you think I'm dumb and old?"

Argumedo extended the flask to Pedro and Pedro took it and drank from it. By the time Pedro returned the flask, Argumedo had gotten peeved at Pedro and Pedro's good fortune. He couldn't help it. Argumedo replied, "The thought had entered my mind."

⊁

The children were in Cota's room smoking. María was in bed anointing herself with mentholated alcohol, wondering what all the talk about a quilt had been. Matías was sitting in the middle of the room, his cigarette resting in an old conch shell that someone had said came from the gulf at Corpus Christi. He fumbled around, searching for the ingredients for his new secret weapon.

From inside his shirt he brought out an ear of corn and from his pocket he took a needle and thread. He began to shell the ear of corn that he had stolen from the fields that Juan Garibay owned. He pierced each kernel with the threaded needle, making what seemed to be the beginning of a long necklace of corn.

Chapter Ten

It was not enough that Argumedo had just insulted Pedro. He continued to question Pedro, and the sacristan became more and more irritable. He demanded that Argumedo stop his interrogation, which he said was making him feel like a prisoner of war. Argumedo insisted, and when he tried to pass the flask to Pedro, Pedro refused, a sure sign that the sacristan had had enough of Argumedo. Argumedo lifted the flask and had a good strong drink from it.

As they walked in the silence of the evening, Argumedo could hear Pedro mumble that apologies were in order for the groom to be. Argumedo ignored Pedro, once again asking about the wedding. Pedro repeated that the wedding would take place in the summer and before the month of rain. To which Argumedo replied that from the information that he had about the month of rain, that date could be set forward or backward by several months. Pedro thought for a few moments. "Still," he insisted, "it will be before the month of rain."

At the corner, just before reaching the center of town, Pedro turned to his left toward the church without a word, hurt that Argumedo had questioned him so harshly. Argumedo leaned the bicycle toward himself, threw one leg over the seat and pedaled away. And although he did not believe Pedro, he felt that there must be some relationship between Pedro and María. What that was and to what extent, he would have to find out. Regardless, what had started as a night full of promise had been ruined by the whole episode and an old fat sacristan.

When Argumedo rode somberly past the depot, Lupito, who was closing up, turned back from the door and shouted at him that he had finally found his true love. But Argumedo was in no mood to talk. The more he pedaled, the angrier he got. Once more his mind carried him to his fateful past, as though he were trapped in remembrances of the revolution. He managed to expel into the night, in one long breath, the disappointment buried in his heart.

So deep in thought was he when he reached the center of town, that he barely had enough speed to keep his balance. Although Don Porfirio had just closed the drug store, the codgers had not yet left for home. When they saw him, they waved at him and shouted greetings. He heard the codgers but chose to ignore them as he had Lupito.

Argumedo passed Celestino, the milkman and his horse Relincho, who were on their way home. Celestino was so drunk that when he tipped his hat at Argumedo, he leaned over to one side and began to fall. Relincho was an expert at keeping his master on the saddle. Shifting his weight, the horse gave a slight jump and caused Celestino to land back on his seat.

Argumedo went into his room through the back way, past the shiny car on blocks, so as not to talk to Genoveva Marín, but Genoveva heard him rustling about in his room.

Argumedo began to reason while he readied for bed. Surely, thought he, someone as beautiful as María could not be the least interested in Pedro. But then, his mind played tricks on him by unwillingly making him think of two examples of the vagaries of love. The wife of Colonel Agustin Mendoza, Panfina Mendoza, the most beautiful woman he had ever seen before seeing María, married to a man who was so repulsive in physical appearance that in the field of battle he had only to show himself and the *federales* would turn and run, thinking that they had seen the soldier of the devil. Had Agustin Mendoza been present at every battle, General Villa had said later, all battles against the *federales* would have been won. And then there was Cleotilde Barrera, married to General Basilio Esparza, a woman almost the equal of Panfina Mendoza, married to a man so ugly and ignorant that every officer thought for sure that she would be prime for a sexual encounter, but she was so trustworthy to her husband, so adoring, that she was nicknamed "The Virgin." That was proof enough.

Confused with the vagaries of love, Argumedo took a swig. He was about to have another drink, when Genoveva knocked on the door to his room.

"Who is it?" asked Argumedo, a frustration in his voice that Genoveva had not yet heard.

"It's me, Genoveva," she replied, placing an ear to the door. "How did it go?"

"Horribly," Argumedo said, sitting on the edge of the bed, taking another drink.

"May I come in?" Genoveva asked.

"Of course," Argumedo replied, buttoning his shirt. Genoveva entered slowly and, upon seeing Argumedo drinking from his flask, covered her eyes and thought that María had thrown him out of the house for drinking.

"What happened to you?" she asked him, taking a seat on the bed next to Argumedo. "When you left here you were the very picture of manhood . . . all pride, happiness."

"I smelled like lemons," Argumedo added.

"You smelled like an orchard in bloom," Genoveva Marín said in exaggeration of her memory. Argumedo leaned forward on the bed and rested his elbows on his knees. He gazed at Genoveva and said, "What exactly is the relationship between María and Pedro?"

"María and Pedro?" Genoveva asked. She had an incredulous look on her face. Argumedo explained that he had seen Pedro walk in and sit down and have a cup of coffee, all with the familiarity of a husband.

Genoveva made a noise like air coming out of a tire. "Oh, that. It's nothing," she replied with a wave of her hand to signify that Pedro was of no consequence. "He forces himself on María. Poor woman. The man is an idiot."

Argumedo felt a sense of relief. Genoveva explained that Pedro had been bothering María since the day after Gonzalo's funeral. It was all a misunderstanding, Genoveva continued, that only a fool like Pedro would have believed to be true. She explained to Argumedo that after Gonzalo's funeral María had had people over to share a meal cooked by the ladies of the church. Father Non had said a few words. Later, after the meal, as any widow would have done after burying her husband, María had said to the women, unfortunately within earshot of Pedro, that she wondered how she was going to survive without a man, meaning, of course, that she needed a man to help around the house. Pedro had been bothering her ever since.

"And Pedro is nothing?" inquired Argumedo.

"Nothing. Nothing. Not a thing," Genoveva almost shouted for emphasis. "And you didn't even get to talk to her?" she admonished him. "Next time, even if Pedro is around, go ahead and take the initiative. Knock on the door."

"I'm not very good around women," Argumedo confessed, sadly.

"She would love you, if she knew you," Genoveva concluded

Blushing, Argumedo asked why she had come to that conclusion, not having known him for any length of time? Genoveva Marín took the flask away from Argumedo and took a hefty swig. She smiled, explaining that it was for her nerves, and said, "You are exactly like Máximo Pérez, my late husband. Honest. Straightforward. And you don't require much food. A perfect specimen for a husband."

)(

Early in the morning, Sheriff Manuel went to see Don Pedrito about the pain from the Capsule of Oblivion. Don Pedrito informed him that the pain in the flank was to be expected. The pain drove away the gulf of miseries by nullifying the memory. When he returned to his office, Sheriff Manuel tried to contemplate the realities of the day. Those being too many and too painful, he reached into his shirt pocket and brought out the vial with the capsules. He contemplated taking another one, then he remembered the man who had killed himself, and he put the vial back into his pocket. The noises of people in the hallway upset him and he left his chair to go close the door. As he stood at the doorway, he could see Herminia at the end of the hall, talking to someone that he couldn't distinguish in the sunlight. He pulled his head back into the office and went and sat down. He rechecked his mail on the possibility that he might have overlooked the letter from Don Jaime, the judge, giving him the authority to take the children away from María. "That would take care of one problem," he said, under his breath, patting his stomach as he felt the release of acid. Don Jaime had not written and Sheriff Manuel, as much as he liked the judge, had to admit that procrastination was something the judge was well known for.

A knock on the door startled him. He jumped to his feet and hid the mail in the drawer. He felt the revolver in his holster and looked toward the door.

"Come in, it's open," Sheriff Manuel called and Father Non walked in.

"I heard the turkey the other day," the sheriff said right off.

Father Non's face glowed with pride. "This is the first time that I have raffled something to eat," Father Non said, sitting down in front of the desk.

"What about the hawk?" Sheriff Manuel reminded him, trying to put on a smile.

"People don't generally eat hawks," Father Non replied, making himself comfortable in the chair.

"The whole town is crazy over the raffle, Father," Sheriff Manuel said.

Father Non smiled and said, "Manuel, this is by far the greatest raffle we have ever had. Why didn't I think of this before? A turkey! How perfect."

The sheriff took the revolver out of his holster, checked it and placed it inside the drawer, and then said, "Sometimes the obvious is hard to see."

"Spoken like an observant man," Father Non replied. "But I guarantee you that from now on, every year we will raffle a turkey. Juan Garibay willing."

"Don't get so carried away, Father," Sheriff Manuel said. "Remember how you are about fads."

"Well, fads or not . . ." Father Non answered him as he crossed his legs and placed his hands on his lap. He looked down at his magnetic ring, studied it for a moment and said, "This is the best I have ever done for this town. All the tickets are sold. And they have been for some time. I can hardly say the Rosary anymore. All I hear are the murmurs of the old women. Louder and louder. Back and forth. Praying to win the turkey."

The sheriff invited the priest to a cup of coffee, but Father Non declined. "I had my two this morning. That's all I drink now, Manuel," he explained. "Remember in the old days when I would drink coffee all day long? No more now." He tapped his chest with both hands to indicate the source of pain. "My heart is giving me trouble. Dr. Benigno agrees. However, he cannot prove it. As you know, he's trying to get into the use of electricity and all that type of medicinal magic."

Sheriff Manuel got up and went by the window to pour a cup of coffee for himself. He felt the surge of bile lessen as he talked with the priest. He probed his stomach and pressed around and under the rib cage.

Father Non could not help but notice the change in the man. He asked, "Don't you feel well?"

The sheriff smelled the coffee, and it made him nauseous. He put the coffee cup down without drinking from it and returned to his seat. "I'm all right," he said.

"You don't look well," the priest continued. "Now that I've seen you by the light of the window, you look sort of bluish. Purplish."

"Give me time. Soon you will see me like a new man. As

soon as I can solve my problems," Sheriff Manuel said.

"Solve your problems? That's a mysterious answer coming from you," Father Non suggested.

Not wanting the conversation to proceed further, the sheriff leaned forward and said, "This coming week is a banner week for this town, eh?"

"The raffle, you mean?" Father Non inquired.

"Well, in reality we are having two raffles."

"Two raffles?" the surprised Father Non asked. "Who else is raffling and what?"

"María and the children. Didn't you know?"

"This is the first I've heard of it," Father Non said, confused. "I . . . I don't understand."

"Well, Father," Sheriff Manuel replied, leaning back on his chair, "the children are raffling a quilt that María is sewing, a beautiful quilt."

"I haven't seen it," Father Non said. "I didn't know anything about this. I'm dumfounded."

"Well, it is going to be raffled on the Friday before the church raffle," the sheriff kept on, "so it won't interfere with your raffle."

"And the turkey on Saturday," Father Non added, the look of concern covering his face. "Am I being unduly concerned? Do you think that's too many raffles?"

"No," Sheriff Manuel replied, "it's just a quilt. What can the children do to upset what you're doing?"

"María's children?" the amazed Father Non asked. "Don't you know? Can't you imagine what they could do?"

"Not this time," Sheriff Manuel said, with a complacent wave of his hand. "This time I'll have my eye on them. No tricks up their sleeves this time. I've already warned them. They know the trouble they will get into by misbehaving."

Father Non continued to ponder the consequences of having two raffles in one week. His first reaction had been one of disappointment, that perhaps his raffle would be diminished. Then, as he thought in silence in front of the sheriff, he began to sort out the possibilities. After rehashing it in his mind he said, "At first I was concerned that anyone would have a raffle without my consent. But now, the more I think about it, it seems just the right thing to do. That will be the preliminary. The turkey will be the featured raffle." He brightened. "What a splendid idea!"

"I thought so too," Sheriff Manuel agreed. "As a matter of fact, I bought tickets for the raffle on the quilt also."

"From the children?" Father Non asked, finding it hard to believe that the sheriff had entrusted María's children with his money. "They convinced you to buy tickets for their raffle?"

A self-satisfied Sheriff Manuel said, "Yes. I'm sure that they think that they have outsmarted me, but now that I have the tickets, I can keep up with them. I will have to know who won the quilt. They will have to tell me."

Said Father Non, "I seem to follow your reasoning. I will pray that everything works out for you and the children. . . . But now, about my raffle."

"That's what you're here for," Sheriff Manuel said, "to tell me what you want. What am I to do?"

"You, Manuel, like always, will be in charge of crowd control. That's precisely what I came to talk to you about. And your beautiful wife, Inez . . . why I would be honored if she were in charge of seating the ladies of the Altar Society."

The mere mention of his wife made Sheriff Manuel get up, excuse himself and walk into the bathroom. "Are you all right?" Father Non asked from the office while the sheriff threw water on his face. Sheriff Manuel wiped his face with an old towel and then studied the towel to see if any of the medicinal dye had rubbed off on it. He felt the battle of acids in his stomach, causing a billowing of his gut, followed by the largest belch that the priest had ever heard. Father Non got up. He felt that under the circumstances Sheriff Manuel would like to be left alone.

On his way out, Father Non could hear Herminia and Don Bruno arguing inside the tax office. Next, he heard a great commotion. He took a peek inside the office and he saw Herminia holding one of the large tax rolls over her head, chasing Don Bruno.

><

Benjamín Argumedo could not free himself of the compulsion to pedal by María's house in the morning. He did not see her. María had gone to clean the mayor's house. Argumedo continued on his way to his original destination—Juan Garibay's farm. He pedaled by the depot on his way and waved at Lupito, who was checking the water level in the cistern. Lupito tried to catch up with him to tell Argumedo of his new-found love, but Argumedo was too far gone. He had turned north into the road that divided Juan Garibay's pasture in half.

Juan Garibay was sitting at the kitchen table, drinking his coffee, talking to Carolina. Carolina had told Juan the night before about Argumedo. She was by the door holding the broom which she had just used to sweep the hallway. She came over to where Juan was sitting and caressed his hair. Juan took her hand and she sat down next to him. She was so happy, she told him, that it made her afraid. "I fear something awful will happen when I get this feeling," she said.

Juan looked at her as though he thought that she was being unduly concerned. "Nothing will happen," he replied. "Nothing ever has."

Juan heard Argumedo's knock and got up. "Who could this be?" he asked Carolina.

Carolina had a worried look on her face. She was holding the corner of the apron up to her mouth. "I hope it's not that the children are in trouble," she said.

"Don't be afraid," Juan scolded her lightly. "Why are you feeling so gloomy?"

Carolina let out a sigh. "I don't know," she said. "Some days I have the strangest feelings."

"Leave them behind," said Juan on his way to the door. "It's probably Argumedo."

Juan Garibay opened the door and saw Benjamín Argumedo for the first time. He was exactly as Don Napoleón, the postmaster, had described him when Juan had gone to pick up his mail. Behind Argumedo he saw the bicycle, as beautiful as Don Napoleón had said. Juan immediately wanted it for his beloved children. It was the most appropriate toy he could ever buy for them.

When Argumedo informed him of the reason for his visit, that he was interested in renting the old barn at the edge of town, Juan Garibay found it hard to contain his joy.

"How did you know the barn was mine?" he asked, diverting attention from the matter at hand, as any astute businessman would.

"Don Bruno told me," Argumedo answered.

Juan laughed and said, "Don Bruno knows everything." He was laughing for joy.

It was the old deserted barn that Juan owned and had not used for years that Argumedo wanted to rent for his far-rier business. In fact, Juan had just recently thought about selling it. When Juan pressed for terms, Argumedo had to admit that he had almost no money. Juan Garibay made his mental calculations, as though he were bartering for a billy goat or a ram. He offered to sell the barn, knowing that Argumedo could not afford it. Argumedo started to leave and was already on his bicycle when Juan stepped off the porch and stopped Argumedo. He said that it would not be a fair trade, that the barn was very valuable to him, but seeing that Argumedo was a stranger and that no stranger had arrived since Father Non, he would trade even for the bicycle. Argumedo hesitated at first, but when Juan threw in the old horse-shoeing tools that he no longer used, Argumedo realized that he needed to make a living more than he needed the bicycle. He agreed. Juan invited him inside and they signed a contract. Argumedo walked back home and, when he arrived on foot, he startled Genoveva.

"Don't tell me you lost the bicycle?" she asked, worried for him.

"No," Argumedo responded. "I traded it to Juan Garibay for the barn and farrier tools. I'm a farrier now."

"Tomorrow, then," Genoveva said, taking off her apron and accepting a drink from Argumedo's flask, "very early, we go see Father Non."

"What for?" Argumedo inquired, taking the flask back.

"You need him to bless the barn," Genoveva said.

In the morning, Argumedo and Genoveva went to see Father Non about blessing the barn. He was not busy, so Father Non, Argumedo and Genoveva walked to the edge of town with all of the codgers following close behind.

"This is the first building I've blessed since the court-house," Father Non reminded Genoveva, who had provided the Queen Anne's lace for the occasion. Father Non stepped into the old dusty barn to be by himself.

From the inside, Argumedo and Genoveva and the codgers, who were standing a few yards behind, could hear Father Non invoke the name of the Lord on all the pieces of lumber, nailed or un-nailed. The priest sprinkled the premises with holy water and prayed that the building and Argumedo would be blessed

Chapter Eleven

María relished the warm feeling of motherhood as she sat at the table with her children while they studied. Juan had tied a string to his pencil and was drawing circles on his paper. He was working with so much intensity that his tongue was sticking out of the corner of his mouth, almost lapping the paper.

"Stick your tongue in, Juan," María said. "It's not a good sign when you do that. The teachers don't like that."

Juan pulled his tongue back into his mouth.

"When I went to school once," María remembered, "Herminia was there and she used to stick out her tongue like that and Doña Chucha would scold her, and when she didn't mind, Doña Chucha would grab Herminia's tongue and pinch it."

"That's cruel," Cota said as she nervously curled a strand of her hair around her forefinger, knowing that the matter of the quilt had not been addressed. She had to wait for an opportunity. Then she wondered, like the other children, whether María had forgotten all about it. Surely, as much as she had reacted at its first mention, she had not.

Matías was attuned with Cota. He understood that they would have to ease their way into the quilt at an opportune moment, something which only their mother could give them. He closed his eyes and said aloud, "An odd number . . ."

And Juan immediately interrupted, ". . . is a crazy number."

Matías kept his eyes closed and repeated the text he was studying. He recited, slowly, "An odd number is a whole number that is not even. A prime number is any whole number greater than one which has only two different factors, itself and one. Examples: two, three, five, seven, eleven . . ."

"Be quiet, Matías," Frances said, having lost her patience. "Can't you see we're all studying?"

"Matías, you're confusing everyone of us," María complained. "What kind of numbers are those anyway? All numbers are good. There are no odd numbers and that is that! Is this another one of the books Mr. Rodríguez lets you have?"

"Mr. Rodríguez loaned it to me," Matías replied, studying the book cover.

Frances tattled: "He bothered Mr. Rodríguez until Mr. Rodríguez had to lend it to him."

"We don't even use the book in school, Mamá," Cota said.

María frowned at Matías and said, "You shouldn't bother Mr. Rodríguez, Matías. God knows, you children drive him crazy as it is."

Cota stopped what she was doing; the time had not yet come. She thought out loud: "Math is for those kind of people who don't know anything, anyway."

"Matías is odd, not the numbers," Juan said, as he traced a circle within a circle. The little snickering sound he made afterwards was meant to irritate Matías.

In the stillness that followed, María soaked in the beautifully intense maternal feeling that her children gave her. "You children don't know the joy I feel when I see all of you studying . . . trying to do well in school. There is no greater thing in this world than an education. Look at me . . . ignorant. Cleaning houses. No money."

"But you're happy, aren't you, Mamá?" Matías asked her.

"I'm happy when I'm with all of you. God gave me a

great gift when he gave me my children. But I'm not happy with the way my life has gone."

Cota stared disapprovingly at her mother. "Gone?" she asked her. "What do you mean, 'gone?'"

"Gone," María said, emphatically, as though closing out her life.

"You're not dead, Mamá," Cota said.

"There's no reason to talk of this," María told them, remembering the pain of her childhood and the years of marriage to Gonzalo. "I'm not happy with the way my life has turned out. But what else could I have expected?"

"You didn't love our father, did you?" Cota asked.

"No," María confessed quietly. "Not at the end."

"At first you did. When we were born," said Juan.

"Yes," María responded, remembering those days. "At first I did. I loved him very much. Then later . . . he seemed to go away from us."

"You have us," Juan said.

Matías raised his eyes to heaven, exaggerating, making fun of Juan.

María noticed him and said, "You don't have to do that, Matías. Juan is right. I do have the four of you. And that is enough."

Cota sensed the opening that María had given them. "That means," Cota squeezed herself in, "that you would do anything in the world for us. Right, Mamá?"

María clasped her hands, gently placing them on top of the table. "Wait until you have children. Then you'll know the love that parents have for their children. There is no greater love. . . . None."

"What about Pedro?" Matías interjected, laughing, stringing out the conversation, giving Cota plenty of time.

"Oh, be quiet, Matías," Cota said, taking her cue from Matías. "He's crazy."

Frances was not as astute. She had heard the opening and could not be patient. "Mamá . . ." Frances started to say.

Before Frances could continue, Cota interrupted her.

"Mamá," Cota said, holding up her hand to stop Frances, "we need to talk to you."

"Well, children," María replied, innocently, "that's what I'm here for . . . to listen to you."

The opening!

What was surprising to the rest of the children was how Cota could manipulate the conversation and then act as though it were a spontaneous happening. "Mamá," she began, "we need a quilt and we need it for Friday. We're desperate."

"A quilt?" María asked. "Did I hear you say Friday? A quilt takes time. Months. Maybe a year. Why would you be desperate? We were talking of love. Now we're talking about being desperate for a quilt?" María glanced around the table. She remembered and it struck her. She said, "This is the quilt that you children were talking about before, isn't it?"

They lowered their eyes, patiently waiting to see what course María was going to take.

Frances could not contain herself. "We need it, Mamá," she cried.

"We need it for Friday," Cota added.

María stared down each one of them and finally said, "You're in trouble aren't you?" She felt her forehead and whispered, "This is making me sick."

Cota blushed and looked down and then raised her beautiful, pleading eyes to María and said, "Yes, Mamá."

María stood up and began to walk the floor. "In the back of my mind I knew it," she cried, tears coming to her eyes. "I knew it. I knew it. I knew it! Dear God!"

Now the children knew what tack María was going to take. They knew how long it would last and they knew the words by heart. All they had to do was wait for María to talk her heart out.

María continued walking around the room, talking to herself. "Answer me, God! Why us?" María sat down and wiped the tears with her apron. "What kind of trouble are you children in now?" she asked as she settled down.

The crisis was over. The children waited for María to regain her composure.

"WeneedtoraffleaquiltonFriday," Cota cried out, running the words together, trying to get that part out of the way as fast as she could.

María was numbed by the bombardment of words. "What on Friday? Raffling? Did I hear you say raffling? A quilt?" María asked them. "Where did you children get that idea?"

Matías had thought out a reply very carefully beforehand and the others had agreed that Matías would be the one to use it when the opportunity came. "From Father Non," he explained, blaming the priest.

"Heaven and earth!" María said, her head in her hands. Then a terrible thought came to her. She didn't want to ask, but she had to. "Did you sell tickets?" she demanded, not really wanting to know.

Cota was content to let someone else answer this question. Juan so far had not taken any lumps, so she looked toward him and Juan replied, "Yes, we made eleven dollars."

María looked to the heavens past the rafters and prayed: "May God have mercy on all of us."

"Lupito," Matías said, "bought tickets."

"Poor Lupito," María said. "As if he could afford it."

"And Herminia," Frances kept on.

"Poor Herminia. You went to everyone who's poor."

"No," Cota said, biting her lower lip. "Sheriff Manuel."

The last bit of information had fallen in place.

"Oh, my God!" María cried out loud. "The orphanage! What have you done? Now he holds in his hands evidence for the judge."

Self-satisfied that the conversation was going as planned, Matías said, "No, he doesn't, Mamá."

"We can make a quilt in four days, Mamá," Cota said.

"Children, be sensible. How can I sew a quilt in four days?" María replied. Then she made a quick mental calculation. "I would have to start tonight," she said. She shook her head at the absurdity of her statement. "With what? I don't have any wool."

"We would help you. Five people working night and day, Mamá," Cota said, desperately. "That would do it."

María replied emphasizing every word, "Don't you children understand that we do not have the wool?"

The children ignored her. They didn't tell María, but they knew that they could get the wool and with Father Non's help. Matías eagerly took out his pattern and showed it to his mother. "Look at this," he said, proudly smoothing out the worn paper on the table.

María looked at it and turned it first one way, then another. She was not able to make heads nor tails of the pattern. Finally, she cried out, "Why must it be so much work? Why not simple?"

"Because, Mamá," Cota said, "that is the drawing that we showed them."

"And that's why they bought the tickets," added Matías.

Cota knew that María would accept any challenge. She said, "Unless you can't make the quilt, Mamá . . . Maybe it's too much."

María looked over the drawing on the table and said, "It's not that I can't do it. It's that we don't have the time." Then turning to Cota she asked, "Do you think you can delay the raffle for a few months? Tell them I'm sick . . . No. That would be lying. Listen to this," she said, excited that she had found a solution. "We'll all go. We'll all go and see Sheriff Manuel—tell him the truth. And Lupito and Herminia. Tell them that the quilt will be ready in six weeks—something like that. Six weeks, at the least. We'll give them their money back if they want it. Everything will be done honestly."

Cota shot up from her chair and raised a hand in victory. The conversation had gone exactly as they had planned it. "I knew my Mamá would help us out," she shouted.

"My Mamá has never let us down," Frances cried out proudly.

"My Mamá is the best Mamá in the world," Juan cried

out also.

And Matías stood on his chair and tooted an imaginary bugle and Juan stood on his chair and acted like he was playing a saxophone. Frances danced around the table, humming a tune, and then broke into a song about how great her mother was. María continued to wipe the tears from her eyes with her apron.

Benjamín Argumedo was standing by the edge of the ditch. Through the window he could see the spectacle of Matías and Juan tooting imaginary horns, Frances dancing around the table singing and Cota raising her fist in victory and shouting out María's name. He wondered what was going on inside. Seeing the happy scene made him happy also. The anticipation of being close to María made him shiver.

Argumedo studied the scene through the window for a while and waited for the celebration inside to end. Then he strode to the porch, climbed the steps and walked to the door. He took off his hat, wiped his mouth with the back of his hand and tasted the bitter lemon that he had anointed on himself after his shower. He took the index finger of his right hand and scrubbed his teeth with it, feeling for the grit of charcoal from the old fire that he had used to clean his teeth. He inspected his finger when he was done, and rubbed it clean on his thigh. He blew air through the small spaces between his teeth, making a hissing sound, like a snake.

When he was sure that he looked presentable, he knocked on the door. While he waited for María, he wet both index fingers on his tongue and very carefully used them to smooth down his eyebrows. He stood rigidly at the door waiting for María. He lost his courage when the door opened. He was about to run off, when he saw María and could not help but be impressed by her. Sensing the goodness in her character made him settle down.

María, anticipating at first that it would be Pedro, had fought the children back and had sent them to their rooms. When she saw Argumedo, she was surprised. She turned back to see about the children. They had left their rooms and were at the far end of the hallway, waiting to insult Pedro.

"Are you the one who set the fire?" María asked Argumedo as he stood at the front door.

Before he could think, Argumedo replied, "Yes. Do I smell?"

María said, "No." Then she took a whiff of him and said, "As a matter of fact, you smell like an orchard in bloom."

Argumedo swallowed the nervous spittle in his mouth and said, "My name is Benjamín Argumedo and I've . . . I've. Well, I've . . . I've . . ."

The children crept up to stand behind María. They were peeking around María's skirts and giggling, making it more difficult for Argumedo to speak.

At last Argumedo said, "This is worse than battle," and the children broke up in laughter.

"Be quiet, children," María scolded them. "Can't you see the gentleman is having a difficult time?"

Argumedo held his fringed hat at his chest with both hands and not knowing what else to do, bowed deeply from the waist, causing the children to giggle even more. "I," Argumedo said through the children's laughter, "I . . . came. Came. Went. No! Came. . . ."

María understood Argumedo's predicament. A stranger in a close-knit town calling on a widow and bashful around women to boot. "What is it that we can do for you, Mr. Argumedo?" María asked him gently, trying to ease the man's discomfort.

Argumedo nodded his head and pushed his wavy black hair back on his head, reviving the smell of lemons in the air. "Yes," he replied and then he remembered that Genoveva Marín had asked him to use her name. "Genoveva," Argumedo informed María, pointing with his hat toward town where Genoveva Marín lived.

"You live with Genoveva?" María inquired, politely completing the thought.

"Yes," Argumedo answered. His forehead felt as cold as

ice. He was relieved that María had understood what he was trying to say.

"Genoveva is a very nice lady," María said and Argumedo agreed. "Are you here on an errand for Genoveva? Do you wish to come in?"

"No errands," said Argumedo, walking in tentatively, taking in the children at a glance, then wondering why the house smelled so much of tobacco and camphor. He would have turned around and gone home at that moment, but his legs betrayed him, trembling as they were.

"You must sit down," María told him. "You look pale in the light. Are you in any kind of trouble?"

Argumedo shook his head and, not wanting to admit his nervousness, said, "No. I'm perfectly well. I'd rather stand for now. If you don't mind."

"We can stand here if you want," María replied with great compassion. In spite of Argumedo's paleness and his composure, María liked him instantly. Like Genoveva Marín, she could sense in Argumedo a man of good character.

There followed a silence in which neither Argumedo nor María had anything to say. They could both feel the attraction to each other. At a loss for words, not wanting the silence to ruin the effect of the moment, Argumedo asked her, "Do you like Mexican candy?"

The children began to giggle again and Cota said, "Mamá, he smells like lemons."

María ignored the children and answered, "Yes. We all like Mexican candy."

Argumedo said, "Me too," causing the children to break out in laughter.

María turned to the children, quieted them down and sent them to Cota's room while Argumedo stood and looked around uncomfortably, feeling like an intruder.

"Don't feel bad for the children. Sometimes I need to be alone with an adult," María explained. "And they don't mind it when I send them away. They just act that way."

"That makes me feel a lot better. I didn't want to inter-

fere with the family. After all, I realize that I came unannounced."

"Don't feel bad about that either," María remarked. "It
seems that people do drop in unannounced in San Diego."

"In all our culture," Argumedo responded, starting to
feel somewhat better.

"That's true," María agreed. She was enjoying making
small talk with the gentleman.

"You don't know how much better that makes me feel,"
Argumedo said. He cleared his throat nervously. "María,"
he confessed, "I came to see you the other day but I could
not get up the nerve to do so. You can see by now that I'm
all thumbs when it comes to women. Well, I almost ran
over you the other day and . . ."

María waited for Argumedo to continue. She did not yet
know whether to be flattered or not by his visit. When she
noticed Argumedo struggling once more for words she
asked, "And?"

Argumedo's words seemed to him to come out of someone else's mouth, not his own, when he said, "And . . . I
thought that you were the most beautiful woman that I had
ever seen."

María tried with all her power not to blush, but her
defenses were no match for such admiration. She turned a
bright red. She felt faint. She felt the ice in her skin. She
moved gently away from the door in case Argumedo still
wanted to leave.

Argumedo could not believe that he had been so bold.
He put his hat back on and tightened the string around his
chin. "There," he sighed with relief, "I said it and nothing
happened. I didn't die. I am amazed. Absolutely nothing
happened."

"You're very forward," María said, having regained her
composure somewhat. "Is that why you came? To tell me
that?"

Argumedo gazed intensely into María's eyes for the
first time and felt the surge of love come over him like a
spiritual wash. For a moment he could not talk, paralyzed

as he was in his tracks, unable to move or breathe. The light-headedness that he had felt when he first saw María at the door was nothing compared to what he was feeling now.

María took him by the hand and led him into the kitchen. By the time Argumedo sat down, he felt his strength back, but his mind was a blank. What he was experiencing was the beginning delirium of love

Chapter Twelve

Argumedo was gradually recovering his senses, focusing on the most beautiful face he had ever seen. He raised his hand as if to make a point, but he could think of nothing to say. Finally his mind cleared. He started with a bashful grin that turned into a smile and that made María feel a certain liking for him.

"Argumedo," María said, "you are a . . ." She paused, not sure of what to say. She did not want to destroy the moment.

"You can say it," Argumedo insisted. "A fool?"

María wrung her hands on her apron and thought for a while, studying Argumedo with curiosity. A fool he was not. "No, you're not," she said, finishing her thoughts. "You're a gentleman. I can tell."

"Thank you, María," Argumedo answered, relieved. He took his hat and spun it slowly through his hands. "You must not think that I'm like this all the time," he said.

"Aren't you?" María teased him, smiling. If she had known him better, she would have burst out laughing.

"No . . . no," Argumedo replied, being so serious that María felt even more like laughing. Then a dejection took hold of him and he said, "I'm afraid I've made a mess of everything."

"No, you haven't," María reassured him. She did not

want him to feel uncomfortable, not in her presence. Trying to make him more at ease, she asked, "Where is the bicycle? The whole town is talking about it."

Argumedo snapped his fingers. "I knew there was something I wanted to tell you. I no longer own the bicycle," he replied excitedly.

María leaned back in surprise. "What?" she asked. "What happened?"

Argumedo sat up proudly. "I traded it to Juan Garibay," he replied.

"What?"

"I am now the proud owner of the barn at the edge of town . . . and the land it stands on. And not only that, Juan Garibay threw in the complete set of tools that a farrier needs . . . old tools, but complete."

María could hardly contain her curiosity. "Are you a farrier?"

Argumedo leaned back, put his thumbs under his arms and said, "I'm a farrier, and I'm a military man."

"How exciting!" María exclaimed. "So you're going to be the farrier in town. We need one."

María got up and brought back coffee for the both of them. She took a sip and looked out the window, but did not see Pedro standing in the darkness.

Outside, the light from the window coming up to his knees, Pedro had removed his hat and was vigorously rubbing his head. He could not believe what he was seeing. His beloved María seemed to him to be very serious conversation with Benjamín Argumedo. She seemed to be enjoying herself. Argumedo was very serious with her, Argumedo drinking coffee from Pedro's favorite cup. Pedro tightened his mouth in anger. He bent over to one side to see through the window at a better angle, his eyes never wavering, studying the scene for any clues as to what was going on. After a short pause, he murmured with contempt, "I hate this man."

Pedro's heart was broken. He took one last look through the window and could hardly stand to see María laughing with Argumedo. Had he seen her touch his shoulder? How unfaithful a woman could be, he thought, as he walked away, his hat in his hand. Although he reminded himself that a man risks losing a woman if he does not strike quickly, when it came to María he could not put into words what his heart felt.

Argumedo could hardly control his excitement on the way home. He knew he could not sleep. When he saw the light still on at the depot, he decided to stop to greet Lupito. Maybe the conversation would settle him down. He walked up the stairs to the loading platform and could see Lupito huddled over the telegraph machine. Next, he heard the clamor from the machine.

Argumedo's years in the revolution had brought him face to face with many telegraphers, but that had not prepared him for Lupito's speed. Argumedo's mind was awhirl, trying to decipher Lupito's message. He could catch a few words here and there: Love. Flor. Laredo. Money.

Argumedo went inside and found Lupito stooped at his desk. And when he asked Lupito if it was closing time, Lupito stared at the wall in front of him and said that the dimension of time was of no significance to him now. What he needed was not time, that he had plenty of. He replied that what he needed for his happiness was money. Lupito's love-by-telegram, Flor, was desperate for money for her sick mother.

Lupito asked for advice. "You have seen the world, Argumedo. But me?" Lupito asked Argumedo. "I know nothing. What is to become of me if I don't send the money? Do you think I should send the money? Should I go to Laredo?"

Argumedo could only admire Lupito's innocence. He said, "Lupito, whether you should or not is not the question. You will. Believe me, you will. You are in love".

"I must get the money," Lupito said, wringing his hands.

As Lupito checked to see that the door was locked, he and Argumedo heard Celestino, the milkman, approaching

114

on horseback through the darkness. They greeted Celestino, who was on his way home from delivering his milk and finished with his nightly drinking bout. Celestino leaned over on Relincho, courteously waving his hat at them. Celestino kept going over to the side, almost falling from the horse, but recovering as Relincho quickly shifted his own weight to throw the rider back on the saddle.

Looking in Celestino's direction, Argumedo and Lupito saw in the distance that Juan Garibay had turned his automobile's lights on at the farmhouse so that his children could ride the bicycle. Shortly, they noticed the squeals of pleasure coming from the children.

"I traded it," Argumedo said to Lupito when Lupito looked curiously at him. "I now own the barn at the edge of town and the land that goes with it. Plus the old farrier tools that Juan Garibay threw in to complete the transaction."

That night Lupito did not sleep. He stayed awake, alternately worrying about his love and then counting the money that he had been so diligently saving for his old age. He also counted the money that he had stolen from under his mother's bed while she was asleep.

Chapter Thirteen

*E*arly the next morning, Juan Garibay was walking in his pasture when he noticed four shorn sheep. Someone had done a horrible job of shearing them and taken the wool. He turned around and headed for home. Before he got there, he saw his children run out of the house. He saw Anna, the oldest, jump on the bicycle and pedal away like the wind, followed on foot by Petra, and then Antonio and then little Gabriel. He hurried to the front yard, between his pasture and the house, and tried to call at his children, but they were gone and the sound of his voice could not reach them. He went inside, took the car keys and went back out to the garage. Carolina was doing the laundry inside the shed next to the garage. She had not seen the children run out of the house.

Juan Garibay poked his head into the shed and said, "The children are gone with the bicycle."

Carolina could not hear over the noise she was making with the washboard. She stopped when she heard Juan Garibay's mumble and looked around to where he was standing at the doorway. "What?" she asked.

"The children," Juan Garibay said. "They are gone. Gone to the dump, I presume."

Carolina massaged the arthritis in her hands. She stood by the wash basin, the soapy water rolling down from her elbows all the way to her fingertips and falling on the wooden floor. "I wish," she said, "that they would not go there. It's such a filthy place. Mark my words, as much as we love them and protect them, they will pick up something one day and get very sick. It's one big worry."

"I know," Juan Garibay replied, already feeling guilty for what he knew Carolina was going to say next.

"You're the one who tells them to be more independent," she admonished him. "You're the one who tells them to be more like María's children. Self-reliant, you say. . . . And look at them now. What are they going to do now that they have the bicycle?"

"I did not mean for them to go to the dump," Juan Garibay explained once more to her. "I wanted them to be more on their own. The bicycle has nothing to do with it. I love to give my children gifts."

"But this is what they figured you meant. And you haven't told them to stop."

"I . . ." he stammered uselessly. He knew that he could not bear to discipline his children, could not deny them the joy of playing in the dump.

"I know you are afraid . . . for them," Carolina came back. She went over to him and reached out and touched his face. She apologized. "I shouldn't get after you. You are such a fine man. I shouldn't say anything. I'm afraid also."

Juan Garibay played with the car keys, looked down at them and said, "Carolina, you are so kind. But I fear for them after I'm gone. What will they do when I die? They are so innocent. A father wants his children to be independent."

Carolina removed his hat and kissed him on top of the head and went back to the washboard. She said, "And where are you going so early?"

"To see Sheriff Manuel," he replied. "Someone has sheared four of my sheep."

⊁

María's children had taken all night to pack the wool from Juan Garibay's sheep in burlap and had hidden it in the shed. They were to take it out in small pieces as time would let them, introducing the wool in small amounts to María.

And when María noticed that the pile of wool being washed, dried and carded in the house was getting larger and larger, she asked where the wool came from. She was told that it was found here and there, stuck to the barbed-wire fences where the sheep rubbed themselves, on the ground where the sheep playfully chewed the wool off each other. "Normal shedding," Matías had explained.

Juan had been instructed to say, "All you have to do is grab a sheep and all this wool comes off in your hand."

"You would be amazed," Cota would say, "how much wool we can find just walking around."

"I wish I had known that before," María replied.

Ж

Lupito sent off his telegram to Flor as soon as he arrived at the depot the next morning. He needed to know how much money she required. Lupito did not have long to wait for a reply. Flor answered immediately:

> HAVE BEEN WAITING ALL NIGHT. NEED FOUR
> HUNDRED DOLLARS. LOVE YOU ETERNALLY.
> WISH I WAS IN YOUR ARMS. YOUR BELOVED
> ALWAYS. FLOR.

Lupito's disappointment made his heart weak as he read the message. He went over and started coffee and then sat at his desk and counted his money once more, as if counting it again would make it grow. The counting was futile. He already knew he was one hundred dollars short.

He sent a message back to Flor informing her of the shortage, begging forgiveness. Her reply was short and to the point. She knew it was a small fortune for a telegra-

118

pher, but she needed the four hundred. She demanded that he look for more.

Lupito sat down with his coffee, looked out the window and saw María's children coming toward the depot. He could see them talking. He did not know that the children had seen Anna Garibay riding the most beautiful bicycle that they had ever seen.

Lupito immediately thought of the quilt when he saw María's children. If he won the quilt, maybe he could sell it and get some money. But then he realized that no quilt would be worth very much. He still needed money from somewhere else.

In his desperation, he thought consecutively of stealing, of fraud, of borrowing. He went to the ticket counter and unlocked the drawer. He counted out twelve dollars—six months worth of tickets. Now he needed eighty-eight more.

The telegraph machine began a slight whir and then came to life with its clickety-clack. Lupito put his coffee cup away and began to write furiously.

It read:

> LUPITO. IF I CAN'T HAVE THE MONEY THEN I
> HAVE A GENTLEMAN FRIEND WHO WILL GIVE IT
> TO ME. BUT HE IS ASKING FOR MY COMPLETE
> LOVE IN RETURN. MUST SAVE MY MOTHER.
> ETERNAL LOVE IN YOUR ARMS EVERY NIGHT.
> FLOR.

Lupito read and re-read the note many times, and each time it affected him more, multiplying his despair. Finally, when he could read no more, he sat down and began to sob quietly.

The children could see Lupito rocking back and forth on his chair in front of the telegraph machine, crying, wiping both his eyes with his fists. Slowly, without making any noise, they walked to the door and opened it. They tiptoed inside, careful not to disturb Lupito, not knowing what Lupito was going through.

Lupito stopped crying and saw them as a haze through his tears.

"What happened, Lupito?" Cota asked, worried about him.

"My beloved . . . I am about to lose her. I need money. I need to send her money. You don't know about problems until you've been in love," Lupito said, his voice cracking.

Juan was too young to understand the vagaries of love. "Why don't you just take Herminia?" he asked Lupito. "She loves you. Why don't you marry her? Why go away for a woman?"

"Because he's in love with this other one," Frances told Juan. "Don't you know anything about love?"

"As much as Herminia loves you," Cota thought out loud, "I bet that she would give you the money."

Lupito could not believe what Cota had said. "Even though it would be for another woman?" he asked, full of astonishment.

"Probably," Cota agreed. "That is what is beautiful about true love, as our mother would say."

"But how could I ask for such a favor?" Lupito inquired. The more he thought about it, the more absurd it seemed. "This is incredible. I wouldn't know how to ask for such a thing."

"I'm not sure if Herminia will lend you the money," said Cota, "but she will think very hard on it."

"She probably will give it to you," Frances said.

"Give it to me?" Lupito asked. Then he remembered the children's penchant for word games. He said, "No. You're trying to make a fool of me. I won't let you."

"Well," Matías informed Lupito, "you do what you want."

"We won't help you if you don't want it," Cota said.

"I'm desperate," Lupito told them. And he was. He thought a few moments while the children watched him crack all his knuckles. He agreed, saying, "As much as I'll probably regret it, I'll accept your help."

Matías saw the opportunity to gather a future favor. He

decided to play with Lupito's emotions. He said, "We don't know. We might not be able to help you after all."

Lupito panicked when it appeared that the children's offer for help was being withdrawn. He pleaded: "Will you help me, please? If you help me I'll do anything for you.

"Anything?" Matías asked. He had already thought of a favor.

"Yes," Lupito cried, holding a hand to his head where his pulse was throbbing. "Anything."

"Anything, anything?" Matías insisted.

"Yes," Lupito cried out. "Anything, anything!"

"Swear it? On a Bible?" Matías forced the issue.

Lupito gulped and said, "Yes. Swear on a Bible."

"You don't have a Bible," Matías said, looking on top of Lupito's desk. "Do you have a Bible in one of the drawers?"

Lupito, in his desperation, said, "All I have is the Telegrapher's Manual in the middle drawer."

"That'll do," said Cota, opening the drawer and taking out the plain brown manual with the drawing of the telegraph key and a finger poised over it. She stuck it in front of Lupito and Lupito swore on the manual that he would do anything the children asked.

⊣⊢

Sheriff Manuel took out his watch and saw that it was close to noon. He stuck his watch back in his pocket and hurriedly searched around the area of Juan Garibay's pasture where the sheep had been sheared.

Ever since they had left the courthouse in two cars and gone to pick up Don Lupe, the mayor, he had been thinking that all he was doing was being courteous to Juan Garibay, thinking that what he and Juan Garibay and the mayor were doing was hopeless, looking for a grain of evidence in a pasture with grass growing almost to their waist.

Sheriff Manuel pushed the grass aside as he walked, looking back to the farmhouse. He saw Juan Garibay slowly picking his way back home. To his left, toward the road that cut through the pasture and about one hundred feet away was Don Lupe, the mayor, looking about. The sheriff could see the short mayor bend down to pick something up, disappearing into the grass every time he did so. Presently, he would straighten out and reappear, look at something in his hand and then throw that something away.

Sheriff Manuel reached the fence on the south end of the pasture, close to María's house. Here he found a small clearing in the grass, the ground showing signs of a struggle. He was studying the site carefully when something unusual caught his eye. He stopped and studied a coiled string partially imbedded into the soil. He knelt down in the tall grass and picked at the string. Gently he took the string in his fingers and pulled on it, bringing it up. He got up and held it in the air in front of him. Sheriff Manuel called for Juan Garibay and the mayor to come over. The three men inspected the string and the kernels and wondered what it was.

"Some type of something," Don Lupe, the mayor, speculated. He was not about to be definite.

Juan Garibay studied the string of kernels and pronounced it to be "an amulet. Something that one would use for a ritual."

"I'll keep it as evidence for later," the sheriff said, wrapping the string around his hand.

Don Lupe, exercising his prerogative as mayor by repeating whatever he heard, said, "Keep it as evidence for later, Manuel."

As it always did, the mayor's repetitive nature irritated Sheriff Manuel. "I just said that," he snapped.

The mayor, not to be outdone, replied, "I just said that too."

Juan Garibay was too serious to take note of the exchange, being more worried about his sheep. He let out an unsettled sigh and said, "Well, we've done about as much as we can do." He turned to Sheriff Manuel and shook his hand and then to Don Lupe and shook his. He walked away slowly, threading his way through the tall grass. At the road waiting for Juan Garibay were his children, who had just run into the pasture back from playing in the dump. Anna was riding the bicycle, having not let anyone else ride it. Sheriff Manuel and Don Lupe could hear the rest of the children complaining to Juan Garibay about Anna.

Chapter Fourteen

When Father Non's old rooster opened one eye, he thought he saw the red brilliance of the early morning sun rays fanning up from behind the steeply gabled church roof. He was, in fact, being deceived by his cataracts. Immediately he dusted himself off, pecked his tail clean and strutted out from under the pomegranates to climb the roof of the hen house. Once he reached the top, he let out a sound, frail and weak, that mimicked his ill health. No one who heard him, especially Father Non, had the heart to tell him that it was early afternoon.

María heard the anemic cry of the rooster while she stacked the last of the dishes in the cupboard. She was thinking of Argumedo and where last night's visit might lead to. Argumedo was certainly a handsome man, sure of himself—not at first, she had to admit, but later he had gained confidence and was very at ease with her. She knew that she was at ease with him. By the end of the visit, she felt as though she had known him for a long time.

Earlier in the morning, after the children had had their breakfast, they asked María about Argumedo. They liked him, they told María. Cota had followed that conversation by giving María a certain look that told María, woman to woman, that Cota approved of Argumedo and that the children would allow their mother to continue seeing him.

The rooster had just finished crowing when the children returned from playing in the dump. On their way home, Don Napoleón, the postmaster, had stopped them to tell them that he needed to talk to María. María knew what that was about. Don Napoleón's Christmas gift for the children had arrived.

The children also brought with them the news of the bicycle that they had seen Anna Garibay riding.

"It looked like Argumedo's bicycle," Frances said.

"That was Benjamín Argumedo's bicycle," María told them.

"We thought we recognized it," a dejected Cota said.

"Now the bicycle is theirs?" Matías asked.

"Yes," María replied. "I was in such a hurry this morning," she continued, "that I didn't tell you. Argumedo traded the bicycle for the barn at the edge of town. And Juan Garibay also gave Argumedo his old farrier tools. Argumedo is going to be the farrier in San Diego."

María had expected that this news would excite the children as much as it had her. But instead, the children seemed preoccupied with something else. It took María's motherly instincts a few moments of silence to figure out what was bothering the children. She could sense their disappointment at having seen Juan Garibay's children with the bicycle.

"Children," she said, "don't be envious of Juan Garibay's children. Look at everything that you have."

Matías said, "We don't have anything, Mamá."

"Nothing," Juan spat out. María could see how disappointed he was.

"Mamá?" Cota asked. "Why is it that some people have everything and some don't have anything?"

"That's not for us to know," María responded. She felt for them, wished that she had it in her power to buy each one a bicycle. But that was impossible. "Maybe Father Non would know. I surely don't. But let me tell you children something. Don't envy the things that people own. There are many other things that are more important."

"You're going to tell us about health, right Mamá?" Cota said to her.

They knew the lecture by heart, having heard it so many times.

María had to laugh at how well the children knew her. "That's the only thing I can tell you. Your health. Education is also so important. I can't tell you how important it is. And look," María kept on, "look at us. We have each other."

"Oh, Mamá," Cota said.

After the children ate, they told María that they would return to play at the dump. All that was left for María to do was to clean the kitchen and then get ready to go see Don Napoleón.

Alone with her thoughts, she brought up Argumedo again, and this time she felt his warmth. Very fleetingly, she gave herself the luxury of thinking what it would be like to be in love, to be loved by a genuine man.

Then, while wiping her hands clean on her apron, she wondered what Sheriff Manuel, Juan Garibay and Don Lupe had been doing walking Juan Garibay's pasture that morning. She had seen the sheriff pick something up from the ground next to the fence, show it to the other two men, then roll it in his hands and stash it in his pocket.

Finally she was through in the kitchen. She went into her room, combed her hair, powdered her nose and picked up her bonnet and her purse, and started off to the post office.

A block from the post office, Pedro startled her by jumping out from an alley between two abandoned buildings that had been destroyed by the month of rain. At first she had thought it was one of the drunken codgers trying to scare her, so she had jumped into the street. When she recognized Pedro, she was so angry that she felt like telling him not to ever bother her again.

"You scared me!" she said, between clenched teeth. "You almost scared me to death." Then the most cutting of remarks: "Why must you bother me so much?"

Pedro winced on hearing María's words. He felt the

pain that they caused his heart. "I've been waiting for you in hiding all morning long," he said with an urgency that almost made him seem comical—his face contorted in mental anguish, his upper lip raised to expose his solitary fang, his little eyes flicking about like an unwanted animal. He was looking into the sun, shading his eyes by pulling the brim of his hat down over them. "Thank God you are here. I thought that you would never show up. I was about to go see you. I was that desperate. Look at me. Away from my duties. If Father Non knew he would be very angry. I couldn't sleep a wink last night, thinking."

"Thinking of what?" María inquired, curious to know what had gotten into the sacristan.

Pedro said, "Look at me. Old and fat."

By now María had gotten back on the sidewalk and had regained her composure. She felt sorry for having hurt Pedro's feelings.

María continued on her way, Pedro walking beside her. He had taken his old hat off and held it over his broken heart. She could hear him nervously sucking on his tooth. "What's gotten into you? Why are you acting so strange?"she said.

Pedro could only wiggle his head. No words would come out.

"Say something," María insisted.

Finally, Pedro blurted out the words. "Last night . . ." he said. "How . . . how . . . how could you? Argumedo. Argumedo in the house with you. Coffee?"

"Sure," María replied. "Argumedo was there. He came to visit. We had a nice visit."

"Oh, María," Pedro cried, "how you have hurt me!"

"Why?" María asked.

"Infidelity!" Pedro shouted. "Can't you see?"

María stopped and turned to Pedro and said, "If you ever say that again, I'll never speak to you. I will never have you in my house again."

Pedro realized that he had gone too far. Infidelity was not the right word. "Unfaithful," he said and María threatened to banish him from her house again.

Pedro knew that he had come to that moment that he had so long evaded. He drew from his heart all the courage that was in him and he faced María and asked, "Do you love me or not?"

"No," María said slowly for emphasis, "I don't love you."

"Then, at least, you care for me?" Pedro insisted. "Give me something . . . some hope."

"I care for you as a friend," María was good enough to say.

Pedro admitted to having a confession. "María," he said, "it looks more and more that you did not know that I love you. That I went to your house to be with you. I would die to be with you, María."

María could not believe what she was hearing from Pedro. Suddenly, he had opened up and revealed his feelings. "You are very forward today," she said to him. "What has gotten into you?"

"The final desperation!" Pedro announced.

"Have you talked it over with Father Non?" María said, trying to get Pedro away from her.

Pedro slapped himself with his hat. "I did, María," he replied. "And you know him. If you only knew what he said, how long the scolding took. The only thing he didn't do was take the broom to me."

"I wish I had known how serious you were, Pedro," María said in retrospect. She was at the post office door. She stopped and Pedro stopped beside her. "I had no idea that you took your visits so seriously. I thought. . . . Well, if I had known, I would have stopped it. The children spoke to me about you, but I put that off as jealousy on their part. I assumed . . ."

Pedro cut her off in mid sentence. "Assumed?" he cried. "What else could you have assumed? Except that I love you so much, María." Then he grew desperate. "What am I to do?" he agonized. And once started, he kept on. "And I had everything wrong about you? You never had intentions of marrying me?" Pedro cried out.

"Never," María replied. She was so emphatic and the rejection was so much for the sacristan that he reeled back on his heels and almost fell backwards. The rejection brought a tear to his eyes.

The old codgers who had been listening from across the street, who had moved there for protection from the afternoon sun, began to talk among themselves, the sounds of their voices like tumbleweeds rolling across the street.

"Give the man a chance, María," one of them grumbled.

"Look at how he cries like a baby," another one of them said.

"That is the problem with unrequited love," Gumercindo said, his shaky voice projecting across the street. "It saps a man . . . makes him cry like a child."

"I don't know who I'm going to marry," María spoke to the men across the street. "If I ever marry. And I don't want anyone asking me about it either. I'll get married to whomever I please . . . whenever I please."

The codgers gave María a warm applause.

"See, Pedro," one of them shouted. "See what you're problem is?"

"That," Gumercindo said to his fellow codgers, "was spoken like a woman of her word . . . a woman that knows where she stands." They all agreed by nodding.

At the post office, María found her box empty, as usual. The only sign of life in the building was the sound of constant snoring coming from Don Napoleón's office. María rechecked the box to make sure she had not missed anything, and then she went over to Don Napoleón's office and knocked quietly on the door.

"Don Napoleón," she whispered through the door, a sense of urgency in her voice. She wanted to get away from Pedro, who was watching her from the entryway.

She waited to hear Don Napoleón snoring once more before she repeated herself, this time with more force. "Don Napoleón!" Then she heard the squeak of the chair spring as Don Napoleón leaned forward. The she heard him grunt as he stood up and stretched. She placed her ear on the door and heard him imploring God's and his long-gone mother's blessings for his wife, for his children, for a long life. María heard him smack his lips as he walked to the door.

"Who is it?" he yawned.

"María, Don Napoleón," she answered on the other side of the door.

"María. María. María. María," he repeated over and over again, and then María heard what could possibly be the longest yawn she would ever hear in her life.

"Yes, María," she said again.

Pedro continued to stand at the entrance. He said, "Knock again, María."

María gave Pedro a disapproving frown and knocked again.

"All right. All right," Don Napoleón was heard to say. "I'm coming."

He opened the door, looked at María standing in front of him and then gave Pedro a sideways glance. "What is he doing here?" he asked María, pointing at Pedro with his thumb.

"I don't want to talk about him," María said, walking into the office.

"It's a shame that we have people like Pedro in this town," Don Napoleón complained, looking at Pedro and shaking his head. "People with nothing else to do than to bother the honest women of this town."

Pedro lowered his head, his hat still at his heart and, as if begging for pity, he raised his eyes and said, "Everyone is against me now."

"Every man creates his own troubles. That's in the Bible. Ask your employer, Father Non," said Don Napoleón.

"He's suffering from unrequited love," Gumercindo yelled from across the street.

Don Napoleón walked to the post office door and escorted Pedro out. He looked across the street and yelled, "What other type of love do you think Pedro could ever have? Who would ever return his love?" Once again the codgers all agreed.

Don Napoleón closed and locked the door. He pointed at the lock with his thumb. "That way," he explained to María, "we won't be bothered by all these people wanting to look into their empty mail boxes."

He extended his hand in front of him and swept it toward the office. "In here," he said. Don Napoleón showed María the chair he wanted her to sit in, right in front of his old desk. He went around and sat at his chair, and twiddling his thumbs said, "I see the children gave you the message."

María's eyes brightened. "Did the postcards arrive?" she asked.

Don Napoleón laughed and said, "What if I told you yes? Would you be happy?"

María leaned forward and smiled. "So happy," she said. "In light of what has happened to them recently, you couldn't understand how happy."

Don Napoleón remembered the day he had told María that he had sent off for the post cards for the children. "How long has it been?" he asked.

Although the memory of that day was painful, María replied quickly. "The day after Gonzalo's funeral. How well I remember walking in here and seeing you. How nice of you to think of us at a time when we needed help. You knew that the children loved to look at the postcards."

"Yes, I did," Don Napoleón said. "I sat here after the funeral, and I could hear Gonzalo's voice. How proud he was of the children. How many times Gonzalo had told me how they loved to look at postcards from far away places."

"It was so very nice of you," María insisted in her gratitude.

Don Napoleón felt defenseless in María's praise. "I did what any good postmaster would have done. I had a unique opportunity to order them."

"Did they arrive? Don't play with me, Don Napoleón," María said, smiling. "Did you get the postcards for the children or not?"

"Yes," Don Napoleón said and opened the drawer at the same time. "At long last they are here."

María asked, "Are they beautiful?"

Don Napoleón handed her the envelope with the postcards of San Antonio that he had ordered for the children. "Beautiful?" he said. "Why they are so beautiful that when I looked at them I wanted to go to see Lupito, get a ticket and ride to San Antonio to see for myself."

María opened the envelope and took out the postcards. "They are beautiful," she said, studying each one of them. Then, while still studying them, she asked, "I wonder why it took so long?"

Don Napoleón, frowned, leaned forward on his chair and said, "That's another story. I'm ashamed to admit it, being in the postal business, but we do have some thieves in our profession. Apparently someone stole my original quarter out of the envelope."

"And they still sent the postcards? Wasn't that nice of them?"

"I sent them another quarter," Don Napoleón explained.

"I'm so sorry for that. The children and I will always be in your debt, Don Napoleón," María said, placing the postcards inside the envelope. "I'll give them to the children for Christmas," she informed him, "and I'll be sure to tell them that they came from you."

"Oh, no," Don Napoleón replied. "Don't mention my name. It was the least I could do for them. You know how much I care for them. I was just thinking this morning that the long delay turned out for the best. It turns out to be their Christmas."

María reopened the envelope and took a peek inside. She said, "They will love these. I can't thank you enough. Now to hide them. You know how they are about finding things."

"Yes. I know. And how are the children?" he asked.

"Oh," María replied, wearily, "you know how children can be. They're in trouble again."

Don Napoleón waved María's troubles away, making

light of them. "Little things," he said. "Nothing big."

"Still," María answered, "I worry."

Don Napoleón did not speak right away, but María could see that he had something on his mind. Then, he opened the desk drawer with a flourish, took out a Bible, threw it on top of his desk and said, "Worry? You think you have problems? Look at the Virgin Mary. Read it in this Bible," he told her, poking his finger on the Bible. "Look at all the problems her son caused her. He was abnormal since birth . . . went around speaking in tongues, saying things that nobody understood. Always answering in parables that we haven't unraveled to this day. Never worked a day in his life. Got up late and came home late. Running around with his friends. Starting a new religion. Thrown in jail. Getting crucified. Life is one big problem, María. Suffering . . . When you understand that life is one big problem followed by another big problem, with a little bit of happiness thrown in between, then you can enjoy life to its fullest."

"Thank you for those words," María said, comforted. "Sometimes, Don Napoleón," she continued, admiring the post master, "you make as much sense as Father Non. You should have been a priest."

"And what?" Don Napoleón asked, smiling, "miss out on parenthood?"

María excused herself, thanking Don Napoleón again for the postcards for the children. Don Napoleón shrugged away her gratitude and told her that it made him feel good that he had done it. He walked her to the door and unlocked it, letting a few of the codgers in.

⋈

The children were not at the dump this afternoon for once. Cota was sitting in Herminia's chair, swiveling from side to side, chewing a piece of gum that she had found underneath the chair. Matías was at Don Bruno's desk asking questions of the bald man with the black cigar. Juan and Frances were sitting in front of Herminia's desk while Herminia was standing at the counter acting as though she were heavily involved in the tax rolls. Her thoughts were with the message that the children had brought: Lupito needed money.

"Don Bruno?" Matías asked him.

Don Bruno was getting impatient with the children. "Don't bother me any more," Don Bruno replied in a huff. He took the cigar out of his mouth to talk. "Can't you see I'm working? And after the news that you children bring? What kind of news is that? That a man needs money?"

Matías ignored the man's irritability. "Don Bruno," he continued, knowing that the question that followed would infuriate the man, "some people say you steal the tax money."

Don Bruno, who had heard the rumor for so many years, turned red with anger, stuck the cigar firmly in his mouth and set his jaw. He spoke in an irritated voice muffled by the cigar. "Tell the people that if they go by my run-down house and see it, they'll know how much I steal. Let them see for themselves. It's all a lie. The people know that we don't collect taxes in San Diego. Then they blame me for stealing something that doesn't exist."

"There is no money to steal?" Matías persisted.

For now, Herminia felt it her duty to support Don Bruno. "There is no money," Herminia said.

"Son," Don Bruno began, "we haven't collected taxes in this town in the fifty years that I have been here."

Cota took the gum out of her mouth, inspected it, made a face and threw it into the trash can under the desk. "Then what do you do with the books?" Cota wanted to know. "You're always looking at the big books."

"We're just playing," Don Bruno said. "It's all a game."

"There are no taxes," Herminia explained. "There is no money."

"There is no money to steal," Don Bruno informed them.

"Still," Juan said, "the people say you steal the money."

"I wish I had the money to steal," Don Bruno replied,

chewing on his cigar. And then he said, "The only money we ever get is from the state. That pays our salaries, meager as they are. Now, run along and get out of here before you make me angrier than I am now. Go and tell Lupito to get his money from somewhere else."

"With all due respects, Don Bruno, we're here to see Herminia," Frances informed him.

"It's up to Herminia," Cota said.

Don Bruno glanced at Herminia to see what she was going to do. He took the cigar out of his mouth and placed it in the ash tray. "Well, then, leave me alone," Don Bruno said and lowered his head to his books.

Herminia came over and sat on the edge of her desk, thoughtfully watching Cota as Cota swiveled in the chair. Herminia was going over the request that the children had brought over from Lupito.

"So Lupito needs money?" she asked, finally, when she could think of nothing else.

Don Bruno perked his ears up. "Don't do it, Herminia," he said, not looking up from his work. "I know I'm repeating myself, but don't do it."

Herminia walked slowly around her desk, rubbing her large chin, contemplating her dilemma.

"The man is using you, Herminia," Don Bruno continued. "He doesn't love you. He just needs the money. As soon as you give him the money, he won't talk to you. As a matter of fact, later on he'll resent you for it."

Herminia kept walking slowly around her desk, ignoring everyone in the room. So deep in thought was she that when she decided to sit in her chair she crushed Cota. Herminia let out a squeal as she jumped up from her seat. At the same time Cota came out of the chair as though she had been thrown. Her brothers and sister began to laugh.

"I'm sorry," Herminia said, sitting back down. "It's just that I can't think straight. This is a problem that I have never had before."

"Don't," Don Bruno advised her.

Herminia sighed deeply as she thought of what to do,

letting out air for the longest time. She said, "If only he was mine. I would do anything on earth for him. I would scrub floors . . . pick cotton. Even kill. Anything . . . if only he were mine."

Don Bruno put the cigar back in his mouth and grumbled, "He only wants the money. You'll never see the money again."

Not only was Herminia confused, she was tired of Don Bruno's advice. "Oh, shut up," she snapped back. "Can't you see that it's tearing my heart apart just thinking about it?"

Herminia leaned forward on her desk and rested her head in her hands. The children, quiet now, concerned that Herminia was taking the situation so seriously, were standing together in front of the desk.

"Maybe it's better if we go," Cota said to Herminia.

Herminia looked up and, with tears in her eyes, said, "No. No. No. Please. Stay. It's not your fault."

"It's just that Lupito begged us to come," Frances told Herminia.

"He was crying," Juan added.

"Poor thing," Herminia reflected.

Cota, trying to make Lupito out as very sensitive, said, "You know how Lupito cries for everything."

"He needs fifty-eight dollars," Matías said.

"If he wins the raffle for the quilt and the turkey," Cota explained.

"And he's not going to win the turkey," Frances reminded them all, "because we are."

"If he doesn't win anything, he needs eighty-eight dollars," Matías said.

Don Bruno made a loud bull-like noise through his nose and said, "A fortune for someone on Herminia's salary. Almost all of her savings for her wedding."

"A human being needs help," Herminia replied. "That's all I can say. If he doesn't love me . . . well, I can't make him. I know I am ugly. But in my heart I care for everyone. . . . If only Lupito could understand that."

Cota wanted to make Herminia feel good about herself,

to show her that what was going on was not Herminia's fault. "He's dumb," she said. "Lupito is dumb. All he knows how to do is send telegrams real fast."

But Herminia was determined in her admiration for Lupito. "In many ways he's very smart, Cota."

"If he has a fault," Don Bruno reminded them, "he takes it from his mother, who always looked for perfect love."

"And he had it so close," Herminia answered, meaning, of course, herself.

The conversation had strayed enough that Cota had lost control. "Let's talk about the money and Lupito crying and all that," she said.

"Tell Lupito that I will give him the money," Herminia replied. "I'll take it to the depot tonight . . . and tell him . . ." she continued and then stopped to reflect.

"That what?" Cota asked.

"Tell him . . . nothing. What can I say that I haven't said already?"

The children began to run to the door when Don Bruno shouted at them, making them stop. "Where is the quilt that you children are raffling? Herminia might have forgotten but I haven't."

Cota stepped forward and put her hands on her hips in a defiant pose. "That's not till Friday," she said, as the other children wondered what she was going to answer. Then Cota hitched up her skirt and they all ran out.

And Don Bruno said, "Oh." Satisfied.

Chapter Fifteen

María was sitting at the sewing machine, pumping away as fast as she could, her two feet moving together in synchronous effort at the ankles. The heavy metal wheel underneath spun furiously like a runaway fly-wheel turning the upper smaller wheel by way of a round leather belt at an incredible rate of speed. The up and down motion of the needle was a blur. Her hands guided the pieces of cloth that she had assembled to sew for the cover on the quilt. She stopped only to gather more pieces of cloth, folding them together, making seams. She looked up to the wall and, taking her eyes off the needle, she saw the model of the quilt that Matías had drawn. "Never has anyone made a quilt that complicated," she said to herself.

The act of sewing, the gathering of the cloth before submitting it to the needle and thread had become so routine for her that her mind could wander to other things. How Gonzalo, her late husband, had been cut into disproportionate thirds by the train. Only Lupito had heard the overpowering screech as the iron wheels ground heavy metal flakes off the rails in the engineer's desperate attempt to stop before running over the drunken man stretched out across the rails. Only Lupito had been there to run out of the depot and had seen the original carnage. It had been up to Lupito to reform the man to look life-like, to pick up the feet and place them under the hem of the trousers, to pick up the head and place it inside the shirt collar.

María lowered her head and stared at the blur of the needle rising and lowering, spearing the thread into the cloth, her thoughts far away.

She closed her eyes in the agony of the thought of her husband's death, and then went back in time to the moment when Sheriff Manuel had knocked on her door in the middle of the night. She had awakened thinking that someone was trying to beat the house down and, alone, without the protection of her husband, she had run into Cota and Frances' room and had jumped into bed with them. The three females then ran into the boys room to wake them up.

The persistent knocking continued in María's head. She felt the house move in tremors. The agony in her heart began to rock her back and forth in the rhythm of the sewing machine. Her eyes clouded with tears from the aching. Her original feeling had been one of shame when she saw Gonzalo stretched out on the floor of the depot. Later, when they had transferred him to Dr. Benigno's office, she had felt awkward at being the center of attention.

With one hand she guided the cloth through the sewing machine. With the other she wiped her tears.

Shuddering at the top of a sigh, she hesitated with her feet, realizing that the cloth would not be sewed perfectly. She tried to stop it as it went under the needle. Her thumb was dragged underneath by the mechanical action of the feeding plate. Her thumb glided under the needle as it ascended, was held there for an instant as María watched in horror, as though it were someone else's thumb and not hers. The needle came down swiftly on the fingernail, through the flesh and bone, penetrating the thumb completely.

María let out a scream that reverberated through the house. Blood spurted from the wound. She tried to move her thumb but it had been impaled by the needle. Desperately, she tried to move the small wheel with her free hand, trying to raise the needle through and out of her thumb. The needle had pierced the bone. It was no use. She could not free herself. She cried in agony, stuck to the machine. She would have to wait for the children.

She passed out. The blood covered the entire table top of the sewing machine, ruining all her work and the hopes for the children's raffle.

)(

Cota sat in Lupito's chair in front of the telegraph machine. Frances was standing behind her, pushing the chair from side to side. Juan was sitting on the floor next to Cota. Matías was leaning on the desk top close to the telegraph machine, inspecting it, wondering how it worked. They were alone in the room. Lupito had been caught in the rest room. The children had laughed when they called him and he had to answer that he was occupied.

Lupito came out readjusting his pants, the starch in his wrinkled clothes gone. He walked over, pushed Cota out of his chair and sat down. He leaned over the desk on his elbows, wringing his hands nervously.

"What did Herminia say?" he asked, fearing the worst. Then, feeling as though his world had come apart, he stopped wringing his hands and announced, "Don't tell me. She refused. She said I was a scoundrel."

"No, Lupito," Cota informed him, "she's coming with the money tonight. She said for you to wait for her."

Upon hearing the news, there was a gradual change in Lupito, from a worried frown to an eventual smile. When the good news had taken hold, he sat up in his chair and grabbed the telegraph machine away from Matías. With a speed that amazed the children, he began to send his message to Laredo. When he was through, he enlarged his smile and waited for the reply. He did not have long to wait.

All of them looked patiently over Lupito's shoulder as

Lupito jotted down the letters clickety-clacking through the machine:

> MY DEAREST. KNEW YOU WOULD HELP. LOVE
> YOU SO MUCH. MOTHER WORSE. IF SHE DIES I
> HAVE NO PLACE TO GO. WILL YOU TAKE ME IN?
> SEND MONEY. LOVE FLOR.

Lupito stood up quickly and, not knowing how to express his great joy, began to pace the floor, his happiness ensured. "If I could," he said to the children, almost bursting with happiness, "I would kiss all of you. But you know that I'm not like my father. I am not a man to show too much emotion."

"Yes," Matías reminded him, "like you weren't showing emotion when you were crying like a dog stuck in a trap when you didn't have the money."

Lupito stopped his pacing, gave them a hard stare, and said, "That was then. This is now." And he stopped to wonder if his mother had found out yet that he had stolen the money. He stared at the telegram and read it over and over, blocking the children's presence from his mind.

"Well, Lupito," Cota said, bothering his concentration, "we've done what you asked. Now it's time for us to leave. We're going to see the turkey. Juan is in love with him."

"Be on your way," the ungrateful Lupito said, shooing them away. "The sooner the better."

But Matías was not one to forget. "Remember," Matías reminded Lupito as they got to the door, "that you promised to do anything we want you to do."

"A promise is a promise," Lupito agreed, waving them away, as though he would not dwell on it.

Cota stopped and reminded him. "Wait for Herminia. Don't forget."

"Forget?" Lupito replied, smiling broadly. "How can I forget?

"You're a fool, Lupito," Frances couldn't help but blurt out. "Herminia is the woman for you."

"No," Lupito answered as he took money out of his pockets and began to count. "She is too ugly."

"How do you know the woman in Laredo isn't more ugly?" Juan asked him.

Lupito, with his perpetual smile, said, "Because I can sense her beauty in her words. It's that simple."

Lupito had made a slight miscalculation while thinking of his good fortune. He had been premature in dismissing the children. Lupito needed one more favor done. He went over and hugged the children one at a time.

They realized that they were being set up again. Cota got her voice up a pitch and whined, "What do you want now?"

Lupito turned serious. "I would want one more favor from you," he said.

"Not another favor, Lupito," Juan complained.

"All we do is do favors for you," Matías said. "Remember that you have to do a favor for us . . . a big favor."

"Anything," a desperate Lupito replied, "if you'll help me one more time . . . just one more time." He was sticking up one finger.

"What do you want now?" Cota asked him.

Lupito swallowed the last fragment of his pride and said, "Go to my house and bring my clothes. I'm moving into the depot to live here from now on."

"You're crazy, Lupito," Cota replied. "What about your mother? We all know she loves you so much. Why, she'll die."

"Worse . . ." Lupito responded. "She may kill me, if I stay."

"Because you stole money from her," Matías said, figuring out why Lupito had to leave his home. "The only money that she has."

"Shut up," Lupito shouted, nervously. "What do you know? You always think you know everything."

"I know you stole the money that you have. I know it," Matías informed him. Matías took out his magnet and held it at arm's length pointing it at Lupito. "This magnet tells

142

me," he said.

Lupito took a good look at the magnet and said, "What can you do with that thing? You always think you know everything."

※

Sheriff Manuel sat forward on his chair. He felt his body aching throughout as though he were coming down with the flu. He felt his forehead and declared himself without fever. At first he dismissed his pain as the aftereffects of the many Capsules of Oblivion that he had taken.

He studied the letter in his hands that Don Napoleón had, at first, refused to give to him, had actually held it behind his back to hide it from him. Don Napoleón had finally handed it over when Sheriff Manuel threatened him with the pistol.

Sheriff Manuel turned the letter over and studied the back. The Judge had sealed it with hot resin and had imprinted the resin with the seal of his huge ring, his initials over the scales of justice. He opened the drawer and took out the letter opener. He stuck the letter opener into the flap of the envelope, cutting through with one violent motion. He blew the envelope open, smelling the garlic in his breath as it rebounded from the envelope. He peered inside and took out the letter. He read it slowly.

"In the matter of María García's children, Cota, Juan, Frances and Matías. From the information that you have given me, it is my opinion that this requires more public policy arguments. For certain, there are circumstances which warrant that they should be taken away and sent to an orphanage. However, I do not make such decisions without a public hearing where both parties are free to present their case. I will, however, make myself available to you at a moment's notice should you need me. And now on a more personal note: I miss the camaraderie. You. Don Lupe, the worthwhile mayor. The old days. The quail should be nesting right now. A good time to kill them on the ground. My regards to your lovely wife, Inez."

)(

The children went to see Mercedes, Lupito's mother, about his clothes. When they told her that Lupito was going to live in the depot, she burst out crying. At first she refused to let them have his clothes. Mercedes made the children sit outside on the porch while she sat inside, babbling about her son.

Finally, she quieted down and came out. She spoke to the children in a voice so thin with anguish that the children felt sorry for her. She spoke of Lupito's ingratitude. Then taking on a ferocious anger, like a wounded animal, she said that Lupito had stolen her money. She forsook Lupito publicly, acting as though she were wrenching him from her breast and casting him away. She ran inside and then came out with a butcher's knife, which the awed children at first thought she was going to use on herself. Instead, she went into the yard and cut the sky with the knife, saying all the time that what it signified to her was that she had cut Lupito away from her soul. Then she had the children go inside with her and she threw Lupito's clothes—washed and unwashed, ironed and un-ironed— into a wooden box and let the children have them. "Tell him that this is what I get," she cried out to the children, "for all my love."

"He's in love with a woman from Laredo," Cota grunted, trying to appease the woman as she helped carry the heavy box.

"Hummmph!" Mercedes snarled. "Love? What does he know of love?"

They took turns carrying the heavy box. When Lupito saw his clothes, he smelled them, trying to capture the smell of his old room: the iron bed, the wooden trunk where he kept his clothes, the chamber pot so clean that he could have sipped water from it, his father's old saddle that sat on the wooden saw horse against the wall, the bridle over his bed, the chest of drawers with the one drawer missing, the dust that accumulated lightly on the window sill, the smell of basil-scented kerosene . . . And, he remembered his mother. His emotions were a mixture of sadness, of joy, of apprehension of the unknown.

"Remember, Lupito," Matías reminded him, "that you have to do us a big favor. I mean big. If not, we will tell the sheriff that you stole your mother's money."

)(

When they arrived home, Cota, as she normally would, begin to call for her mother. Juan and Matías went to their room to roll a cigarette. Frances went into her room and began to change. Cota walked into her mother's room and did not find her there. She called her mother again, went into the kitchen and noticed that María had not started supper. She called again as she walked into the hallway. She went into her room and asked Frances if she had seen their mother. "Something is wrong," Cota said when Frances told her she had not seen María. Both went into the boys' room, where they found them smoking. They had not seen María either. The boys put out their cigarettes quickly as Cota, fearing the worst, ran toward the sewing room.

Cota opened the door and saw her mother slumped over the sewing machine. She walked toward María slowly, calling her name. Cota could see her breathing slowly. She said, "Mamá? Are you all right?" and María did not answer.

By now the other children were inside the room, following closely behind Cota.

Cota, being ahead, was the first one to see the blood covering the top of the sewing machine. She let out a scream. "Blood!" she yelled and all of them ran to María.

"Her hand!" Matías yelled as he pointed at the thumb impaled by the sewing needle.

Cota grabbed María's hand and held it down as María moaned in agony.

"Help me hold the hand down!" she cried to Juan and Juan pressed on the thumb while Cota held the hand down at the wrist.

"Frances and I will move the wheel!" Matías cried out quickly.

Matías and Frances grabbed the wheel and began to turn it as Cota held the hand and Juan, the strongest of the four, held María's thumb down. Slowly they turned the wheel as María cried out in pain.

"God in heaven above!" she screamed. "What agony is this? Not even childbirth!"

The needle began to move slowly upward, trying with all its might to pick the thumb up with it. Juan was putting the whole weight of his body on the thumb. Cota was standing on her mother's lap, trying to put all her weight on the hand. Matías and Frances had hold of the wheel and they turned it slowly with all their strength. María, in so much pain, could only weave her head from side to side, gasping, trying not to alarm the children by screaming.

But it was too much pain. As the needle finally came out through the bone, María let out a scream that pierced the children's ears.

Later, after the children had carried her to her room, she cried out even louder when they held her down and poured the camphorated alcohol into the open wound.

And in the afterglow of the pain, María tried to equate her misfortune to someone in town. Her first impulse was to think of her husband, Gonzalo, but she reminded herself that he had never known what hit him, that the moment the head came off the body he had left this earth in a strange but painless way. Thus she transfixed the rosary hanging on her headboard with a painful stare and, speaking to the crucifix, she said, "Now I know, dear God, what Mercedes felt when she had Lupito feet first."

She was too young to have been around when Pedro was born sideways.

Chapter Sixteen

María was in so much pain that she could not eat. She had tried valiantly not to make the children feel bad about the simple food that they had prepared: refried beans and left-over rice. Cota had made the dough for the tortillas but had forgotten to add salt and, when everyone started to eat the tortillas, they made faces and acted as though they were about to puke.

"Now, now," María had scolded them softly, afraid that if she raised her voice the thumb would hurt her more, "don't make fun of anyone." And then she inspected her thumb and said, "I have never been in that much pain in my life. Now I know what Mercedes was trying to explain to me about Lupito's birth."

"It's a good thing we found you, Mamá," Cota said. She slowly and meticulously carded a small piece of clean wool. She had pried the piece off the small pile of wool set up in the middle of the table after the meal.

María's thoughts went back to the afternoon and she remembered the children, Cota standing on her lap applying all her weight to her hand. "I'm glad you children cleaned up the blood," she said. "I don't think I would have had the strength to do it."

María began to feel the throbbing in her wound once more. She gently squeezed the thumb at the base and the pain subsided. "Maybe I'm talking too much," she said. "It hurts when I talk."

Matías said, "Anything you do makes it hurt, Mamá."
"Keep squeezing it, Mamá," Frances advised her
as she carded wool to Cota's rhythm.

María said, "What a tragedy this has been." She looked at her thumb, sadly, and thought of the lost opportunity. "There will not be any quilts for a long time," she remarked. She sighed for the hundredth time and asked, "What do we do now?"

"Nothing," Cota replied.

María grew thoughtful, checked her thumb against the lantern, and repeated, "Nothing. Isn't it awful to do nothing?"

"Not me," Matías informed them. "I'm going to start on a new necklace." He reached into his pocket and took out an ear of corn that he had stolen from Juan Garibay's field and began to shell it on top of the table.

María stared with curiosity at what Matías was doing, saying, "God only knows what this child does with those necklaces. What happened to the other one?"

"I used it," Matías answered and, before María could ask where he had used it, he said, "But this one is going to be smaller. I don't need a longer one."

María wanted more information. "What happened to the magnets?" she wondered.

"I have them in my pocket," Matías replied. He reached into his pocket and asked, "Do you want to see them all?"

"He pointed one at Lupito, Mamá," Juan told on him.

"I don't want to hear about it," María replied. "I'd rather not see the magnets and the iron filings and all that mess . . . ungood numbers and all that. I'd rather talk of something else."

"Well," Cota said, casting an eye at María, "we can talk of Mr. Argumedo."

The rest of the children started to laugh at María.

"You children," María replied, "can be so meddlesome!"

"We saw Argumedo today, Mamá," Juan said. "He was carrying all his tools to the barn like he was moving in."

To a Widow with Children

Benjamín Argumedo's moon that had seen the pain of many deaths was visible to him through the window of his room. He undressed and bathed. Afterwards, he reached for the lemon that Genoveva Marín had given him and cut it in half with his pocket knife. He squeezed a half lemon into the palm of his hand, laid the lemon down and mixed the juice in both his hands and then rubbed it briskly into his face. For sure this would take out any remaining smell of the old barn.

Genoveva was waiting for him as he walked by the porch. She whistled her approval. "Now that's a man," she exclaimed and then she beckoned him to come to her. He walked over to where she sat. She motioned for him to bend over toward her and she tilted his hat slightly to one side. "There," she said, studying him, "now you look more romantic. You remind me so much of Máximo Pérez, my husband." She winked at Argumedo and said, "If only I was younger and didn't have to compete with María . . . ah!"

Ж

By the time the children ran to the depot, after leaving María asleep, Herminia was inside talking to Lupito. Very quietly they crawled on the platform to sit under the open window to hear what was being said.

They could hear Herminia counting. "Ninety-five, ninety-six, ninety-seven, ninety-eight, ninety- nine." After a silent pause, they heard the noise of coins falling from her hand onto the table. "And thirty-five cents," Herminia said.

Lupito did not want the coins. They could hear him shoving the coins out of the way.

"You can have it all, Lupito," Herminia said.

"I don't want the coins," replied Lupito, in a voice that the children sensed was lacking in compassion for Herminia. "They bother my pockets."

"Please," Herminia insisted. "I don't mind, Lupito."

Lupito insisted that he didn't want the coins. "How many times do I have to tell you?" they heard him say, highly irritated. They could hear him gathering the money and counting it out again. "As you can see," the children heard him continue, "you have me at a disadvantage. I hope you don't expect anything from me for giving me this money. You are seeing me in a desperate moment."

"You're in love, Lupito. I know how you feel. That's why I feel so much compassion for you," Herminia said.

"You're making me feel less than a man. Here," they heard Lupito say, "take this. I only need eighty eight dollars."

Herminia sighed heavily enough for the children to hear and said, "Take the money, Lupito. You need it more than I do."

They could almost sense Lupito changing his mind. They heard Lupito say that, since he could not predict what the future might hold, he might need the extra money.

Herminia wanted to hear the truth from Lupito. She asked, "What you are going to do with the money?"

Lupito said, "I'm giving the money to the woman that I love."

"The one María's children told me about? The one in Laredo?" Herminia asked.

"Yes," the children heard Lupito answer in a voice that choked.

"I wanted to hear it from your lips," Herminia said.

Lupito remarked, "Now you've heard it."

"And how are you getting the money to Laredo?" Herminia inquired. "Have you thought of that?"

There was silence and the children waited for Lupito's answer. They were as interested in what Lupito would say as was Herminia. They heard Lupito walking and then heard the creaking of the chair as he sat down.

"That, I haven't figured out yet," he replied. Then, after careful thought, he added, "I may have to leave with it."

The combination of hearing Lupito say that he might be leaving and being in Lupito's presence for an extended time was more than Herminia could bear. "Oh, Lupito," Herminia suddenly cried out, "things could be so different." And the children heard the footsteps as Herminia ran toward Lupito. The chair squeaked violently as Lupito shot out of it to avoid Herminia's long arms. Lupito was pleading for Herminia to leave him alone.

The children got up to peer through the window. Herminia was trying to embrace Lupito. She cried out, "I want you in my arms. Please God! How wonderful you must feel."

Lupito was trying to run away from Herminia's grasp. "Leave me alone, please, Herminia," he cried out. "I don't love you."

Herminia turned Lupito loose when she heard what he said. She composed herself, straightened out her dress and said, "Dear God, I don't want to beg."

Lupito said, "I can't help it. I don't love you, Herminia."

"Take the money. I'll never beg you again," they heard Herminia say, angrily, and they ran off when they heard her walking heavily to the door.

Had Herminia observed carefully as she slammed the door, she would have barely seen Benjamín Argumedo to her left in the evening dew walking toward María's. And at the same time, if she had turned her gaze to the right, she would have seen Pedro, a misty shadow, stooped in his disappointment, walking on the tracks, heading toward the street and Argumedo. Pedro was also on his way to see María, hoping that if he apologized, it would give him one more chance with her.

Instead, Herminia, consumed with rage, kicked the pail of water that Lupito kept on the edge of the platform to extinguish the cinders coming off the train. She jumped down to the tracks without bothering to use the steps and started to run back home, crying all the way. At home, she would collapse in her mother's arms.

The children had run off toward Juan Garibay's pasture. From there, by the light of the depot, they could see the eerie spectacle: Argumedo walking briskly, Pedro coming from Argumedo's right side, stumbling on the railroad track, mumbling to himself.

Argumedo could barely make out the figure coming from his right, having difficulty with the light from the depot shining into his eyes. He thought he could make out the aura of a man. He raised one hand to shield his eyes. He could hear the figure jabbering, as could the children in the field.

Pedro had yet to see Argumedo, so intensely was he mumbling about his fate. When he could not hold back his anger he shouted, "I hate Argumedo!" not realizing that Argumedo stood not ten feet from him.

"We hate you!" Juan shouted from the field.

"We all hate you," Matías yelled alongside Juan.

"Dumb," Cota and Frances shouted, as one.

Pedro stopped, confused by the sounds coming from the field. He looked around with his mouth open.

"Who's there?" Pedro demanded to know. "Who's calling me names? Show your faces . . . whoever you are."

And he began to dance around, jabbing at the air. "Take that . . . and that . . . and that. Come closer, Argumedo. Don't run. Take it on the chin like a man." Then he stepped inside his invisible opponent's reach and threw a few body blows. "There," he said to his satisfaction, "that will kill the legs . . . hurt the liver." Argumedo heard the voice of the man in front of him, saw him fighting an imaginary foe. He heard voices from the field.

"Who is it?" Argumedo demanded.

Pedro heard Argumedo's voice, stopped and looked up to see Benjamín Argumedo standing in front of him.

Pedro rubbed his eyes in disbelief. "Argumedo!" Pedro cried out. "God help me! Now I must fight!"

Pedro lowered his head and charged at Argumedo. Argumedo stepped deftly to one side with the precision of a bull-fighter while Pedro stumbled past him. Once Pedro fell to his knees on the tracks, Argumedo saw his face.

"Pedro," he said slowly. He tried to help Pedro up, but the dew on the tracks made Pedro slip. Every time that Argumedo had him up, Pedro fell again, until Pedro reared backwards, lost all his footing and fell like a rock, hitting his head on the track.

The sound of Pedro's thick skull hitting the iron track was heard even by Lupito, who later said that he had thought that one of Juan Garibay's pigs had broken through the fence and, while foraging by the railroad tracks, had slipped on the dew, falling on the tracks and cracking his skull.

The children ran to Argumedo, who was kneeling over Pedro. They could hear Pedro moaning in pain.

Argumedo propped him up and said, "You're all right, old man. We need to take you home. You've had enough for tonight."

Argumedo took out his flask and offered Pedro a drink. Holding his throbbing head with one hand, Pedro took a large swallow and thanked Argumedo.

The sound of the late train from Laredo forced Lupito out of the depot. He came out onto the platform and stepped down to the tracks to walk for a short distance. He held the lantern high to illuminate his way, looking for what it was that had hit the track. He found Argumedo and the children giving Pedro a lift.

"I'm too old to be doing this," everyone heard Pedro say with much difficulty.

"That's why you ought to be seeing the widow Doña Juan," Frances advised him. "She's more your age."

"Come," Argumedo said, "I'll walk you home."

"To the hen house," Pedro corrected Argumedo.

"To the hen house, then," said Argumedo and he and the children walked Pedro back.

Chapter Seventeen

María looked around her at the bareness of the sour-orange trees, the dying grass, the buzzards soaring effortlessly high in the sky, the stifling gloominess of the morning. She had never seen the sky so gray. "There will not be a cloud in the sky until the month of rain," she said as she stopped at the courthouse steps.

She felt her forehead. "I've never been so nervous in all my life," she said. "Not even for Gonzalo's funeral." And she began to nervously adjust the clothes on her children. "Why must you always have your skirt so low?" she complained to Cota as she yanked up Cota's skirt. She walked over to Frances and said, "Frances, when are you ever going to learn how to dress? And you Juan, look at you. I hadn't noticed that you didn't wash your face. You've got old white saliva on the corners of your mouth. Here . . . come over here. Let me wipe you."

She picked up her skirt by the hem and wet it with her tongue and rubbed the crust off the corners of Juan's mouth. "I don't know what I'm going to do with you children. Matías, come over here. Over here by me. Let me see you." Matías was trying to hide behind Juan and Cota. "Come over here I say. Look at you. Look at both your hair and Juan's hair. If you two ever ruin your hair again, I'm going to whip you. I've never hit you children, but if you ever do that again, I'm not going to contain myself. Dear God," she said looking up to the heavens, "look at my hands trembling. I have to get control of myself. Let me stop to say a prayer." She bowed her head, closed her eyes and fell silent for a few moments as the children watched her.

"I want to pray, too," Frances said.

"Be quiet," Cota answered. "Leave Mamá alone. Can't you see she's falling apart?"

María ignored them as she continued with her prayer. Presently she opened her eyes. "I hope that this prayer does it," she said. "Matías, quit pushing your hair down with saliva! That's dirty. Leave your hair alone. It will never look good. Not the way it was cut. You ruined your beautiful hair."

Matías wet his lips and dried his fingertips on his pants. "It's good luck," he answered.

"Oh, be quiet," María told him. "And take off the necklace. You look like a girl. And besides, it's made of corn. How do you come up with these things, Matías? You drive me crazy. God in heaven help us."

"You're nervous, Mamá," Cota said, trying to calm María down.

Instead, María became even more irritated with the children, hearing Cota speak the obvious. Her thoughts were that she had a right to be nervous, that it was their fault that she was nervous. She said, "I'm nervous, Cota says. What else can I be? Look at what you're putting me through. This is more than I can handle. This raffle for the quilt. The sheriff and his orphanage. Just when I think I have one problem solved, then another one comes up. And now . . . this. Nothing less than a full confession about a quilt that doesn't exist—a raffle that doesn't exist."

She opened the courthouse door and held it open for the children to go in.

"We're going to take you to San Antonio after all of this is over," Cota said, hoping that those words would soothe her mother.

María looked at her and said angrily, "Oh, be quiet. We

can't get out of the house without getting into trouble and you want to go out of town."

"We're going to take you, Mamá," Frances said. "Just you wait."

"Be quiet," María replied, ignoring what the children were saying to her. "Don't make any noise. We don't want Herminia to know we're here just yet. After we talk to the sheriff, we'll apologize about the raffle to her. Give back her money."

The children followed their mother quietly past the tax office, looking in and seeing Herminia hard at work turning the pages of the large tax rolls, studying an item on a line, following the column across the page with her finger.

"Here is another one," they heard Herminia say to Don Bruno. "Another delinquent account."

"Leave them alone, I tell you," Don Bruno advised her. "Leave things the way they are. They are all delinquent."

"No taxes," Herminia said to herself, closing the large book.

"No one has paid taxes since I've been here," they heard Don Bruno say, "and no one will. I'll swear to that."

María knocked gently on the sheriff's door. She knocked again and listened. From within came Sheriff Manuel's muffled voice.

"Come in," they heard, "it's open. Don Juan? Is it you? Have you found out anything about the sheep?"

María and the children walked in silently. They could hear the sheriff gargling in the rest room. He had just taken his capsule.

"It's us," María said meekly. "María and her children."

Sheriff Manuel stuck his head out. He had been sure it would be Juan Garibay to report on the stolen wool. When he saw María and the children for the first time, it took him a few moments to adjust his sight. Then gradually he came to recognize the family. "Oh, it's you," he said so coldly that María trembled slightly with fear. He finished cleaning his face with a towel and threw the towel into the rest room. Slowly he came to his desk and sat down, placing his hands on the desk top in front of him. "Well," he continued, "I suppose you want to sit down."

María and the children came over timidly. María took the chair in front of the desk.

"Well?" Sheriff Manuel asked María as he began a slight rocking in his chair. He stared all the children down. On Matías he noticed for the first time the corn necklace, identical to the one he had found at Juan Garibay's pasture.

María looked nervously about before speaking, trying to find the exact words. Cota was standing next to her at her right. Frances was at her left, leaning against her, trembling in fear like María. Juan was behind the chair and to her right, behind Cota. Matías was behind Frances on her left.

Matías was intent on studying the sheriff's every move. He was remembering what he had heard the codgers talk about. "You don't look like you're turning blue," Matías said to him, and that brought a renewed cold stare from Sheriff Manuel. Matías slipped behind his mother.

"If the truth be known," María said, nervously, in a frail voice, "this year has been bad for us. Gonzalo . . ."

The sheriff jumped up at the sound of the name. "Don't mention his name in front of me," he growled, pointing a finger at María.

"I didn't mean to offend you," María replied. "I had no idea you hated my husband. I don't know what goes on between men in this town. Maybe he owed you money. It was just my way of introducing our problems to you."

Sheriff Manuel sat, rolling a pencil between his fingers. Now he noticed that María's thumb was bandaged. "And the thumb?" he asked María, thinking that perhaps the children had injured their mother, something else to add to the charges against them.

"Another one of our problems. I pierced it with the sewing machine," María replied, studying the thumb. "You didn't see it when it happened. It's looking so much better now."

Sheriff Manuel dismissed the thumb and said, "Today is your raffle. Am I correct? Do I have the right day?"

"First of all . . ." María began.

The sheriff leaned forward and stopped her. "I hate to interrupt you, María, but there is a lot of talk in town. You were the cause of the fight between Pedro and Argumedo."

"That was not a fight," Cota shot back quickly.

"Pedro fell down," Matías added.

"Typical of your children to interrupt, María," Sheriff Manuel said. "But mainly," he continued, "there is the matter of the children. They run wild. You cannot control them. They steal." He opened the drawer and took out the chewed corn necklace that he had found in the pasture. He held it up for María to see. "This object is identical to the one that Matías is wearing around his neck . . . except that this one has been chewed. This was found in Juan Garibay's pasture the morning after Juan Garibay found several of his sheep naked. Without any wool."

María panicked at the sight of the chewed necklace dangling from the sheriff's hand. She felt the blood draining from her head. She tried to reply, but she had been caught completely by surprise. She had not expected this turn of events. All that she had practiced with the children had been their apologies for not having the quilt ready for the raffle. Now she understood how the children had gotten the wool. She covered her mouth and the only thing that came out was, "God in Heaven above."

"I cannot legally accuse Matías of stealing the wool," Sheriff Manuel kept on. "But I'm saying that things are very, very suspicious. I will have to find the wool." He let the words sink in. Then he said, "And I will. Believe me."

He reached into his drawer again. This time he pulled out the letter from the judge. "This is the letter from Don Jaime, the judge," he said, pointing the letter at her. "It's possible Don Napoleón has told you about it? He seems to care so much for you and the children."

María felt more and more light-headed. She placed her cold hands up to her forehead and she felt the perspiration on her brow. "No," she replied, acting more disoriented. She could feel a wave of nausea. "Don Napoleón has not told me about the letter."

The sheriff felt the power of having the upper hand. He said, with a sneer, "Hoping not to worry you, of course."

"I suppose so," María responded, feeling weaker and weaker, casting her gaze down in submission.

Sheriff Manuel read the letter from Judge Jaime to María and the children. When he was through, he leaned back comfortably in his chair, raised his arms over his head, and then clasped his hands and brought them behind his head. He waited for their reaction. María was stunned and pale. He could tell that she had no idea that he had written to the judge for the judge's opinion. The children were very quiet, as quiet as he had ever seen them. They appeared to him to be at a loss for words, to be thinking of the pain of being separated from their mother.

Fully in control, Sheriff Manuel said, "Now to something else." He unclasped his hands and leaned forward. He wagged a finger at the children. "You don't make a fool of me like you do everyone else in town." He flashed them a devilish smile and asked, "The raffle? Today is the day of the raffle. I have it right here on my calendar. You think I would forget? Who won the beautiful quilt?"

All María could hear was the buzzing in her ears. María blinked rapidly as she looked around for help from her children. The children could see the terror in her eyes. They hated to see their mother helpless like this. The turn of events was something that they had not rehearsed while smoking in their room. Juan looked at Cota for help. Frances looked at Cota. Matías punched Cota in the back and that brought a series of events flashing before her mind's eye. Cota cleared her throat and hitched up her skirt. Her mind spun for an instant and stopped on the most logical of names. "Lupito," Cota said without flinching. "Lupito won the quilt."

María tried to stand when she heard the name. The children pushed her down and held her.

The name stunned Sheriff Manuel, but not as much as it had María. Sheriff Manuel made a face of disapproval. "Lupito?" the sheriff repeated as the children struggled with their mother. Then accepting the winner and his own bad luck, he said, "How lucky."

"Very lucky," Matías replied, holding on to his mother. "Lupito is lucky in raffles, but unlucky in love."

María stood up and was about to speak the truth when the small amount of blood in her head finally drained to her feet and she felt the room going around and around. She collapsed back into her chair and went completely limp.

Cota and Frances began to pat their mother on her hands. Juan and Matías grabbed the papers on top of Sheriff Manuel's desk and began to fan María with them. María was out, sprawled on the chair, toppled over to her right. Cota and Frances set María upright, continuing to pat her hands.

By this time, Sheriff Manuel had gotten up and had walked around the desk and was standing in front of María. "What's the matter with her?" he asked the children.

"She's, she's almost dead," Cota replied, stopping her patting to put her little ear to María's chest. "Her heart!" she cried out, grasping the opportunity to scare the sheriff.

"She's had a heart attack!" Juan cried out, picking up on Cota.

Matías was always one to exaggerate. He ran to Sheriff Manuel and cried out, pointing his finger at him, "If my mother dies because of you, you are going to be in big trouble. We will get Argumedo to kill you!"

Sheriff Manuel didn't wait for Matías to finish his threat. He shoved Matías out of the way. He said, "Don't you threaten me, young man. That would be all you need to be sent to the orphanage." Sheriff Manuel reached down, picked up María's hand and took her pulse. "She's all right," he said. "She fainted."

"Because of you," Frances told him.

Cota produced a solitary tear and she let Sheriff Manuel see it. She sensed the upper hand. She said, "I hope

God let's us keep our mother."

Sheriff Manuel helped the children carry María out of the office.

Herminia came out to see about the commotion. When she saw María being carried out she screamed, "My God, it's María," waking up Don Bruno. Don Bruno came out to see the collection of people carrying María out of the courthouse. He joined them, supporting one of María's arms, patting her hand. "What in heaven's name happened?" Don Bruno asked them, taking the cold cigar stump out of his mouth and putting it in his pocket.

"María," Sheriff Manuel responded, puffing with María's weight, "was so excited that she fainted."

"What was she excited about?" Herminia wanted to know, looking for a part of María that she could help carry.

"I don't know," Sheriff Manuel replied. "That Lupito won the quilt, I guess."

Herminia showed the happiness in her face. "Oh," she said, holding on to one of María's legs, "I feel so happy for him."

And they carried María to the sheriff's car and laid her out on the back seat and the sheriff took her and the children home, but not before taking her to see Dr. Benigno, as the children had insisted. Dr. Benigno was about to attach María to his electromagnetic machine when she regained her senses. Dr. Benigno snapped his fingers, cursed under his breath. He had been kept from trying out the newest of medical gadgets.

And in the confusion, Juan had stolen the letter from Judge Jaime to Sheriff Manuel.

Chapter Eighteen

After Lupito sent his telegram he sat back, rested his chin on the palm of his hand, and waited for a reply.

Presently the reply came:

> DEAREST HEART. I FEEL SO UNWORTHY. DON'T
> TROUBLE YOURSELF COMING. JUST SEND THE
> MONEY BY TRAIN. DON'T DESPAIR. WE WILL BE
> TOGETHER SOON. I PROMISE. ALL. ALL MY LOVE
> WILL BE YOURS FOREVER. FLOR.

Lupito wrote furiously as the words flowed out of the machine. When the machine quit its clickety-clack, he read the message at a more leisurely pace. He wet his lips at the part where she promised him all her love. Lupito was about to send off another message, when he heard the door open. He turned in his chair and saw María's children rushing in. Lupito had never seen them look so determined. He did not know that the children had just put María to bed and had run to see him before Sheriff Manuel could get to him first.

"Has Sheriff Manuel been here?" was the first thing Lupito heard from Cota.

The question baffled Lupito. "No, why? Why would Sheriff Manuel be looking for me?" Lupito asked, nervously thinking about the money he had stolen. He noticed the obvious lessening of tension in the children. The determined look left their faces and they were back to being their old selves again. "What do you children want from me?" he asked them.

"A lot," they answered.

Cota walked in front. Matías was right behind her, followed by Juan and then Frances.

"Lupito?" Cota asked, clearing her throat, preparing Lupito. "Remember that we went to talk to Herminia and had her come to give you the money you needed? Remember when we had to go and drag your stinky clothes over here? Remember when we asked you to swear that you would help us out?"

Lupito immediately sensed that they were in trouble again. He didn't want to be a part of it. "I didn't say about what," Lupito replied, raising his hands in front of him, trying to ward off the children's advances.

"You promised, Lupito," Matías said, walking toward the telegrapher. "I made you promise and you said you would do anything we asked. You were in trouble."

Lupito hated himself for being so vulnerable. He had to admit that he had promised to help. "It depends," Lupito replied, acting vague. "What if you want me to kill someone? What if you want me to steal?"

"You already stole," Juan said.

"Remember that you stole from your mother?" Matías made sure to remind him.

"That's right," Frances chimed in.

Cota jumped in. She said, "That's right, Lupito. Your mother knows. She told us."

"You stole," Juan said.

"We can go to the sheriff right now," Matías said and they all turned around and started for the door.

Lupito ran to stop them. He reached the door before they could and he barred them. He said, "Matías, don't be so jumpy. We don't need the sheriff."

"Maybe we do," Frances said.

"Get out of our way!" Juan cried out.

Lupito had a desperate moment in which he knew that the children would go straight to the sheriff. He let go of the door handle and said, acting defeated, "I did promise, didn't I?"

"You promised. And now you've got to help us," Cota said. "We're in a little trouble."

"But you're always in a little trouble," Lupito complained, leading the children back to the desk. "I don't know of a single day that you children are not in a little trouble."

"That's not true," Frances said, "sometimes we get into big trouble."

"You promised to help," Matías said, picking up the telegraph machine and studying it. "You've got to keep your promises, Lupito. You've got to grow up." Matías set the telegraph machine down on the desk. "Men keep their promises," he reminded Lupito.

Invoking Lupito's manhood, frail as it was, was enough to get a response. "Well, what is it?" Lupito asked.

Cota sat down on the desk while the rest surrounded Lupito. Lupito felt uncomfortable being so closely watched. He stood up from his chair and walked to the toilet door and stood there. Matías took the opportunity to sit down in Lupito's chair.

"It's not so bad, Lupito," Cota said. "We just told fat Sheriff Manuel that you had won the raffle for the quilt. That's all."

"I won?" Lupito asked, happily, his eyes wide with joy.

"Well, Lupito," Matías said. "Yes and no. You won but you didn't."

"What do you mean?" Lupito asked. "I won but I didn't?"

"There is no quilt. We couldn't make a quilt in time," Juan said.

"You remember that Mamá hurt her thumb, Lupito? We couldn't do it," Frances said.

Cota sighed and took on a more solemn air. "We had to lie to the sheriff," she explained.

"What else could we do?" Matías asked.

To a Widow with Children

Lupito looked at them each one at a time, not being able to hide his disappointment. "Then I didn't win anything?" he whined.

"That's right," Matías replied. "And if the fat sheriff asks you about the quilt, you say you won it and we gave it to you. If he asks you to show it to him, you tell him you sent it to Laredo to that awful woman, the one that's after your money. You sent it by train."

"I could get in trouble for lying," Lupito said, choosing to ignore Matías' comments about his love.

Matías warned him: "You'll be in a lot more trouble . . . for stealing."

"The way I see it, you don't have any choice, Lupito," Frances said.

Lupito thought for a moment and had to come to the same conclusion. He had given the children the opportunity to trap him. Thinking of any future trouble that the children might get into, he said, "Well, just this once and that's all."

"You owe us a lot more than this, Lupito," Matías informed him, but Lupito disagreed. "You'll need to help us out again," Matías said, "and soon."

"No, I won't," Lupito told Matías.

Matías replied, "Yes, you will. You wait and see."

Cota got off the desk. She was curious about the cardboard box sitting at one of the corners. She walked over and looked in. "I see you're packing to leave," she said.

The children followed Cota out of the depot. When they got out onto the platform, they decided to go see Argumedo. They found Argumedo in his undershirt, cleaning the small barn. He was walking a tight-rope on the rafters, dusting with a broom when the children walked in looking for him.

Argumedo heard them talking below and greeted them. Very carefully he climbed down and cleaned his hands on a rag before shaking each of the children's hands. He was perspiring and dirty from the dust of so many years and the cobwebs of so many spiders.

"This is a nice place," Juan said, looking around.

"Thank you," Argumedo replied. "It will need a lot of work, but I can do it. You should have seen it when I first moved in. I could not walk through here because of the caked mud."

"That's from the month of rain," Matías informed him.

"It rains for a month," Cota said.

"That must be something," Argumedo murmured, walking to the back door of the barn and looking out into the brush. He was used to the sameness of the scene.

"And the bicycle?" Cota asked him, as though none of them knew what had happened to it.

Argumedo came back and sat on a half barrel. The children sat on the ground in front of him. He said, "I traded it to Juan Garibay for the barn. He wanted the bicycle for his children. It was a good opportunity for me. If I'm going to stay here, I have to make a living. And you children know a man has to make a living."

"Well," Cota confessed, "we did see Anna Garibay riding the bicycle like a cow all over town and her sister and her brothers running after her crying. She won't let them ride the bicycle."

"She looked like a spider with her long legs," Frances broke in.

"Might you be envious?" Argumedo asked, feeling the children's mood.

Matías said, "We never get to have anything."

"Some people have everything," Juan complained.

"Mamá says that some day we will be able to have any bicycle we want," Frances remarked.

"But when?" Juan asked, always the skeptic.

"Your mother is right," Argumedo reminded them. "She has the experience to know. And look at you children. You have the most wonderful mother. Isn't that enough?"

Frances said, "We would love a bicycle. Something that we could own."

"Be patient," Argumedo advised them. "Some day you will have everything you wish. But for now, the most important thing you could ever have is a good mother. And you have her. So what's to complain about? And let me tell you something else. The Garibay children will tire of the bicycle. They will use it and fight over it and someone will always be crying over it until Juan Garibay and his wife—what's her name?"

"Carolina," Frances responded quickly.

"Until Juan Garibay and Carolina cannot stand it any more."

"Really?" Cota asked, thrilled that the Garibay children would soon have trouble with the bicycle.

"Yes," Argumedo replied. "Most important in life is people, not possessions."

"Anyway," Matías said to him, "we would like to have something. Like go to San Antonio. Like win the turkey. And have a bicycle."

"Do you have a bicycle?" Argumedo asked them.

They told him the story of the old bicycle and how María had fixed it for them. They laughed about the box María had tied to the frame for them to use for a seat. They laughed about the handle-bars made from a broom stick. And they laughed the loudest about Juan and Matías and the laundry and the destruction of the bicycle.

"See," Argumedo pointed out. "You had more fun with the old bicycle than Juan Garibay's children will ever have with theirs. It is people who are important. You children can have more fun without any toys. Don't you play at the dump? What kind of toy is that?"

"We love playing at the dump," Cota said. "We have freedom there. Except when Juan Garibay's children come over to bother us."

"Exactly what I'm telling you," Argumedo said. "Make your own toys."

"The town dump," Matías said proudly, "is the best toy there is."

Frances gave Argumedo a loving look and said, "I just love talking to you."

"We all love talking to you," Cota added.

"You need to come see Mamá," Frances said. "She stuck

the sewing machine needle through her finger."

Argumedo made a face showing pain. "Poor her. How is she?"

"She's fine now," replied Matías, "but she's in a lot of pain."

"I feel for her," Argumedo remarked.

"Will you come and visit us?" Matías asked.

Argumedo accepted the invitation. "But only," he reminded them, "if I get to talk to your mother and you children stay in your room."

"Oh no!" Frances cried out.

♓

María awoke to find the children in bed with her, each one trying to get as close to her as they could, nudging María in every direction. When she felt her head against the headboard, María lowered herself. But then Cota squirmed her way in between the headboard and María's head. Frances squeezed in on María's right side. Juan stayed on María's left side. Matías crawled around and curled himself up by María's feet. The others were trying to be quiet when Matías began to make a noise by sucking on his necklace.

"Stop that, Matías," said Cota. "Can't you see that Mamá is trying to rest?"

"I do need rest, Matías," María murmured in a tired voice.

"Mamá?" Cota began.

"What is it now?" María asked without wanting to know. She was just now getting over the effects of having fainted at the courthouse.

Cota had wanted to set her mother at ease. "Nothing," she said, "just to tell you that we already went and saw Lupito. Lupito is going to tell anyone that asks that he won the quilt—including Sheriff Manuel."

"Bless Lupito," María replied. "You children think of everything. In a way I suppose that's good. But what if

Sheriff Manuel insists on seeing the quilt?"

"Lupito will tell him that he sent the quilt to that awful woman in Laredo," Cota replied.

"Thank God for that," María said, covering her mouth as she yawned.

Matías asked, "Mamá, how did you feel when Cota told the sheriff that Lupito had won the quilt? Tell me exactly."

María took her time about answering. She moved about in bed first, trying to capture the feeling of that moment earlier in the day. Then she said, barely audible, that she never had felt so hopeless and scared in her life. She had felt as though she were treading through a dream, as though Cota was speaking and there was no one there. She could not believe what she was hearing.

"I didn't know what to do, Mamá," Frances said, cuddling up to María. "I thought I was going to faint just like you."

"I got scared," Juan said. "That's all that I can say. I thought I was going to die. Did the sheriff go for his gun, Mamá?"

"No," María responded, "Manuel might not be the best man in the world, but he wouldn't harm anyone. At least, I don't think so."

"You're so good, Mamá," Frances told her. "You always find something good in everyone."

"Manuel has been good to us in some ways," María reminded them. "Look at how he helped us with Don Chema, the tailor. When Matías and Juan fell from the bicycle with all those clothes . . ." María yawned. ". . . He kept us out of trouble then."

Matías sat up and cocked an ear. He scanned around the room as though he were looking for something.

María said, "What's the matter now, Matías?"

Matías turned his head toward the door. "I hear something," he said.

Cota sat up. "Someone's at the porch, Mamá," she said, "I can hear it."

María was out of the room before the children could get

out of bed. She hurried to the door and opened it expecting to find Pedro. She wanted to give him a good scolding and then to send him on his way. Instead, she found Benjamín Argumedo, smelling of lemon.

"The children invited me over," he said, smiling.

Chapter Nineteen

The day of the raffle had arrived. Father Non looked out over the yard that would be full of people in a short while. He checked his watch and noted the time. He called for Pedro and saw the sacristan come out running from inside the hen house. While he waited for Pedro, he had the opportunity to look to his right, and there under the pomegranates was the old rooster, covered in dust, lying in the hole that he had scratched for himself. The rooster opened one weary eye and, thinking that he was on top of the hen house, opened his beak and a sound came out of it as if someone were shaving ice. It was a rasping sound so coarse that Father Non for once showed his concern by not laughing. From under the house he saw the young rooster come out strutting, shake the dust off his feathers and nod his head toward Father Non several times, as if he were informing Father Non that he was soon to take charge.

Father Non could not help but smile at the sameness of life where the old must give way to the new. He even recalled that the young rooster had been hatched from an egg fertilized out of town.

The young rooster had not been out but a few seconds when two hens came running out behind him, gawking and clucking. Behind the hens came Pedro, at a trot, his head bandaged.

"You're very nervous, good father," Pedro said, before he reached the priest. "I can tell."

"Be quiet and do as you were told," Father Non snapped at him. Pedro lowered his head and very seriously ran toward the church. "That puts him in his place," the priest said, satisfied, walking back inside the house.

He went up to his room and sat on the edge of the bed and wondered why he had inherited the obsession for raffles. He began to unconsciously twirl his magnetic ring and soon he was lost in a long revery of previous raffles—his own and the ones he had heard about from the people.

Shortly before eleven, he recovered his senses, checked his watch and walked downstairs to his office. At eleven, he sat at his desk and studied his fingernails. When he tired of this, he gazed out the window at the town and remembered the day he had arrived and found no one at the depot. From the bottom drawer he took out Father Jaillet's chapbook and read from it. At eleven thirty, he could sense the people forcing their way on the street toward the rectory. He took out his watch once more and studied it for a moment, shook it and brought it up to his ear. He heard the tick-tock. He noted the time and placed it back in the watch pocket of his black wool trousers.

He went upstairs to his room, over to the bureau and took out the clean shirt that Doña Juanita, Herminia's mother, had washed and ironed for him, and he put it on over his old night shirt. He chose one of the best collars that he owned and buttoned it around his neck. He took the coat from the hanger on the closet door and put it on. He adjusted the coat several times, shrugging his shoulders. He pulled the shirt sleeves out beyond the coat. He turned around, studied himself in the mirror from head to toe and thought himself as ready as he was going to be. All this time he could hear the rumble of the people outside, the murmuring, the codgers shouting gleefully above the gobbles of the turkey.

Father Non swallowed the last of his saliva and re-adjusted his coat. He walked over to the night table by the bed and picked up the cigar box full of raffle tickets and with much ceremony flipped the box under his arm.

From the hallway downstairs, through the screen door, he could make out the crowd of people who had gathered for the raffle. Father Non purposely rattled the screen door. Immediately the crowd became quiet, anticipating, waiting nervously for Father Non to make his appearance. Father Non could see Pedro carrying the turkey from the hen house through the crowd, heightening the excitement. He could hear the shouts of glee as Pedro struggled to hold the turkey above his head, showing the turkey around.

"Long live Father Non!" one of the codgers shouted and that started a wave of applause from the front of the crowd to the rear.

Father Non adjusted the crucifix on his chest. He sighed deeply in his joy of the moment. He then took a giant step forward as he opened the screen door and the crowd broke out in applause, shouting his name.

He walked through the applause until he came to the edge of the porch. He called out for the mayor and the sheriff to come and join him, and they walked up and stood next to the priest. Father Non showed them their seats by the wall. He looked around for Juan Garibay and could not see him. He called out for Juan Garibay, and Don Bruno cried out that Juan Garibay had left town for the morning, gone to buy still one more billy goat. The crowd laughed. Father Non expressed his regret that Juan Garibay could not be there, feeling slighted that Juan Garibay did not take the raffle as seriously as he.

He took the cigar box and placed it on top of the little table that Pedro had brought from the church. Pedro was standing at the end of the porch, holding the turkey while the turkey tried its best, with much force and flapping of its large wings, to escape.

"Hold on, Pedro!" Don Porfirio shouted.

"If you let him go, then he'll belong to the one who catches him," Gumercindo said, making his own rules.

"Is that right, Mamá?" Frances asked María.

"Don't pay attention to those old men," María replied, not taking her eyes off the turkey. "I hope to God that we win," she whispered so that only her children could hear her.

"We are going to win, Mamá," Juan said out loud and the crowd began to laugh.

"Don't laugh," Cota yelled out. "We are going to win. You just wait and see."

Cota made the crowd laugh even louder.

"Be quiet!" Don Chema, the tailor, cried out to silence the crowd. "Here comes the raffle."

Father Non took a step forward. He raised his hands as the crowd applauded, asking for silence. "Before we proceed," he said, "remember that mass tomorrow is at the same time as every Sunday. I don't want anyone thinking this raffle counts for mass. Before you ask . . . it doesn't."

The faithful in the crowd groaned.

"Now, now," Father Non scolded them gently, "none of this groaning and moaning. It doesn't speak well of you. And now!" he shouted, "the raffle."

The crowd grew silent. Don Lupe, the mayor, and Sheriff Manuel leaned forward in their chairs. Father Non walked slowly, deliberately, to the table and stood by the cigar box. The crowd, not able to contain itself, broke out in excited applause.

Father Non raised his hands and again demanded quiet. He picked up the box and, holding it high over his head, he began to shake it gently and then more forcefully until his whole body shook from his head to his feet to the rhythm of the box. The crowd was working into a frenzy, shouting and applauding. The children were jumping up and down and their parents tried to stop them.

Father Non lowered the box and shook it a few times more for the benefit of the crowd. He was delirious with joy. He looked over the crowd and everyone and everything became an unrecognizable blur. He jerked his head several times and the perspiration from his brow flew off in a salty spray. He was working his way up to the final delirious moment.

Trembling, the priest raised the cigar box over his head with both hands and held it there. The crowd, seeing the elevated cigar box, grew quiet. At the same time, Pedro, taking his cue from Father Non's wink, pinched the turkey and the turkey gobbled with so much power that the mesmerized crowd reeled from being brought back to reality, all eyes glued to the box in Father Non's hands.

Father Non opened the box gently above his head. The lid flopped over. He stuck his hand inside and stirred the raffle tickets one more time. The crowd watched opened-mouthed. Father Non's hand finally stopped. They could see his fingers searching for the ticket. Father Non's hand came down, a ticket in his grasp. The crowd watched motionless, completely awed. Father Non took the ticket and studied it. He looked out over the crowd and read the numbers very deliberately.

"Zero . . . zero . . . one . . . three . . . four . . . eight," he read, and then he repeated the six digits.

He waited for the shouts of victory. He waited for the crowd to applaud. An eternity passed, by his standards.

Don Lupe, the mayor, stood up and walked up from behind and tapped Father Non on the shoulder. "No one has the number, Father Non," he informed the priest.

"Then," Gumercindo cried out, "Juan Garibay is the winner," while the stunned Father Non stood helpless before the crowd.

Frances could not control herself. She bolted away from María and yelled out for all to hear, "I hate Juan Garibay!"

Sheriff Manuel, sensing the unruliness of the crowd, stood up and walked to Father Non's side. Despite the protests from Father Non, he took out his revolver and fired it several times into the air. "The raffle is over," he shouted. "Juan Garibay has won." The crowd began to disperse slowly. María gathered her children, except for Matías, who was not to be found. He had run off toward the hen house when Juan Garibay was declared the winner.

On the way home, María tried as hard as she could to keep the children's spirits up. "I know you are disappointed," she said, "but the raffle is over. We did not win."

Cota said, "We should have won, Mamá."

"I thought we were going to win," Frances said, sniffling.

"We were going to win," Juan cried out. He was so disgusted that he picked up a rock and threw it toward the rectory.

"Don't do that, Juan!" María said. "That is an insult to Father Non and Father Non is a fine man." Then she spoke of the raffle. "There are no guarantees in this life, children. That is why you need an education . . . so that you don't rely on chance." She took in her brood and asked, "Couldn't anyone find Matías?"

Cota sighed and remarked, "No. We looked everywhere."

"I wonder what he's doing?" María asked herself, thinking that his absence was not a good omen.

"You never know about him, Mamá. He said he wanted to see the turkey," Juan said, holding another rock in his hand. But we looked for him at the hen house and couldn't find him."

Frances rubbed the sniffles from her nose with her finger. Her voice had grown hoarse from crying, "He told me he was going to go see Lupito by himself," she said.

"Oh, that child," María complained, worried at what Matías would do. "I wish that we had found him."

⋊

Matías had sneaked over to the hen house and, without anyone seeing him, had fed the corn necklace to the turkey in case Juan Garibay did not return to town and the turkey had to spend the night in Pedro's care.

After he had hidden from his mother and his brother and sisters, he ran to the depot and found Lupito in such a state of despair that he was afraid Lupito might throw himself under the train that night and end it all. When he asked Lupito why he was so unhappy, Lupito, speechless, pointed to the telegraph machine on top of the desk. The telegraph machine was broken, he finally managed to blurt out. He could not communicate with his love, could not tell her that he was planning on leaving with the money early the next morning.

Matías calmly played his last card with Lupito. If Lupito agreed to one last favor, he informed Lupito, he would fix the telegraph machine. Lupito, of course, agreed. He would have agreed to anything at the moment. Lupito recovered his senses enough to ask what the favor would be, and Matías walked Lupito into the toilet and told him that tonight Lupito would find out. Matías insisted that Lupito stay in the toilet while he fixed the telegraph machine. Matías went out and took the telegraph machine, turned it over and removed the iron plate with a screw driver from the drawer, the same one he had used to undo the plate. He shook the magnet out of the machine and replaced the plate. As soon as he set the machine down on the desk it began its clickety-clack.

Chapter Twenty

 $\mathbf{F}$ ather Non was in his office thinking of the events of that morning. Except for Juan Garibay winning his turkey back, he felt satisfied that the raffle had gone well. He did not, however, approve of Sheriff Manuel pulling out his revolver and firing it into the air. He knew that he had done it for the first time with the old codgers. Now he had done it for the second time, and only God knew when he would do it again and with what frequency. After reprimanding the sheriff, he had sent Pedro to inform Juan Garibay's wife, Carolina, that they had won the raffle.

Before he left, Pedro said, "Carolina knows. The Garibay children were at the raffle, good father."

Father Non was still irritated at Sheriff Manuel and showed his temper to Pedro. "I could see them," he said through clenched teeth. "Do you think I'm blind? I still have the obligation to inform an adult member of the family. So don't be correcting me. Go right now."

By the time Pedro arrived, Carolina's children had told her.

Father Non was busying himself sorting out the old raffle tickets when Pedro returned through the porch and the back door.

Father Non heard him. He said, "Pedro? Is that you?"

"Yes, good father," Pedro replied.

"And?" he asked from inside the office.

"Juan Garibay won't return until tomorrow," Pedro said walking into the office.

"And Carolina?" Father Non asked, wondering if perhaps she could take the turkey off his hands.

"She does not want the responsibility, good father," Pedro informed him.

"Good," Father Non replied, changing his mind when he sensed the opportunity to punish his sacristan. "Then you can sleep with the turkey tonight."

"It will be cold tonight," Pedro replied as though he were predicting and not complaining. "My wound on the head may hurt in the cold."

"Cover up then," Father Non answered as he got up and walked past Pedro.

⋇

María's children were waiting for Matías in the front yard. After what they thought was the longest time, they saw him running toward the house. They could hear, as he came nearer, Matías' heavy breathing and the swishing sound that his cotton trousers made as the legs rubbed against each other.

Matías jumped down into the ditch and stayed there long enough to worry his brother and sisters. When they ran to the ditch to see what was keeping him, he came out and very dramatically ran past them and into the shed. Cota, Juan and Frances took off running after him. There they gathered to be brought up to date on what Matías was doing, and to smoke.

They showed both admiration and unhappiness with his plan. Admiration at the boldness of it: the punishment that it meted Pedro for insulting their mother and Juan Garibay for acquiring the bicycle for his children. Unhappiness at Matías' secrecy, for they had not been included in it from the beginning. However, when Matías explained that the complexity of the plan cried out for only one operative, they happily agreed to go along with him.

After supper they ran to hide behind the church to wait for the first opportunity to steal the turkey. They spied Pedro getting himself comfortable on the hen house floor, covering himself with the bedding and straw that he found around him. They heard Father Non call for Pedro to ring the first bell for the rosary.

"There's no rest for me," Pedro complained quietly, throwing off the old rags that covered him. Then, for Father Non's ears he said, faking a yawn, "I thought I was ready to go to sleep." He crawled out of the hen house and asked toward the rectory: "What time is it, anyway?"

"Be quiet and ring the bell," the children heard Father Non reply. "Don't be so presumptuous as to ask me for the time."

The children were still in hiding when after the rosary they saw Father Non walk out of the sacristy and go by the hen house to visit with Pedro.

Father Non found Pedro wrapped in old rags and straw asleep next to the turkey. Father Non smiled and thought that the image made by the two sleepers, Pedro and the turkey, was worth remembering. He went into the rectory and went straight to bed, feeling very tired with the events of the day. Before he fell asleep, he recounted the raffle in his memory and smiled.

Outside, Pedro, who had feigned sleep, was standing under the priest's window, waiting for him to fall asleep. He reached into his pocket and brought out a small pebble and he threw it up against Father Non's window on the second floor. When the priest did not respond, he knew Father Non was asleep. He turned on his heels and hurried toward María's.

When they saw Pedro hurry off, as they knew he would, the children ran to the hen house.

In the darkness, Matías felt for the turkey while Juan guarded the gate from the inside. Cota and Frances stood halfway between the hen house and the rectory, keeping a close eye on Father Non's bedroom window. Matías went around on his knees feeling through the straw for the old rags that Pedro had strewn on the ground for his bedding.

"Hurry up," Juan whispered.

The turkey remembered Juan's voice and got up from his perch in a hurry. He rustled his feathers, beginning at the neck and working his way toward the tail. Matías could barely make him out in the darkness.

"I can see him a little," Matías whispered.

"Get him," Juan whispered back. "Let's get out of here."

The turkey, hearing Juan's voice once more trotted toward the door. Matías reached out and grabbed him by the neck. The turkey was so full of corn and string that he could only let out a muffled gobble, but it was enough of a disturbance to Father Non's sleep that Father Non turned in his bed. Father Non listened for a while. Not hearing the turkey again, he tried to return to his sleep. Finally, giving in to worry, he got up and went to the window and stuck his head out. He looked down into the darkness of the night and yelled out for Pedro. "Pedro? Are you all right?"

Juan answered, imitating Pedro, "Yes, good father," he replied, giggling foolishly as Pedro would have done.

Father Non then said, "Be careful down there. You stay with the turkey and keep him company. We wouldn't want anything bad to happen to him. You'd be in the hottest water imaginable if it did. Hotter than hell, Pedro. I warn you."

Juan replied, "Yes, good father," in Pedro's voice.

"Now go to sleep," Father Non said, sticking his head back inside.

Matías and Juan held the turkey down while Matías groped for the turkey's mouth. Matías forced it open and felt inside with his fingers until he found the end of the string from his necklace protruding from the gullet. He wrapped the end of the string around his fingers and pulled on it and felt the resistance. They went quickly on their knees to the gate, leading the turkey behind them. Cota and Frances had moved over by the gate in case they had to run. Cota and Frances helped to open the gate and saw

Matías come out first, holding the end of the string with the turkey at the other end. Juan was right behind the turkey.

Once outside, the turkey saw the children plainly for the first time, and recognizing them, he let out another muffled cry, a happy greeting. That was enough of a scare to send the children running, the turkey alongside them. Cota was looking back to see if Father Non had come out of bed. He had. She could see Father Non standing at the window, looking down, yawning.

They ran as fast as the turkey would let them, and when they arrived at the depot, Lupito was already asleep, anticipating a full day to come. He heard the knock on the depot door and at first was afraid to open the door, thinking that perhaps it might be his mother or, heaven forbid, Herminia again. Then he heard Matías asking for him to open the door.

"What is it?" he asked, turning the lock.

Without answering, the children ran in and slammed the door shut.

Lupito saw the turkey and had to scratch his head in amazement.

"Don't say a thing," Cota warned him, wagging her finger at him.

Matías moved toward Lupito, forcing him toward his chair. He said, "Earlier today, when I fixed the telegraph machine, you promised that you would do anything for me. Well, this is what I had in mind."

"No one is going to have this turkey." Juan threatened.

Then Matías said, "This turkey is going with you."

"With you," Frances repeated, wagging a finger at Lupito.

"I'd like to see Pedro get out of this one," Cota remarked.

In the morning, when the train to Laredo arrived, they loaded Lupito's cardboard box full of his belongings and a wooden box with the turkey.

The children stood on the platform and waved Lupito off to Laredo to find his love and his happiness. Lupito, a tear in his eye, pressing his face against the window, waved back. The feelings that engulfed him were staggering. He had never been out of town. He viewed, for what he thought was the last time, the depot where he had worked all this time. He could not help but feel a love for the place, for the town. And as the train began to veer to the left toward Laredo, he opened the window, stuck out his head and shouted, "Tell my mother that I'm safe. That maybe someday she can forgive me." After the turn, in the early mist, Lupito could see the houses of all the people he knew. Close to the tracks, off the center of town, he saw Celestino walking in front of Relincho, delivering his milk. He thought he could hear the familiar clinking of the milk bottles, but he knew that that was his imagination.

María was already cooking breakfast when she was surprised to see the children walking on the road coming toward the house. She had supposed that they had been in bed asleep. When they came in, she asked them where they had been so early in the morning.

"To church," Cota replied.

"To church?" María responded in that familiar state of confusion that the children kept her in.

"Yes, Mamá," Matías agreed, "and we saw Lupito."

"Lupito?" María asked. "What about Lupito?"

"He took the train to Laredo, Mamá," Frances informed her.

"Heaven on earth," María cried out softly, feeling sorry for Mercedes, Lupito's mother. "Only a mother knows what pain Mercedes will be in when she finds out."

Chapter Twenty-One

The month of rain came early that year. The rain began lightly, falling on the parched ground, causing puffs of white dust as the first drops fell on the dry limestone.

María was hanging out the wash when she smelled the moisture in the earth from far away. She looked up and she saw the rolling clouds gathering strength, moving toward the town. Then she heard the distant thunder. Immediately, she took the wet clothes off the line and ran inside the house. She took out the make-shift line that she used every year, and she stretched it across the kitchen, through the door and into the hallway, where she found the nail still imbedded in the wall. By the time she hung the clothes, the rain began gently pelting the tin roof. She worried about the children in school.

Mr. Rodríguez was with the children at recess in the morning when he smelled the moisture in the air. He had not seen the clouds yet, but having been raised in the town, he recognized the smell and he stopped the children from playing and all of them listened carefully for the rumble of the thunder. It was not two minutes before they heard the noise, and Mr. Rodríguez led the children into the building. Once inside, he closed the door and checked the roll to make sure everyone was there. When he could account for all the children, he let them go. And the children ran home in the rain, shouting happily that school was out.

Cota, Frances, Juan and Matías were running at the head of the pack. At the center of town Juan Garibay's children caught up with them. María's children looked across the street and saw Anna pedaling Argumedo's traded bicycle in front, followed by Petra and then Antonio and, bringing up the rear, was little Gabriel. When María's children turned right, toward home, they saw Juan Garibay's children turn toward the dump. Cota turned around and yelled at them, warning them that the dump was not safe if the rain penetrated their diggings. Juan Garibay's children stopped and listened to the warning that the dump could collapse under the weight of the rain. They took Cota's advice and they all headed for home.

⋇

Father Non, Sheriff Manuel and Don Lupe, the mayor, were in Father Non's office at the rectory. They had spent much of their time going from house to house, checking every room, every corner in town, looking for the vanished turkey. Even after all their leads were exhausted, they persisted as if they had been handed a personal challenge. They were meeting at the rectory once again to see if they could figure out who had stolen the turkey and how.

Just as they began to discuss the theft, Father Non turned up his nose, sniffed and said, "I'm beginning to smell rain."

"Don't be ridiculous, good father," Don Lupe, the mayor, interrupted, squinching his nose like a little possum, trying to detect the moisture in the air. He was sitting in front of the desk alongside the sheriff.

"It's rain," Father Non replied, standing up from behind his desk and walking to the window. "I may not be very good at some things . . . but rain I know. You have to grant me that. I will swear on my ring that it is rain."

Sheriff Manuel shifted his heavy bulk forward and said, looking Father Non in the eye, "That's impossible. The

185

month of rain is at least two months off."

Father Non walked back to his desk from the window and noted to himself how much weight the sheriff had put on since Christmas. Sheriff Manuel had always been a big man but now he was huge.

Father Non took his pen and crossed out another suspect off his sheet. He whispered the name to himself, "Don Chema, the tailor," and then he crossed out the succeeding name. "His wife, Marilisa," they heard him say. Then he directed his full attention to the window and said, "Impossible or not, it's here," and he said it with such a definite air that Don Lupe and Sheriff Manuel had to agree.

"And we haven't found the turkey yet," Don Lupe mused.

The sheriff, barely able to lift his leg to cross it, asked, "I wonder how they did it?"

"They? Still with the plural, Manuel?" Father Non asked him.

"Yes . . . they," the sheriff responded.

Father Non stroked his chin and then said, "You're being stubborn, Manuel."

"I still believe María's children had something to do with it," he replied. "And that's not being stubborn."

Don Lupe, the mayor, said, "That's not being stubborn."

Father Non brushed Sheriff Manuel's comments aside. He said, "That's impossible. We've checked every corner of the house. The shed."

The mayor leaned over to rest his elbows on Father Non's desk. "It was an act of genius," he pondered. "You have to admire the thief."

"Thieves," Sheriff Manuel corrected him.

"And now the rain," Father Non said, suddenly losing all hope. "We'll lose all scent of the trail."

"Pedro?" Don Lupe erupted with the name, eyeing everyone for approval. He had forgotten that they had gone over Pedro as a suspect before.

Father Non flung the pen on the desk and stood up once again, walked to the window and opened it. He took a long whiff of air. "We've been over this many times before, Don Lupe," he reminded the mayor. "How many times do I have to tell you?"

The mayor sat up straight to accept the scolding from Father Non. "I'm sorry," he apologized. "I just keep going back to Pedro. My mind . . . I have a repetitive nature. If you've noticed."

"Pedro has been crossed off. We couldn't prove anything," Father Non re-explained. Father Non looked out of the window far out into the distance. The other two men could tell that he was thinking deeply and was not to be interrupted. Father Non said, "It was someone. Someone that could imitate his voice . . . but who?" The priest continued his thoughts back in time for a few moments and could hear the voice all over again. "Now that I replay the voice in my mind's eye," he said, the fingers of his right hand thoughtfully playing with his lip, "I should have known right then. The voice sounded more like Pedro than Pedro."

"The voice sounded more like Pedro than Pedro? How could that have been?" the mayor sought an answer. "To imitate a voice and sound better than the original?"

Father Non lowered his head and thought again for a few moments. Dumfounded, he replied, "It defies the imagination."

"It does," the mayor said. "It defies the imagination."

Father Non sat down and studied the names on his list. He looked out through the open window at the shadows that the distant clouds were beginning to cast on the church wall across the yard. The other two waited for him to look down at the paper with the list of suspects once again.

"I can guarantee you, good father," Sheriff Manuel said, interrupting Father Non's interlude, "that it was not Pedro. Whoever planned this was as cunning as a snake, as sly as a fox." "We are dealing with a cunning mind," Don Lupe repeated the sheriff's thoughts.

"That is why from the outset I knew it could never have been . . ." Father Non said, stopping short. "I just don't know what to do about Pedro," he continued with his thoughts. "Sometimes when I think about it I want to . . . well, what is a priest to do? I had to let him go."

"I haven't seen Pedro in several weeks," the mayor remarked.

"He's around," Sheriff Manuel informed them. "He spends his time at the taverns."

"Like he did before I found him," Father Non reminded them. "But," he kept on, "let us talk of more pleasant things."

"If this is the start of the month of rain," Don Lupe worried, "then we will have lost all our clues."

Irritated to hear his words again, Father Non said, "That's what I said."

"Without a doubt," Sheriff Manuel replied.

"Without a doubt," Don Lupe whispered so that no one would hear him.

Father Non looked out through the window again and his mind drifted back to the torrential rain of that year when he had seen Gonzalo's mule, broken off from her halter, running toward the rectory. She was blinded by the driving rain, galloping ever forward until she fell into the ditch and drowned. His conscience bothered him once more when he remembered that he had not gone out to help the men resuscitate the mule, nor had he come out to give it its final rites, so afraid had he been of the rain.

"The rain, Father," he heard Don Lupe in the background.

Father Non sighed heavily. "Yes," he said, "the rain. It's here."

⊁

María by now was hurrying to bring the children home, when she saw Cota and Frances and Juan and Matías running toward her. She yelled against the wind for them to run faster. The drops were beginning to get bigger, and the ground was turning to mud. At the same time she could see

Pedro running toward her from the right, from the direction of the taverns. He was yelling at María in a slurred voice for María to go home, that he would take care of the children. But María would have none of that.

She ignored Pedro as he ran toward her. Pedro staggered forward, his pants hanging so low that María felt they might fall down with every step he took. She was trying to run and at the same time cover her eyes so that she would not see his underwear if his pants should fall.

The children saw Pedro coming from their left, and they began to yell to their mother not to talk to him.

María met and embraced the children just as Pedro came up. He was so drunk and exhausted that he was barely able to stand against the wind. Before he could insist on helping them, María and the children ran home, leaving Pedro standing alone. Seeing that he was not wanted, he staggered back to the taverns from where he had come.

As they reached home, María and the children encountered their neighbor, Martina. She was out on the porch holding her bonnet down to protect it from the wind. Martina shouted at María that Francisco, her husband, had decreed that the month of rain had officially started and that he was already in the process of anointing himself with mentholated oils to protect his skin from the moisture.

The whole town began closing. Don Napoleón had been caught napping at the post office. The rain drops of the second hour awoke him. He shot out of his chair and locked the post office and rushed home. Across the street Don Porfirio took in his old magazine rack and locked up. He ran home. Don Chema, the tailor, hurried to the fire station to wake up Don Antonio, the siren master, from his late morning nap so that he and Don Antonio could crank up the siren. Together they cranked the handle and the siren blew like it did only at the beginning of the month of rain.

From the rectory, Sheriff Manuel drove one more time to park in front of María's house, hoping to catch the children with the turkey. He gave up his vigil when the rain fell so hard that he could not see across the street. He returned home to find that Inez had cooked tremendous volumes of food in preparation for the month of rain. He looked for her in the kitchen, but Inez had gone to hide in her side of the house. He sat down to eat.

Argumedo had eaten breakfast and was back in his room preparing to go to work on the barn when he heard the ruckus in the kitchen. He could not imagine that Genoveva Marín was looking for the largest butcher knife she owned. By the time he stepped outside, Genoveva had found the butcher knife. She was standing in the middle of the backyard flailing away at the clouds, cutting at them with the knife, trying to keep the clouds from forming into the torrents of rain that were to come.

"It's the month of rain!" she shouted, looking back at Argumedo.

Argumedo could feel the coolness in the wind. He ran inside and picked up the tools he was using to clean the barn. Genoveva advised him against going, but he was determined. He could not lose the only thing he owned. He ran to the barn.

By the time he arrived, the rain had started in earnest. He had never seen raindrops as large as these. Inside the barn he could hear the barrage of rain, like artillery fire, pummeling the roof. Rain was beginning to drift in through the roof, through the walls. The water was rising. The remaining dust that he had not cleaned was reconverted to mud. The winds gained strength, and when he thought that the rain had lessened, it would return stronger than before. He spent the night at the barn and felt he would not live through it. He had little to fear. Never had anyone died from the month of rain.

María and her children, like the whole town, had been caught unprepared, but that did not create any hardship. María and her children were used to being alone, working, talking among themselves and enjoying it. They used their time to tend to the work inside the house—ironing, washing clothes in the tub in the hallway or on the porch, gathering rain water from the buckets on the porch to scrub the walls and the floor. Together they dumped the mattresses on the floor and took out the iron beds and springs, leaned them against the porch wall, scrubbed them with water and lye to kill the yearly accumulation of bed-bugs. Then they rinsed them off with buckets of rain water. They killed the bed-bugs on the mattresses by touching them with rags soaked in kerosene.

The rain did not bother María as much as it did the children who, in spite of their chores, craved to be more active. After the first week, they had grown tired of sitting at the table at night and staring at the postcards of San Antonio that Don Napoleón had given them for Christmas. They were anxious to leave the house, to go to the dump to play, to go visit Argumedo at the barn, to go visit Father Non. They did not miss school. "That is what you children should be missing," María reminded them when they started to complain.

At night, Matías devised simple little mathematical games for them to pass the time, showed them the magical properties of magnets and iron filings. Cota and Frances put on fashion shows, taking out all the clothes that they owned and some of María's, walking around the house modeling. Juan played for them on his imaginary saxophone, sitting in the hallway, making sounds through his nose. When they grew tired of playing, they carded small bits of wool that they took out from under their bed, still hoping that they could sew a quilt.

If the truth were known, Father Non enjoyed the month of rain. During this time no one could make their way to church. There were no masses in the morning, no stations of the cross or rosary in the evening. He could sleep late. He could read. He could play with the lariat, roping the furniture. He could play the mouth harp. And most important, he could play with his magnetic ring and entertain himself with the magical properties of iron filings.

At the end of the second week, Genoveva Marín was so worried about Argumedo that she put on a pair of old rubber boots that belonged to Maxímo Pérez, her late husband, covered herself with an oil cloth and went to look for him. She trudged through the mud and rain and found Argumedo inside the barn, completely wet and wrinkled, trying to nail pieces of lumber from the walls to the roof, trying to keep the barn from collapsing. She convinced him that he needed food to survive and she brought him home. "No barn is worth your life," she told him.

Juan Garibay had set up the bicycle on blocks for the children to ride inside the house. No sooner had he finished the job, than the children began to fight over who had ridden for how long. Carolina had brought over a clock and each child was supposed to ride for a certain time. Anna did not play by the rules. The children were complaining, whining all day long.

Juan and Carolina Garibay became depressed at not being able to appease their children. After three weeks, Juan Garibay could take no more. He exploded and raised his voice to his children for the first time in their lives. He grabbed the bicycle away from the children, carried it on his back through the rain and mud to the washing shed and locked it.

When he returned he said, "The bicycle now belongs to Father Non. Let him raffle it."

⨯

At the end of the fourth week, María sensed the lessening of the rain. She felt the sun coming through. She got the children out of bed and they all went to stand at the porch to view the destruction. Large pieces of debris floated by in the ditches. The road in front of the house was covered in water. Don Pedrito's dog came floating by on an old wooden door. He barked at them.

The next day the old rooster crowed a mildewed sound that seemed to come from deep inside his throat.

Chapter Twenty-Two

Juan Garibay was as good as his word. As soon as the rain stopped and he could get out of the house, he loaded the bicycle in his car and drove it to the rectory. Father Non was sitting at his desk wondering what it was that Juan Garibay was unloading. When he saw Juan Garibay walking the bicycle toward the rectory, Father Non thought that it was being brought to him to be blessed.

On the contrary, it was Father Non who would be blessed. He would have the best raffle that the town had ever seen. And this time there would be no theft.

"I," he promised Juan Garibay, "will take care of this beauty."

"And Pedro?" Juan Garibay asked. "Will Pedro guard it?" He was one of the few people in town who did not know that Father Non had fired Pedro over the theft of the turkey.

"Pedro is gone," Father Non said.

Juan Garibay begged to differ. "I saw him just now sitting on the stairs of the church," he told Father Non.

"Impossible, Juan," Father Non insisted.

"Impossible or not," Juan Garibay said, "I just saw him. Just as I was unloading the bicycle."

"Then," Father Non thought out loud, "the infidel is back."

"I should say so," said Juan Garibay. "I did not know that he had been relieved of his duties, but I hope that whatever he did, you would find it in your heart to forgive him."

"It was you that he offended, Juan," Father Non reminded him. "It was your turkey that he allowed someone to steal."

Juan Garibay was more sensible in these matters. "Possibly," he told Father Non, "whoever stole the turkey had more use for it than I. I should hope so, anyway. And feeling like I do, I hold nothing against the thief or Pedro. Just as I hold no grudge against that someone that stole the wool off my sheep."

"That makes it easier for me to forgive the scoundrel," Father Non said.

⋊

Argumedo was in his barn working. He had reinforced the walls, had nailed lumber across and at angles connecting the walls to the roof. He had cut cedar shakes with Genoveva Marín's axe and had patched the roof. He had covered all the holes in the walls and re-nailed the siding. Inside, he had removed the mud and set his forge at the far corner and to his right. He was lighting the forge to reset some horseshoes for Juan Garibay when the children walked in.

So glad was he to see them and so glad were they to see him that both thought about embracing each other, but then thought better of it. Instead, the children eased over to him, and he sat at the half barrel and they sat in front of him to talk.

The children had prepared well during the month of rain. They weaved the conversation as one would take a dog through an obstacle course.

Argumedo showed his anger by biting his lower lip. He said, "I did not know that Sheriff Manuel was intent on sending you to an orphanage. I don't know what to say. Are you children sure?"

"Yes," Cota answered. "We are sure. He has talked to Mamá many times about us. Like he doesn't like us or something."

Argumedo asked, "Why hasn't Genoveva Marín told me about this?"

Matías replied, "He is smart. He only tells some people. Not everyone. Don Napoleón at the post office knows. You can ask him. He knows about the letter from the judge. The mayor knows. Inez, Sheriff Manuel's wife. She knows."

"Dr. Benigno knows," Juan said. "Remember Sheriff Manuel asked him about sending us to an orphanage when we fell off the bicycle?"

"What about Father Non? Does he know?" Argumedo asked.

Cota answered, "Yes, he knows, but he doesn't believe anything will come of it. He thinks Sheriff Manuel is not serious."

"I would not take a chance," said Argumedo. "I have known people like the sheriff. They need to be watched carefully. You can never trust a man like that."

"He hates us," Cota said.

Frances could not hold back the excitement that her infatuation with Argumedo produced. "Cota is right, Mr. Argumedo," she said. "Sheriff Manuel hates us. And we don't know why."

"What have we ever done?" Matías asked, innocently.

Juan said, "We've never done anything. Sure we play at the dump. But that's all."

"Now, we ask you," Cota said, with all sincerity. "Why would he want to separate us?"

Argumedo fumed over the injustice. "He must be crazy," he said.

"That's what we think too," Frances said.

"This is infuriating me," Argumedo said. "But don't you children worry. I am here now."

Ж

Father Non made his announcement at the Rosary that night. Juan Garibay had donated the bicycle that Benjamín Argumedo had brought from Mexico, and he was preparing for the biggest raffle in the history of San Diego. The congregation could hardly sit still while Father Non explained how the raffle was to take place.

Father Non had worked all afternoon and into early evening trying to outsmart the town. He wanted no repeat of the episode with the turkey. Therefore, he had come up with a fool-proof plan that would preclude any cheating.

There would be no tickets sold. The raffle would be for free so that everyone in town would have a chance at the happiness that the bicycle would bring. To insure that there be only one entry for each person, Father Non had come up with the idea that each person's name would be written on a small piece of paper that he would cut. The name would have to be in ink to prevent erasures. Father Non would write in the names of those who could not write. After the raffle, Father Non was to inspect every piece of paper to make sure no one had entered more than once. "Only the winner's name will be missing," he explained. Anyone trying to enter more than once would be dealt with by Sheriff Manuel. The winner had to be present and would take possession of the bicycle immediately. "He will ride it off the porch right then and there," he said.

The following morning when Father Non set out to cut the pieces of paper and write the names, he realized that the job would take longer than he had anticipated. He would need help.

He could see Pedro standing by the church wall, his hat in his hands. It was too much of a distraction. He called the sacristan over. "Come here, you fool!" Father Non shouted through the window, and Pedro's ears perked up at being talked to. He ran toward Father Non's window.

"Am I forgiven?" Pedro asked, running.

"Yes, fool!" Father Non cried out. When Pedro arrived at the window he said, "Get María's children. They, of all people in town, will be able to help me."

To a Widow with Children

Pedro lowered his gaze and twirling his old hat at his waist, said, "I've always said it, good father. María's children might be the devil in disguise, but they are smart. Why, I have known them to do things that defy the imagination. And I just happen to know where they are right now. I saw them when I was coming here. They and Juan Garibay's children are at the dump, digging tunnels."

"Go get them quickly," Father Non ordered.

"I will, good father," said Pedro. Then, to show his appreciation for having been forgiven he said, "I will work for free. If I don't get paid, I don't mind. As long as the good father forgives me for what happened to the turkey. And the way I figure it, working for you, good father, is its own reward. Payment enough. You know that I will never stray again. Just last night I prayed to the Virgin to guide me, and she says that liquor will never touch my tongue again. And I believe it, good father. And I told . . ."

"All right. All right," Father Non said from inside his office. "I can't stand listening to you anymore. As of today you will get paid."

"Father Non," Pedro responded in an aside to an imaginary companion, "is a saint if there ever was one."

"Go for the children," Father Non ordered him. "Go without delay."

Within an hour María's children had arrived running, Pedro running behind them like a shepherd. Father Non insisted that they wash their hands. Afterwards, they returned to sit around Father Non's desk, folding papers and cutting the strips that Father Non had decreed for the raffle. On top of Father Non's desk was a list of people that had not been able to write their names. Father Non was patiently scribbling the names on the raffle strips with his fountain pen.

The conversation between the children and Father Non ranged from questions about the priesthood to Pedro and his being rehired; they talked about school, Argumedo, Sheriff Manuel and his behavior toward them.

"You have got to remember," Father Non told them

about Sheriff Manuel, "that he and your father never got along."

"We didn't know that," Cota replied.

"And what does that have to do with us?" Matías asked.

"Human nature," Father Non explained. "Some types of anger take strange forms. This is one of them."

"He still wants to send us to an orphanage," Juan said. "Well," Father Non replied, "how can one be sure? You can never tell. One cannot predict what a man will do."

Frances gave Father Non a squinting glance and asked, "Not even you, Father Non?"

"Of course not," Father Non said, writing down a name. "I'm only a priest and priests are notorious for not being able to predict anything."

"Like when somebody is dead," Matías said.

"The people say that about you, Father Non," Juan told him. He wanted to get one more dig into Pedro. "Pedro says that you don't know when someone is dead."

Father Non knew what the people said, the rumors that they carried around. He was used to them. "Pedro is a scoundrel," Father Non said, not caring any longer what his sacristan said about him.

"You never say when someone is dead," Cota remarked. "Why?"

"Well," Father Non responded, "I love life so much that I just don't like to say that someone is dead. It's against my priestly nature. You see, children, I want everything to live. To live forever."

"We will all live forever," Matías reassured him.

"Ah," Father Non said, smiling faintly, "that that were true. That God would hear you."

Cota asked, "Why can't we live forever and ever? Why must we die?"

Father Non himself had asked that question many times, and the answer had always been the same. "We must die," he said, "to make room for the new order. So that others may live after us."

"I don't want to die," Frances said to him. She was cutting a piece of paper, her tongue sticking out.

"I'm scared to die," Cota said and then shuddered.

"Dying is beautiful," Father Non reassured them.

With the certainty of youth, Matías said, "I'll never know. I'm never going to die, Father Non."

"Oh, Matías is crazy," Juan said.

Cota agreed. "Don't pay too much attention to Matías, Father Non. He'll drive you crazy."

"I wish he would," Father Non replied, smiling.

"Argumedo is going to help us," Frances said.

The remark caught everyone by surprise. Even Frances surprised herself. She covered her mouth with her hand and began to giggle.

It took Father Non a while to recover from Frances' words. Then he asked, "How is he going to help you children?"

Cota replied, "He's going to protect us against Sheriff Manuel."

Father Non gave the children a disapproving glance. "Argumedo should not get involved," he said. "Sheriff Manuel is a formidable opponent."

"You mean strong?" Matías asked him.

"Yes," Father Non answered. "He is very, very strong."

"With the codgers and the women and children," Cota reminded him.

⋊

María was sewing alone at the table that evening when Argumedo knocked on the door. The children were in the girl's room and they ran out to see who had knocked. When they saw Argumedo, they greeted him warmly and held the door open for him. María was standing in the doorway, allowing Argumedo to pass on by.

"Now children," María said, "let's not be so noisy. Mr. Argumedo is not used to all this noise."

"I'm getting used to it," Argumedo said, warmly.

"I know," María said, laughing. "As much time as they

199

spend with you at the barn. How are the repairs on the barn coming along, by the way?"

"Doing very well," Argumedo replied.

He had followed María and the children into the kitchen. María asked him to sit down. Argumedo hung his hat on the back of the chair and sat down.

He continued: "Also, the farrier business is doing well. Juan Garibay sees to it that I stay busy. Today, Don Chema brought in the wheel from a sewing machine for me to fix. So it goes well. Very well."

"We're so glad," María said. "You never know how a business is going to do when you start."

Argumedo agreed. "That's true, María," he said, looking into her eyes. He felt the surge of love at the pit of his stomach ascend to his heart. "One never knows what is to be— whether one is a success or whether one is a failure. All we have is hope."

"Hope," María repeated. "What a beautiful thought. We have hope, the children and I."

María brought coffee, and the children returned to their rooms.

Argumedo continued, "The hope that you and the children have may be destroyed."

"By whom?" María asked.

"Sheriff Manuel," Argumedo responded.

"The children told you," remarked María. "Somehow I knew you would find out."

"It was just a matter of time," Argumedo said. María let out a sigh. "I don't want you getting involved," she cautioned him. "I will handle this problem by myself."

Argumedo responded by straightening up in his chair. "I would have to get involved," he said. "I do not condone an injustice, no matter what."

"I beg you," María told him, "not to get involved. I will handle this."

Argumedo remained silent. María knew that he had not agreed. She inquired, "What is the dearest thing to your heart?"

"Besides you, María, and the children," he responded, "it would have to be the memory of my mother."

"I want you to swear by that memory," said María, "that you will not get involved."

"If not?" Argumedo asked, wanting to know the consequences.

"If not," María answered him, "you will never set foot in this house again."

"Then," Argumedo said, "you make it impossible for me to get involved. Although it will kill me, I swear to you."

Chapter Twenty-Three

F ather Non abandoned his thoughts to glance at María dusting the bookcase. He heard the young rooster crowing. Not two seconds afterwards he heard the coarse voice of the old rooster trying to answer. "Two idiots," Father Non said, dismissing the petty rivalry. "And an example," he said softly to himself so that María would not hear, "of the excesses of self-importance . . . every little piece of feces wants to weigh a half a pound."

He blew on his magnetic ring, shined it on his shirt and admired it. "For some strange reason," he said to María, looking at it at arm's length, "this ring has increased its potency ten fold. Actually, I have to be careful where I walk. It keeps getting stuck to any metal nearby." He did not know that Matías had glued his most powerful magnet inside the ring.

"Your strength is in the crucifix, good father," María said. She had picked up the broom from the hallway and was sweeping his office.

"You're right, María, as usual," Father Non agreed. "It's just that . . ."

"You love your magnets," María finished the sentence for him. "Just like Matías."

"As a matter of fact," Father Non remembered, "he loves magnets as much as I. He loves to play with my ring.

To a Widow with Children

Whenever I allow him to, María."

"I can tell you love him," María said.

"All of them, María," Father Non assured. "I love all of them." He stood up quickly and stretched. He walked over to the window and peered out. He saw the old rooster chasing the younger one under the church. "It's time," he said, looking over to the door to check the clock in the hall way.

María went over to the desk and opened the drawer and took out the cigar box. She placed it on top of the desk. "Here it is," she said. "The papers for the raffle."

Father Non came over to sit down at the desk. He studied the box and said, "Today is the day. I somehow feel bad about it . . . mixed feelings, I should say." He paused to organize his thoughts. "You know, María, I've always loved a raffle. I know the people make fun of me because of it, but it's true. I love a raffle. Some say that the fathers before me enjoyed raffles, but I love them." He ran his finger around the lid of the cigar box. "Today," he continued, "seems like this may be the last one. Oh, I can't hide the years. The irremediable accumulation of sadness that one goes through in life. We must all look into God's eyes for love. There is where one must look. But, God, I do love a raffle!"

"Control yourself," María scolded him gently. "You never know what life is going to bring you."

"Like you, María," Father Non continued, "what a hard life you have led. You have taken everything God has thrown at you, and you have not bent one inch. You are the same person you were as a young girl. I can't tell you how much I admire you for never having compromised your principles. What an incredibly strong woman you have become. But still, you must be sad at times."

María was standing in front of the desk and said, "Oh no, good father. On the contrary. I am very happy. I am grateful for my children. God gave me something precious that he doesn't give to everyone. Some day they will be grown and proud. In the meantime, they are enough to keep me from worrying about anything else. I have to stay alert just to stay abreast."

Father Non said, smiling, "If I know them, you will be well taken care of in your old age."

María turned to hear the clock chime. "You've got one hour," she said, picking up her broom and walking out of the office. "The crowd will be here before you know it."

Father Non picked up the box, shook it and left it closed. He felt the heaviness of the names of all the townspeople. He could hear María in the kitchen preparing coffee.

By the time he was through sipping his coffee the crowd began to gather at the back yard. He got up and went to the window and noticed the early arrivers—the codgers, mainly. They were sharing a bottle of liquor, passing it among themselves. It surprised him to see Don Porfirio and his wife, Diana, with them, although when the bottle was offered to them they shook their heads to refuse. Next to the codgers, accepting their offer of liquor, was Pedro. Father Non saw him take a big swallow, so big that Gumercindo poked him in the ribs and got him to choke. Father Non went back and sat down, not minding anything that Pedro did anymore. "Who will the winner be?" he asked, without giving Pedro a second thought.

⋊

Cota, Frances, Juan and Matías got up late. They read the message María had left on top of the kitchen table. She had gone to clean the rectory for Father Non. They fixed breakfast, ate and went outside to play. When they saw the neighbors across the street, Martina and Francisco, come out of the house, Francisco with his hat on, they knew it was time for the raffle.

On the way over, Frances said, "We're going to win this time, aren't we?"

"No, we're not," Juan replied, full of gloom. "We never win." He was leading the pack.

"Oh shut up, Juan," Cota scolded him, following closely behind Juan. "You're so negative. You remind me of Pedro."

"But it's true," Juan cried out. "We never win."

"We're going to win this time," Matías said, quietly. He was bringing up the rear heavily in thought.

"How can you know?" Juan sneered, without looking back, his way of ignoring Matías. "You're not God."

Matías picked up a rock and threw it as far as he could and said, "You don't have to be God to win a raffle."

"You're crazy," Juan said to Matías. "No one knows who's going to win."

"I do," Matías answered.

Cota stopped and turned around and said, "If you're so sure, why didn't you say something before?"

"Because," Matías stopped and replied. "It's like stealing the turkey. If I say something someone is going to spill the beans or Juan is going to say it's not going to work. Or that I'm crazy. This is too important, so I just kept it to myself."

"Again?" Cota asked, finding it hard to believe that Matías had kept another secret from them.

"How are we going to win?" Frances demanded, walking backwards to face Matías.

Matías said, "It's my secret. But I know we're going to win. Just watch Father Non's hand when he pulls out the paper from the cigar box. Just watch."

"And just what are we supposed to see?" Cota asked him, not knowing whether Matías was telling the truth or not.

"If my calculations are right," Matías said, now walking with the rest of the group, "and if Father Non does what I think he'll do, then you will see something you have never seen before."

"What if Father Non doesn't do what he's supposed to do?" the unconvinced Juan wanted to know.

Matías jerked his little head and said, "Well, I tried. And we don't win."

"See," Juan complained. "I knew it. He's going to blame it on Father Non if we don't win."

"Does Father Non know about this?" Cota asked Matías.

"Because if he does, he's in trouble."

"No," Matías replied. "He doesn't know."

"Matías, you're crazy," Frances said to him.

"I told you he was crazy," Juan reminded them.

"Matías," Cota warned him, "you better be telling the truth."

⋈

At exactly twelve o'clock, when the chimes from the clock finished sounding, Father Non got up from the metal chair on the porch and quieted the crowd. Seated with him on the porch were Sheriff Manuel, Inez, Don Lupe the mayor, María, Juan Garibay and his wife, Carolina. Behind Carolina stood their children—Anna, Petra, Antonio, and Gabriel. Father Non asked the mayor to address the crowd. Don Lupe stood up, went to the edge of the porch and said a few words that no one heard, since the codgers were talking loudly at the same time. Don Lupe sat down and Father Non got up and scolded the codgers, told them that if they could not stand to be in the company of good and decent people, they should go back to the gutters of the town. The rest of the crowd applauded. Next, Father Non acknowledged Sheriff Manuel and his wife Inez. Father Non thanked Juan Garibay for donating the bicycle.

Cota, Frances, Juan and Matías had worked their way up to the front of the crowd to be next to Benjamín Argumedo and Genoveva Marín. Once in a while they would wave at María. María would wave back at them. She could see them laughing, pushing each other around. Argumedo waved at her and she waved back, smiling.

"Now," Father Non said, standing at the edge of the porch and very solemnly crossing his arms, "for the event we have all been waiting for. The raffle."

Father Non hesitated, smiled and looked over to the back door. Pedro had been listening from inside. When Pedro felt the pause in Father Non's voice, he took the cue. He pushed the bicycle out of the rectory and onto the porch.

Pedro lowered the kickstand and leaned the bicycle on its side, and then, after facing the crowd for an instant of eye contact, he lowered his eyes, giggled a few times and exposed his fang. The crowd cheered. Never had the bicycle looked so beautiful. Its color seemed to glow.

Father Non stood in front of the crowd and drew out all the emotion that he could from that moment. He cleared the phlegm from his throat. Father Non stepped back and got the cigar box from María's lap. He brought the box back to the edge of the porch and lifted it high for everyone to see. Juan Garibay's children were mesmerized by the occasion—the box, the brightness of the bicycle that had once belonged to them. Ignoring Father Non completely, one by one—Anna first, and then Petra, and then Antonio, followed by Gabriel—they walked over to touch the bicycle. Carolina frowned at Juan Garibay, and he stood up, apologized to the crowd for his children's greed, gathered them and brought them back.

Cota elbowed Juan and showed him that she had her fingers crossed. Juan crossed his fingers and elbowed Matías, who in turn crossed his fingers. Matías elbowed Frances and showed her his crossed fingers. Frances crossed her fingers and her legs.

Father Non shook the box violently over his head, tantalizing the crowd. He felt the force with which he held the crowd. He continued to shake the box until Herminia yelled for him to stop, that she could not take it anymore. Father Non held the box perfectly still over his head. He opened the box, his eyes still fixed on the crowd, enjoying the thrill that every second brought him. He knew at that instant that he would never forget this raffle. He was in rapture. He reached overhead into the box and mixed the papers inside, slowly stirring them. "Who will the lucky person be?" he shouted at the crowd as he continued to slowly stir the papers inside the cigar box.

The crowd was completely enthralled, watching Father Non's swirling hand inside the cigar box. Father Non's hand came out with two papers instead of one, if the crowd had been close enough to see—one paper between his fingers, the paper he had grabbed, and then the other, the one that fascinated Father Non. Right in front of his eyes he noticed this strange paper, resting like a white butterfly stuck on top of his magnetic ring. Mesmerized himself with the oddity of what he was experiencing, his hand went up of its own accord and Father Non dropped the piece of paper clasped in his fingers back into the box. As Matías had predicted, Father Non's love of things magnetic had betrayed his better instincts. His hand came back out and there, still perched like the white butterfly, was the piece of paper attracted to his magnetic ring. Father Non studied the picture silently, showed the ring and paper to the crowd, and the crowd "ooooed" and "ahhhhed" at the spectacle. Father Non reached for the paper, unstuck it with difficulty from his magnetic ring, opened it and stared at the name. He could not see the iron filings that Matías had mixed into the ink. "Matías García," he shouted and, when the force of reality struck him, he had to hold on to one of the support timbers on the porch to keep from fainting.

María, at first heard the words and did not realize that Matías had won. For some reason—the expectation of not winning, one would suppose—she had not connected the name with the winner. She smiled at first, and then, when the realization set in, when she looked at her children in the crowd and saw them jumping for joy, shouting happily, slapping each other on the back, especially Matías, she felt the rush of blood from her head, the identical feeling that she had had when Cota had announced that Lupito had won the quilt. She touched her forehead and felt the same cold perspiration, and the next thing she knew she was on her back on the floor of the porch. The last thing she remembered was Argumedo rushing to her side to hold her head.

By this time, amid the great confusion that swept the crowd, Matías had run up on the porch, had grabbed the paper out of Father Non's hands and the bicycle away from Pedro, had walked it down the stairs and had pedaled off.

Cota and Frances and Juan ran after him while the crowd remained in a great turmoil.

It had been ten years since Father Non had arrived in town, the day when he found no one in the streets, when everyone had been at Father Pedro's funeral, ten years since he had seen the Bishop. Ten years ago he made his way to the rectory, bowed by the weight of carrying his own suitcases, as if he were bearing a cross, coming to the realization that his life had been a disappointment and that probably he would have been better off selling shoes in Guipuzcoa, Spain, his native region.

Ten years later he felt the same way.

Chapter Twenty-Four

Judge Jaime was smoking out his bee colonies in the early afternoon when he heard the faint ring of his telephone. He put down his smoker and ran inside the house to answer the telephone, expecting the call to be about the honey that he had promised his neighbor. He picked up the telephone and said, without thinking, "I know . . . I know. I'll have the honey as soon as I can get the bees out of the hives." He wiggled his moustache, preened it to both sides of his mouth and listened as he heard the urgency of the voice on the telephone. Sheriff Manuel was asking him to take the next morning train.

"I've finally got them," he heard the sheriff gloat. "All we need is to present the evidence in a hearing."

The judge scratched his head and said, "All this for a pint of honey?"

Sheriff Manuel stopped and identified himself. The judge sat down and heard out the story. "And you're sure that this time you have sufficient evidence?" he questioned the sheriff. "You know I hate to do this if I don't have to."

Sheriff Manuel replied, "Absolutely."

"Very well," Judge Jaime said. "But," he cautioned, "you had better be right about this, or it will be a sad day for all of us."

Sheriff Manuel slammed the receiver down. He did not

appreciate Judge Jaime's superior attitude, the judge questioning the evidence.

Sheriff Manuel began to think that this day had been full of irritations. María's children winning the bicycle had upset him to no end. Had it not been for Inez, he would have taken his revolver out and fired a warning shot at Matías when Matías pedaled off with the bicycle. Inez had grabbed his hand and would not let go of it. It was only when Father Non had noticed the scuffle between the two during the rest of the melee that Sheriff Manuel had relented, but not before giving Inez a look that Inez knew could very well lead to further trouble.

After the phone call to the judge, Sheriff Manuel became terribly disturbed by Inez's incessant sounds in the kitchen, as though Inez were throwing pots and pans around to aggravate him. Then there was a silence, and he heard Inez walking toward his room.

Inez was in no mood to be pushed around. She stood defiantly in front of him and said, "I heard the conversation with the judge. I don't approve of what you are doing. I think you are crazy to want to inflict so much pain on María and her children."

"What would you know about pain?" Sheriff Manuel asked. "The pain I have suffered will not be any less than María's!"

Said Inez, "You have got to stop this madness. It's killing you."

Sheriff Manuel's anger rose. "I won't stop," he said, clenching his teeth. "I won't stop until I inflict pain on María and her children for what her husband did to me!"

"Well then, I'm leaving," Inez responded with as much anger in her voice as her husband. "If you cannot get over this madness . . . if you cannot get María and her children out of your crazy mind, then I won't live with you."

Inez turned abruptly and walked away from him to go hide in her half of the house.

Early in the evening, when Sheriff Manuel went for his early rounds, Inez gathered a suitcase full of clothes, a few of her favorite pots and pans, a few of her favorite recipes and walked to the rectory. She found Father Non sitting at his desk, checking the names on the papers from the raffle. He was more than happy to take Inez in, agreeing, after hearing Inez's confession, that Sheriff Manuel had been going crazy for some time.

⊁

As the sheriff had asked, Judge Jaime, short and fat, arrived the next day on the morning train. He got off the train, looked around for the sheriff, nervous like a squirrel, and failed to notice the loneliness of the place. Everyone had gathered at the courthouse. He strolled the platform a bit waiting for Lupito to come out to unload his baggage. Impatiently, he whistled for Lupito. When he saw that no one was coming out to help him, he walked over, went inside and found the office abandoned. He scratched his head and said, "Lupito? Are you here?" He couldn't help but notice the disarray. "What happened to all your neatness?" he inquired. He smelled the mustiness of abandonment, saw the old boxes strewn around the floor, saw the telegraph machine covered in cob-webs. "Son, you were the paragon of cleanliness. You were as clean as a drop of water," he murmured, walking through the debris, lost in thought of what could have happened to Lupito until he heard the impatient whistle from the engineer. He went to the baggage car, rolled out his own law books in their dolly, went back into the train and came out with his suitcase. He waved at the engineer. The engineer looked out to see if the tracks were clear. He waved back at the judge, and slowly started the train moving to San Antonio.

Don Jaime did not have time to put his suitcase down when the sheriff arrived in his car. Sheriff Manuel was not angry with Don Jaime anymore after having taken out his frustration on Inez.

The judge walked to where the sheriff had parked and said, "Where's Lupito? The place is a pig sty."

"Lupito is gone," the sheriff informed him, sticking his head out of the car window.

"Gone?" Don Jaime asked, as though that would be the last thing he expected from Lupito. "Left his mother? What was her name? I clearly remember the lady."

"Mercedes," Sheriff Manuel responded. He had gotten out of the car and was on his way to help with the baggage.

"Mercedes," the judge repeated. "What happened?"

"He fell in love," the sheriff said.

"Not a good affair, I assume?" the judge asked.

Sheriff Manuel picked up the suitcase and tossed it into the trunk. "No one knows," he replied.

"Poor man," Don Jaime said, putting his law books and the dolly in the back seat.

They got in the car, sat silently for a while as the judge contemplated the decision that he was about to render. "You are sure?" he asked Sheriff Manuel one more time. "Personally, Manuel, I need to be absolutely sure before we do what we are to do."

Sheriff Manuel turned the key and pressed on the starter with his foot. The engine turned over and he pumped the accelerator. When he had the engine going smoothly, he looked at the judge and smiled. "This time they've really done it," he informed the judge.

Don Jaime covered his ears. "Don't tell me. I don't want to hear," he said. "You know that my trademark is my objectiveness. I have never been reversed."

Ӿ

María and the children spent a fitful night after Sheriff Manuel informed them that Don Jaime was coming in the morning to hold a hearing on whether the children should be placed in an orphanage. While he was there, Sheriff Manuel took the opportunity to search the house for Matías' slip of paper. He could not have imagined that Matías had chewed on it until it became a frothy pulp, had shown the mess to Cota, Frances and Juan, and then swallowed it. When Sheriff Manuel arrived, María's neighbor, Martina, had been there to admire the bicycle and to tell María about Inez's leaving after Sherifff Manuel left with the bicycle. It was Martina who María sent to town to alert whomever she could about the hearing.

Argumedo arrived later to congratulate the children, but instead found them without the bicycle and despondent. He tried to cheer them, and promised that he would come by in the morning to accompany them. He asked María if she needed help and María refused.

Argumedo felt the frustration of not being able to do anything. "I have my revolver," he said to María, "in case you want me to stop him."

María declined. "That would be insane," she said. "That would leave my children scarred forever."

"You are right," Argumedo said.

"God will find a way, Argumedo," María reassured him.

In the morning, María and the children said the Rosary. Martina came in and told María she had informed everyone who was home. Those people had promised to pass the word. Furthermore, Father Non was to make an announcement at the early masses. María thanked Martina, and Martina went back home to feed Francisco so that he would be in a good mood for the hearing. The children ate breakfast after washing their faces. Argumedo arrived, looking more serious than María had ever seen him. They started for the courthouse. Midway, they met Pedro and he walked with them, silent for a change.

Inez and Father Non were waiting for them at the courthouse door. In the hallway they were joined by Herminia and her mother, Doña Juanita. Don Bruno, upon seeing the group, followed them, but not before first locking the tax office and securing his precious records. People from all over San Diego were coming up to the courthouse and standing in small groups.

Sheriff Manuel and the judge arrived to find the crowd at the front steps. They got out of the car, unloaded the judge's law books and walked inside, parting the crowd.

The judge, in a reminiscent mood, shook hands with the people he knew and exchanged greetings. He followed Sheriff Manuel inside, and the crowd followed them.

When Sheriff Manuel opened the door to his office, he found María sitting with her children up front. Cota and Frances were sitting on her left, Matías and Juan on her right. Father Non, looking very apprehensive, sat next to Juan. He was saying his Rosary. Among the people in the row of chairs behind María, sat Argumedo, Herminia and her mother, Doña Juanita. Pedro had sneaked over to the back wall to be among the codgers and Don Porfirio and his wife, Diana. Juan Garibay and his wife, Carolina—without the children—were sitting in the row behind Argumedo and Herminia and her mother. Next to Juan Garibay sat the mayor, Don Lupe, and his wife, Celia.

Sheriff Manuel went and sat behind his desk. He waited for Don Jaime to rest his books against the wall behind the desk. As the judge took his seat next to the sheriff, the rest of the crowd followed in.

When the crowd had settled down, Don Jaime stood up and went behind the chair and brought back one of his law books. He placed it on top of his desk, opened it and began to read it to himself.

Father Non put his rosary in his pocket and stood up, faced the crowd and asked for quiet. "I realize," he began, "that this is not my realm. I am not the authority here in this room. Don Jaime, the judge, is. But I feel an obligation to represent the moral environment of this town. I feel that I represent the spirit of the law if not the intent, which are not always one and the same.

"If it is proper at this time, I should like to say a few words about María and her children." Father Non looked down at the floor and remained silent for a while, sorting out his thoughts. "It's hard for me to imagine that we are even here," he began. "When I found out about this hearing from Martina last night, it was hard for me to believe it.

"There are a lot of rumors about the children, I know. The turkey and the bicycle are the two most prominent ones. I cannot believe that they would have anything to do with the turkey. Furthermore, I do not believe that they would have done anything to alter the results of the bicycle raffle.

"They are mischievous, for sure, but what a delight they are for anyone who knows them. I beg of the judge to find in favor of the children and let them stay with their mother."

The crowd broke out in applause. The judge looked sternly at Father Non, and Father Non sat down.

The judge banged his gavel on the desk top and, when the crowd settled down, he said, "This is a hearing and there are certain rules that we must abide by. Father Non's comments are taken in good faith, but he was clearly out of order."

That silenced the crowd. Father Non sat down quietly and crossed his legs. He put his arm around Juan.

The judge preened his moustache with the fingers of both hands while looking at the crowd over his glasses. Then he cast a quick glance at Sheriff Manuel sitting to his left and cleared his throat, a sound meant to tell the sheriff that the hearing had begun.

Sheriff Manuel got up and walked around to the front of the desk. He began to walk back and forth in front of María and her children and Father Non. He began to tell the town of the trouble the children had caused. One by one he brought out the litany of their crimes. The judge, in the meantime, wrote everything down.

"I have seen them steal the bitter oranges from the courthouse trees," the sheriff kept on, desperate, as if that were a crime. "They are very unstable, always wanting to leave for other places, never satisfied. They endanger their own lives as well as the lives of others by riding under the train in order to leave for other places." And when he couldn't think of anything else to accuse them of, he told the crowd of the suspicious quilt. He cleared his throat as if to gain confidence and said, "Lupito is gone, of course. And I cannot prove that there was not a quilt. But neither can they prove that there was a quilt. María knows. Why don't we ask her?" He rubbed his chin, walking back and forth. "The turkey," he thought out loud, "what happened to the turkey? Surely it was them," he said, "and now the bicycle. No one here can tell me that Matías did not cheat. How he did it . . . well, we may never know. We can't find the paper with his name on it. I have gone through every inch of María's house. And, if that were not enough, they stole, I'm sure, the letter that the judge had sent me. Where that letter is, I don't know. You would have to ask them. And God knows how many other things they've done. For example," he said and went over behind the desk, excused himself with Don Jaime and opened one of the drawers. "Look at this," he said, taking out the half-eaten string of corn that Matías had made into a necklace. "Who but these children would make something like this? Juan Garibay and Don Lupe are my witnesses that we found this in Juan Garibay's pasture. I know how it was used. It took me some time but I figured it out. It was fed kernel by kernel to several sheep and while the sheep ate the string of kernels, the children sheared the wool off the animal. When they were through with a sheep, they would pull the string out and feed it to another sheep. This device was used to steal wool from Juan Garibay."

María saw the necklace once more and couldn't help but gasp. She was about to jump to her feet and say something, when Father Non placed a finger on his own mouth, signaling her to be quiet.

"All this evidence keeps mounting," the judge interrupted, not quite finished writing down what the sheriff had said.

"Where did you find that?" the judge asked, pointing at the string of corn with his pen.

"Don Lupe, the mayor, Juan Garibay and I found it in the pasture," Sheriff Manuel replied, "just after several of Juan Garibay's sheep had been sheared."

The judge finished writing, and he turned the pages on his law book and read for a while. The crowd watched in silence as he stopped, scribbled some more and then nodded his head toward the sheriff.

"They are a menace to the town," Sheriff Manuel continued and went and sat down. "Incorrigible," he said to finish off the condemnation.

Juan Garibay stood up and asked Don Jaime for permission to speak. He said, "Your Honor, I relinquish all claims to the turkey and the wool. And I hope that that would satisfy Sheriff Manuel."

Don Napoleón was next. He said, "I will personally pay for any damage, real or imagined, that these children have done." Don Napoleón turned around to face the crowd in every direction, looking for someone to lay claim for any damage done them by the children. No hands went up. He sat down.

Father Non stood up and said that he had checked all the names in the raffle slips and the only one missing was Matías García. The raffle had been honest.

Don Antonio, the siren master, stood up after Father Non sat down and said, "I am responsible for taking care of the sour orange trees. I relinquish any rights to the sour oranges on those trees. I encourage anyone to take them, they are of no use and so bitter. María's children are the only ones who eat them."

The judge looked over his glasses at María and the children and asked, "Well, what do you have to say for yourselves?"

María started to get up, but Matías jumped up before she got to her feet and he said, "No one can be made to say anything against himself. My teacher, Mr. Rodríguez, says it's in the constitution."

María got to her feet, forcing Matías to sit back down. She said, simply, "I have no defense except to tell everyone here that I love my children and I will fight to keep them."

The judge looked through his book. He bit his lip under the moustache, knocked the gavel on the table a couple of times and said, "We need a recess." Saying that, he got up, adjusted his clothes and then followed Sheriff Manuel into the restroom.

The crowd started to buzz. Father Non got up and embraced María. "Don't give up," he said. "I've been praying for you and the children."

Argumedo came over to María and the children. The children embraced him. He gave María a very stern look and asked her if she realized what she was doing? María said that she did. Herminia and Doña Juanita came over to tell her that they were praying for her and the children.

The other women were trying to get up front to hug María, when the cries from a little child could be heard outside in the hallway. Don Napoleón and Don Bruno ran to the door and yelled that one of Juan Garibay's children was running up to the sheriff's office. Juan Garibay shot up out of his chair followed by Carolina, who had cried out when she heard the news. They ran to the door to where Don Napoleón and Don Bruno were standing.

It was little Gabriel, crying, covered in mud. The cave at the dump had collapsed on Anna, Petra and Antonio. Only he had managed to get out.

The crowd left the sheriff and the judge in the rest room.

Argumedo, thinking that the children knew more about the dump than anyone else, managed to get the children, himself and María into the car with Juan Garibay, Carolina and little Gabriel. All the way over, María kept consoling Carolina, who could not stop crying for her children. "They are dead!" she cried out. "I knew it. I knew that we had too much happiness."

Argumedo said, "Try to think that good things will happen, Carolina."

Juan Garibay was not crying. He was intent on driving as fast as he could. He would take corners at a great speed, tilting the car toward its side.

They were the first to arrive. They ran out of the car to the dump and saw what had happened. The whole dump had collapsed on the children. María's children began to walk about, checking out what had happened.

"Hurry," Juan Garibay pleaded with María's children. "What must we do?"

Carolina was hysterical by now and was trying to help her children by climbing up to the top of the dump. She did not know it at first, but she found the end of one of the breathing tubes that María's children built into the caves. Cota asked her to talk into the tube.

Argumedo asked the children to hurry.

At the same time María had gone to bring Carolina down from the top of the mound of trash.

Carolina was crying out that she had heard her children whimpering under the rubble through the tube. She had talked to them. This gave Juan Garibay hope. "Thank God," he prayed. Then he thought enough to reassure his wife. "They will be all right, Carolina," he said. But Carolina, in María's arms, was inconsolable.

After a quick discussion, the children agreed on the location of the cave. Cota decided that only one of them was to dig his way. Matías volunteered. He felt that Juan was too big to fit through the narrowed tunnels. Cota agreed and Juan, sullen because he could not go in, finally agreed. All four began to dig to find the exit tunnel, which they found without any difficulty. As they had imagined, the hole on the outside was partially collapsed also. They were able to shove Matías into the tunnel and he told them how dark it was and how narrow it was. "This is going to be hard," they heard Matías say. But soon enough they saw his little feet disappear into the tunnel.

At the same time Argumedo, Juan and Cota and Frances were clearing out the debris around the hole, trying to get air into the tunnel for Matías.

The rest of the crowd arrived exhausted, followed by Sheriff Manuel and Judge Jaime in the sheriff's car. Sheriff Manuel strode slowly to the scene. Judge Jaime, more excitable, ran to Juan Garibay's side. "What happened?" Judge Jaime asked.

"A catastrophe," Juan Garibay replied, solemnly.

Carolina let out another sob. "My children are trapped

under the collapsed rubble."

"Heaven help them!" Judge Jaime exclaimed.

"It's María's children's doing again," Sheriff Manuel said, walking up. "They are the ones who dig these caves."

"They are the ones trying to save my children," Juan Garibay told him, very sternly.

Juan could not stand for Matías to be struggling alone in the tunnel. He was thinking that he could follow Matías, enlarging the tunnel as he went. He could pack the trash against the wall, the floor, the ceiling and then make it easier for all of them to come out. He talked to Cota and explained what needed to be done and Cota agreed. In a second, Juan dove into the hole and disappeared.

The enormous heap of trash gave out a groan and collapsed even more. The crowd screamed. María ran to the hole to see if she could talk to Matías and Juan. Juan Garibay was running around trying to pick up trash and wildly throwing it about. Carolina was trotting after him. María could not hear a word from Matías or Juan from inside the cave. Juan Garibay ran to the top of the dump to the air vent.

Argumedo took off his shirt and ran to the hole and dove in and disappeared. Cota cried out and tried to jump in after him and then so did Frances, but María snatched them back, telling them that there was not enough room for everyone.

Argumedo could barely see inside the tunnel. He could hear voices up front—Matías and Juan. He spoke quietly, fearful that any noise might bring down the whole pile of rubble on them. Matías and Juan heard him coming and answered. They were working their way slowly.

Then Argumedo heard Juan say, "We're trapped."

Argumedo crawled on until he could touch Juan. "It's me, Juan," he said, patting Juan's foot.

"Argumedo's here," Juan passed the word to Matías.

"Good," Matías replied, quietly. Then he said, "If the tunnel collapses . . . we're all dead."

Argumedo reached a point at which he could not

advance. He said, "You boys are going to have to do this alone. I cannot fit anymore. I'll wait for you here."

They could hear Matías say, "I have got to do it." And he was able, with great effort to free himself and continued to dig his way toward the cave in the darkness.

Matías did not have to go two feet when all of a sudden the wall in front of him fell on him. He cried out knowing that for sure he had started an avalanche and that he and Juan and Argumedo were going to die. He felt his heart pounding. He remained perfectly still, not wanting to cause any more debris to fall on him. Outside they could hear María's faint crying, Cota and Frances encouraging them on. Then Matías and Juan began to hear the muffled cries of the trapped children. Matías closed his eyes and said a prayer as more rubbish fell on top of his head. Matías could hear Juan cry out to him. Juan could not see Matías anymore. Matías had disappeared in the trash.

Luck was with Matías. The avalanche was the debris falling down from the hole that led to the cave. After he uncovered himself, he plunged forward and fell into the cave that he and Juan and Cota and Frances had made from glass bottles. As soon as he fell he knew where he was. Juan Garibay's children heard him fall in and they let out a frightful scream. Matías yelled out in the dark that it was him, come to rescue them. He crawled around and found Anna, Petra and Antonio, huddled at the center of the cave. He talked to them, asking them to hold on to each other and that he would lead them out.

They could hear the voices from the crowd outside coming through the air vents. They heard Juan Garibay at the air vent begging God to save his children. Anna screamed at the top of her lungs that Matías had reached the cave. Immediately they heard Juan Garibay pass on the word and they heard the reaction from the crowd.

Then Juan fell into the cave. He had not been able to turn around and had to continue forward. It was decided that Matías would lead in front, followed by Anna, then Petra, Antonio behind Petra, and then Juan, all of them holding on to the ankle of the person in front.

Matías found some light at the widening of the tunnel. Midway to the opening, Matías heard Juan's screams at the rear. Matías stopped. He was able to hear what Juan was hearing—a rumble. The tunnel was collapsing behind them. Juan kept on screaming. It was all that Juan could do to keep from getting buried. He was fighting for his life. He kept telling Juan Garibay's children to pass the word to Matías to hurry up because he didn't think they could make it at that pace. Matías heard the crashing sounds of the tunnel giving way behind them. They were far enough along that they could hear the crowd saying that the whole dump was on the verge of collapsing and that the children would surely die.

Argumedo, as promised, was waiting for them. He had Matías grab him by the neck and Argumedo dragged the whole string of children out just in time to see the tunnel collapse behind them.

)(

That night Juan Garibay had the town over to his farm for the biggest celebration the town had ever seen. He had ordered five goats and ten geese slaughtered, five large buckets of beans, a whole barrel of prickly pears steeped in vinegar, one hundred pounds of prickly pear leaves cooked in butter and eggs, two ten-foot mounds of lard tortillas and a six-by-eight-foot prickly pear pie. The crowd ate it all. To Argumedo, Judge Jaime, and Father Non, who sat by his side, Juan Garibay offered the finest brandy that he had. To the rest of the men he offered the wine that he had bought in Laredo ten years earlier.

Judge Jaime spoke after the meal. All the charges against the children had been dropped. There were no more complainants. "I convinced Sheriff Manuel of the folly of sending these beautiful children away from their mother. The evidence anyway, I informed him, was purely circumstantial and not admissible as evidence under the statutes of Texas law. I had warned him beforehand that his evidence must be based on facts. Pure facts. Some of you here were present when I scolded him publicly. He'll never attempt this again."

Don Lupe, the mayor, could not resist. He got up, holding on to a piece of prickly pear pie, and announced to the crowd that the evidence as he saw it was not admissible under the statutes of Texas law.

Father Non ate and drank so much that the children made fun of his stomach. "It is not very often," he said, laughing, when it was his turn to speak, "that one gets to celebrate such a beautiful conclusion to a day. As you know, ten years ago I got off the train to find no one at the depot. The good Father Pedro was being buried as I know that I will. That is our fate. I just want you to know how much I love every one.

"And now, to praise the valor of María's children and of Argumedo, all of whom risked their lives to save Juan Garibay's children. What great love and kindness María has instilled in her children," he said, wiping a tear from his eye. "And to think that they were almost taken from us. And what can we say of Benjamín Argumedo? We love him now that he has become one of us," he concluded.

Juan Garibay got up from his chair and walked to the front, while Father Non sat down. He raised his arms in the air and asked for quiet. "Please," he cried out. "Please. Not too much noise or I can't be heard. My voice is not the best tonight. As you know, I have been screaming all day. . . . I will never be able to repay what was done for me this morning. I could live ten thousand times and I could not repay." He pointed to Cota, Frances, Juan and Matías, who were standing in the crowd next to María. "To these beautiful children I owe my eternal gratitude. What bravery. What heart they had. To risk their own lives to save my beautiful children." He pointed to his children, who were standing subdued next to Carolina. "I now must confess in front of my beloved children that what happened today was my fault. I feel responsible. I had implored my children to be more independent. Fearing, of course, what every parent fears, that in dying I would leave behind children who were not self-sufficient. What a worry that must have been to Gonzalo when he died and left his children. What parent has not done that with a child? As the saying goes: So much does the parent love his children that he kills them. And now, seeing my children alive and well, I can't say what it means to a father at a time like this. I am now announcing that as a reward I will personally pay for María and her children to visit San Antonio. There they will be the guests of my sister and her husband."

The children began to dance around María as the crowd applauded.

Juan Garibay held up his hands for quiet. The crowd quieted down. "We all know how hard these children have worked trying to get their mother and themselves a trip to San Antonio. Now they can all go. . . . And also," Juan Garibay continued, "I have decided that that is not enough. I am giving María's children the billy goat and the wagon so that they may have some form of transportation in town. Furthermore, I do not want a repeat of this episode ever again. The children should have a place to play. Accordingly, I am giving Don Lupe, the mayor, the authority to plan a playground for the children on the vacant land that I own next to Argumedo's shop."

There was more applause. Father Non stood up and once more walked to the front. He stood there in silence until the crowd acknowledged him. "We must remember Sheriff Manuel in our prayers," he said. "Deep down he is a good man. We may live from raffle to raffle and we may not have much," he reminded them, "but we have it in us to love and forgive each other all the time."

After the celebration, María and the children and Argumedo took a plate of food to Sheriff Manuel. They found him on the porch in his rocking chair, sullen. María and the children were in fear of him. Argumedo walked up to him and set the food on the porch.

On the way home, they heard the train from Laredo

approaching and sounding its whistle.

"A passenger," Argumedo said, half aloud.

"I wonder who it could be?" María asked.

"Some crazy person," the children replied.

It was Lupito, returned, broke and a lot wiser in love. His only remaining possession was the turkey.

They heard the train leave, taking Judge Jaime back to Corpus Christi.

In the morning Inez packed her belongings and left on the train for San Antonio.

Chapter Twenty-Five

On his way to the barn several days later Argumedo encountered Father Non. Father Non, sensing in Argumedo the frustration of unrequited love, walked alongside him and asked him gently if there were something that Argumedo would like to get off his chest. Argumedo began his confession of love but ended abruptly when Father Non replied that love must be spoken in order to be achieved.

"Your trouble, Argumedo," Father Non said, "is that you do not feel worthy of love. When you do, you will be able to ask María for hers. In the meantime, you must change. Remember that your handsomeness is in your bearing, your integrity . . . your being, and not in your physical appearance."

A bewildered Argumedo asked, "What should I do?"

Father Non put his arm around Argumedo and said, "My dear Benjamín, if I knew that, I wouldn't be a priest."

María was sweeping the floor that same day when she saw Father Non coming toward the house. Father Non crossed the ditch and asked María for some moments of her time. His mission was for Sheriff Manuel. He wondered if María could find it in her heart to forgive the sheriff. And if María could, would she please go to the sheriff's house and clean it. Father Non had been, he explained to María, to see Sheriff Manuel and the house was in such a state, so much

227

debris was on the floor, that he could not completely open the door to walk in. He had not, in any case, he told María, been able to talk to Sheriff Manuel. Sheriff Manuel refused to talk to anyone.

María informed Father Non that she would forgive the man and went in and dressed and walked over to Sheriff Manuel's house. She found that she could hardly let herself in for all the trash on the floor. She recognized the trash to be Inez's possessions, ripped and torn apart and scattered all over the house. She found the sheriff hiding in the back room, not wanting to see her or anyone else.

As she came by to clean day by day, María came to understand that whatever satisfaction Sheriff Manuel had achieved in having Inez leave was not enough to offset the pain of being publicly humiliated by Judge Jaime.

He had stopped going to work and had stayed inside the house most of the days. When she did see him go out, it was to walk around the yard for a few moments. Then, when he felt the presence of someone on the road, María would see him run in, not wanting to talk to anyone.

María would hear him speak to Don Lupe, the mayor, once in a while on the telephone. And so it was that at María's urging, Father Non began to telephone every day.

It was after Father Non's phone calls, imploring him to get out, face reality once more, that María began to see the change in him.

When Father Non went by one day, he took Benjamín Argumedo with him. Sheriff Manuel answered the knock on the door while María worked in the kitchen. He was surprised to see the two men there, especially Argumedo. After a moment of awkward silence, Sheriff Manuel was about to confess Inez's infidelity when Father Non put his finger up to his own mouth, a gesture to Sheriff Manuel that he should be quiet. "These things," Father Non explained to the sheriff, "are better left unsaid."

Sheriff Manuel then went into one of the rooms and came out with the bicycle and handed it over to Father Non. They left Sheriff Manuel feeling better about himself, which had been their mission.

That day, Sheriff Manuel experienced the grief of remorse and began his transformation.

Because of her daily visits, these daily changes became more fascinating to María, and a source of joy. The Sheriff began to talk to her. He asked about the children and how they were getting along.

One morning he informed María that he felt some pain in his side where he imagined his spleen to be. He felt the pain growing during the day, and he tossed about in bed that night, feeling restless, unable to sleep, agitated. He dreamed of devils running after him on the railroad track. That night, he got up and ate some hardened left-over pomegranate pie that María had found in the old oven, a relic from Inez. He felt better immediately. And although he tried to fight it by biting his lower lip, tears came to his eyes as he walked around the old kitchen where Inez had slaved for him. He could see in the darkness of the house the ghost of her presence bending over the stove. He began, night after night, to see her chopping wood, cutting up pomegranates, prickly pears, wild cucumbers, shaving rabbit ears, stirring the caldron of soup, dressing armadillos, kneading dough for tortillas, pie crusts, biscuits and cakes. One night, he scratched the stubble on his chin thoughtfully and asked in a lamentable voice, "What have I done?"

On a Sunday after church, María and Argumedo and the children went to see Sheriff Manuel and found him outside on the porch, rocking himself. He was inconsolable. The more they tried to convince him to go after Inez, the more he wished that she had not gone. By night fall he had cried and worried himself into exhaustion, and only then could he fall asleep.

Finally, one morning as he lay in bed looking out through the window, he saw what he believed to be Inez standing on the road in front of the house. His joy was immediate. He got up in his underwear and ran outside to her, only to find that she had disappeared. Feeling her loss once more, he realized then how much he loved her. That was the instant when he forgave her. He had no cause to cry again. He rushed into the house, looked for the Capsules of Oblivion and threw them away.

⑂

The morning after he returned, Lupito came to ask a favor from the children. In spite of all the questions they had for him, he refused to answer, telling them he did not have time. Right now what he wanted was a favor. The children agreed on the condition that some day Lupito would tell them all that had happened to him in Laredo. Lupito agreed. They went with Lupito to his house, took the turkey and turned it loose in Juan Garibay's pasture.

That afternoon, Lupito was at work, starched so heavily that he had had to walk to the depot without bending his knees. His mother had cleaned out the spiders in his lunch pail and had packed it with food she'd learned to cook from Inez's recipes.

Before leaving, Lupito had given his mother his instructions. Mercedes was to go visit Doña Juanita to prepare for his visit to ask for Herminia's hand in marriage. And when Mercedes started to object, Lupito raised his hand to quiet her down and said, "Mother, please."

Lupito's gesture, his words, reminded Mercedes of Lupito's father. She smiled and said, "Wait until you get hit with love. You'll be sitting at the outhouse door protecting Herminia from any intruder, like your father used to do with me."

Mercedes walked the mile to Herminia's house and knocked on the door and greeted Don Juanita when she opened it.

"I've come to talk to you about Lupito," she said.

Doña Juanita reeled slightly, holding on to the door jam, bringing one hand up to her forehead. It made her dizzy to think that for the first time in her life someone was showing any interest in her daughter.

"We have a groom's dowry," Mercedes informed her.

Doña Juanita collected herself rather quickly, not wanting to show too much emotion. She showed Mercedes in. They sat in the parlor, both waiting for the other one to talk.

"Herminia is a virgin," Doña Juanita volunteered, not being able to think of anything else to say.

"I supposed that," Mercedes replied. "My Lupito would not have it any other way. He is a virgin also."

Doña Juanita cast an unbelieving eye at Mercedes and said, "One then supposes that he didn't do anything in Laredo with that ugly woman?"

"Ugly man," Mercedes corrected her.

"Man?" Doña Juanita asked, looking perturbed.

"Lupito was made a fool. It was not a woman. It was a man," said Mercedes, shrugging her shoulders.

"So there was no woman?" Doña Juanita inquired.

"No," Mercedes replied, half aloud, not looking into Doña Juanita's eyes. "He swears it on his father's saddle."

Doña Juanita chose to ignore the response, not wanting to press the matter of virginity, Lupito's escapades, and the saddle any further. "When does he want to come?" Doña Juanita asked.

Mercedes let out a pitiful sigh to show Doña Juanita that she was on a mission that did not please her. She said, "Tonight, if at all possible."

Doña Juanita went to the lamp table, opened the drawer, took out an old appointment book that she had bought for Herminia many months of rain ago and she opened it and said, "Let me see if Herminia is free for tonight."

Doña Juanita's leafing through the appointment book irritated Mercedes. Mercedes said, "Herminia has been free for all the nights that she has lived. Does Herminia have a dowry?"

Doña Juanita sat down with the appointment book in her hands. "Yes," she replied, "my daughter will bring a dowry with her. But we must be formal about this. Both you and Lupito must come and ask for her hand in marriage. I would have preferred that your husband had been able to come."

"If only God could hear you," Mercedes replied. "He was the light of my life. As it is, we would have to dig him up."

"It must be formal," Doña Juanita insisted.

"We wouldn't have it any other way," Mercedes responded, got up, shook Doña Juanita's hand and prepared to leave.

At the door Doña Juanita said, "I have waited many years for this moment."

Mercedes, not in a forgiving mood, said, "I can imagine."

"And Lupito's one testicle?" Doña Juanita inquired, although it offended her to bring up the subject.

Mercedes replied, "Dr. Benigno insists that Lupito's remaining testicle could father a whole town."

⨯

Late that afternoon, by the light of the fading sun, Juan Garibay counted his livestock and found that no matter how many times he counted the turkeys, he appeared to have gained one.

Chapter Twenty-Six

María was swaying gently in her seat to the rhythm of the train when she was awakened from her reverie by Cota's voice.

"Mamá," Cota said, "did you like San Antonio?" Cota was lying on the seat and had her head on María's lap.

María said, "Oh, I liked it a lot. We had a good time."

Cota picked up her head, and looked María in the eye and asked, "But did you like it, like it? Like love it?"

María thought of how, when one gets older, that things are not as satisfying anymore, that the anticipation is better than the deed. And yet she did not want to ruin the children's mood. She said, "I loved it . . . for a while. It's not that important to me, Cota. I guess I don't like big cities. And things are never as good as you think they're going to be."

"You didn't like it," Frances said it for her.

"I liked it," María answered. "Now go to sleep."

"We can't sleep," Cota said, trying to reach the seat across with her feet.

"Matías acted crazy," Frances reminded them. She was sitting across from María and Cota. Her legs were long enough that she had her feet on the seat across from her, where María and Cota sat.

"Oh, leave him alone," María told her. "Matías will grow up some day."

"But when, Mamá?" Cota asked.

"He kept looking up at the tall buildings and then going round and round and then falling on the sidewalk," Frances said. "You didn't see him, Mamá."

"Juan was crazy too," Cota said.

Matías and Juan were sitting at the end of the passenger car, far from María and Cota and Frances. Matías was acting as though he were asleep and snoring, imitating the only other passenger on the train, an old man that was on his way to Corpus Christi. Juan was sitting across from Matías, his legs crossed, swinging his foot just hard enough to hit Matías' foot with his. Matías acted like it didn't bother him.

"I had only seen giraffes in pictures in the books," Frances said to her mother.

"I'm glad all of you got to see them," María said.

"And elephants, Mamá," Frances kept on. "I couldn't believe them. They were so big. The biggest thing I ever saw."

"Mamá?" Cota said, thinking to herself, "I don't like to ride in the wagon with the goat that Juan Garibay gave us. The people make fun of us."

"The men laugh at us all the time," Frances said. "They laugh at us when they see us in the wagon and the goat pulling it."

"Well," María said, "let Juan and Matías ride in it and you girls walk."

"Argumedo promised to take us to see the ocean," Frances remembered. "He promised, Mamá."

María looked at her reflection on the window and said, "If Argumedo promised, I'm sure he'll take you."

"All of us, Mamá," Cota reminded her. "He'll do it," Cota then said, starting to fall asleep.

"Knowing Argumedo," María thought out loud, "he will."

The conductor walked by and smiled at María and the children. Matías and Juan came over and sat with María and Cota and Frances.

"Isn't it true, Matías," Cota asked, "that the people in town make fun of us when we ride the wagon with the goat?"

Matías said, "I don't care. They can laugh, but I'm the one having fun."

"Matías acts crazy on the wagon," Juan said.

"No he doesn't," Cota said, "you do. You act crazier than Matías."

"That's true, Mamá," Frances tattled. "Juan acts a lot crazier than Matías."

"You and Cota act crazier than anyone," Juan accused Frances, defending himself and Matías.

Matías had to lie down to put up his feet on the seat across from him where Juan was sitting, placing one foot on each side of Juan's legs. "One building had five stories," Matías remembered. "I counted them."

"Mamá," Cota asked, "the snake that was in the cage . . . could it ever get out?"

"I don't think so," María replied. "Those people know what they're doing."

"I liked Juan Garibay's sister," Frances said.

"Her husband was nice too," Juan added. "I liked his car. One day I'm going to have a car like that one."

"Only if you go to college like he did," María reminded them.

"Where did he go to college?" Frances asked.

"He's a dentist," Matías replied.

"He takes care of teeth," Juan said, baring his teeth at Matías. Matías bared his teeth back.

"He was old, Mamá," Frances said.

María looked past her own and her children's reflection on the train window into the darkness of the night. "Oh, he's not old," she replied. "Old is like Juana or Doña Juanita . . . that's old."

"You're going to get old, Mamá?" Cota asked her.

"Yes," María replied, giving out a laugh at the innocence of youth. "I hope so. Some day when all of you are gone and I'm old, I'm going to visit you. It won't be long either. When you grow up, you'll know how fast life goes. It seems like yesterday that I went to see the ocean. I was six years old."

"Oh, Mamá," Cota said, "we're not going to leave. We'll always be together."

"No you can't. Everyone has to leave their mother," María said, stunning the children.

María realized that she had upset the children. While the children thought of the pain of leaving their mother, María took out her rosary and began to pray. "Let's be happy for today," she said, before starting.

"I liked it when we got to see Inez," Frances said.

"Who would think," María remarked, putting down the rosary, "that we would run into Inez at the restaurant?"

"At least she found a job," Cota said. "But I don't like the stuff she cooks, Mamá."

"It's horrible food, Mamá," Frances said, making a face.

"I didn't eat mine," Matías confessed. "I threw it under the table when no one was looking."

"Matías made a mess on the floor," Juan said. "I ate mine. I like that kind of food."

"You would," Cota said. She got up from María's lap, straightened out her skirt and then layed down with her head on her mother's lap once more. María pulled Cota's hair back and stroked it. Frances got up to sit on the other side of María, laid her head on María's lap next to Cota's.

"I want you to promise me," María said to Juan and Matías, "that you will never cut each other's hair again with the shears. People kept looking at both of you like you were crazy. I was so embarrassed."

"Juan started it," Matías said.

"I didn't. Matías started it," Juan said.

"I don't care," María warned them. "I don't care who started it. I just don't want you two cutting each other's hair. Now let's all go to sleep."

Cota moved her little head on María's lap, trying to get comfortable. "Do you think Inez will come back?" she asked her mother.

María replied, "Oh, yes. Of course. She'll tire of the big city. I was tired after one day."

"Her food is horrible, Mamá," Matías said without opening his eyes.

"But you don't complain when you are someone's guest," María said. "They were nice enough to take us to the restaurant."

"We didn't complain," Cota said.

"I know," María answered, "and I was proud of all of you. It wouldn't have been good manners to say anything . . . poor Inez."

The conductor got up from his chair and teetered over to the other end, stopping to talk to the old man, who was now awake. He held on to the back of the wooden seat in front of the old man and he leaned over and rolled with the train as he bent over to say something. When he was through, he straightened up and staggered, holding on to the seats, to the back of the car and he sat down, closed his eyes, clasped his hands over his ample stomach and almost immediately began to snore.

At ten o'clock, as it always did, the train whistled to alert Lupito, as if Lupito could not hear the distant huffing sounds of its engine. Lupito got up from his telegraph machine and went out on the platform. He went down the stairs and checked the water gauge at the foot of the cistern. He undid the rope that held the water pipe and lowered it to where it would be just above the engine. He climbed back on the platform and saw for the first time the train's searchlight, swaying from side to side, scanning the track.

The train came to a slow stop, and María and the children got off. Lupito ran to greet them. "How was it?" he asked, as the engineer loaded water.

"Very nice, Lupito," María replied, dusting herself off, "except that I could never live in a big city. Too many people. Too much noise."

"Did you see everything?" he wanted to know.

"Everything," Cota replied, yawning. "We saw everything that could be seen."

"And you didn't get into any trouble?" Lupito asked, rubbing Juan's and Matías' heads.

"No . . . heavens no," María replied. "We didn't get into any trouble."

The train spun its wheels, throwing red iron filings into the night. It began to move slowly and the engineer spun the wheels one more time. The train gathered speed, and slowly made its way into the night.

"We saw Inez," María told Lupito.

"You did? How wonderful. Is she ever coming back?" Lupito asked.

"I think so," María replied. "I don't think anyone can eat her cooking except Manuel. They were meant for each other."

Celestino rode by on Relincho, tipped his hat and bowed from the saddle almost all the way to the stirrup, losing his balance. He was so drunk that he almost fell off. Relincho, sensing the shift in the weight, adjusted his trot and allowed Celestino to straighten himself up. Once in the saddle he asked María how the trip had gone. María replied that they had had a wonderful time, and then she asked for Rebecca.

"She should be putting the cows to sleep," Celestino told them, above the clinking noise of the empty milk bottles.

"He's drunk," Lupito told them.

"Yes, we know," Cota said.

Matías, Juan, Cota and Frances were standing on the ground next to the tracks. María went down the steps with Lupito's help.

"Thank you, Lupito," she said.

In the distance they could hear the faith-healer Don Pedrito's dog howling at the creaking noises made by the breeze as it blew in the trees next to the creek by his bed. Inez's dog answered him. Relincho snorted out the heavy mucus that had accumulated in his nostrils from trotting all day from house to house. They heard Celestino talk to the horse, trying to pacify him. They heard the fading jingle jangle of the empty milk bottles striking against each other, as Celestino disappeared from the depot light into the darkness, like the train.

"These are beautiful sounds," María said to her children.

"Do you love Argumedo?" Frances turned around to ask.

María continued to walk. "What kind of question is that for children to be asking their mother?" she said. "I can't believe you would even ask. I like him a lot. I know that. I love you. I couldn't love anyone else as much as I love you."

"Do you think you ever want to get married, Mamá?" Matías asked her. He was now walking by himself ahead of the rest.

"I don't know," María sighed. "I don't think I ever will. What a question. Nobody has even asked me yet."

Matías sensed the discomfort that his mother was in. They heard Matías up front say, "Leave Mamá alone." Then Matías started running to get to the house first.

María said, "Pay attention to Matías. Leave me alone. Don't you children understand that I need to have my very own dreams? Matías, don't run so far ahead," she continued, but Matías was well beyond the reach of her voice.

"You have dreams, Mamá?" Juan asked her, surprised.

"Sure I do," María replied. "I'm human."

"Pedro asked you to marry him, Mamá," Cota said, teasing her mother.

"No, he did not!" María shot back rather loudly.

"And you think we'll go away and leave you, Mamá?" Frances asked from up front in the darkness.

"Oh, yes," María replied, "you will. Some day you will."

Cota said, very seriously, "I don't want you to ever say that you're going to get old like you said on the train. Do you understand that?"

María laughed and said, "All right, Cota. Whatever you children say. I will never be old."

"Mamá will live forever," Juan shouted, and the rest of the children began to yell their happiness.

At the end, Cota said, "Mamá, you may as well know it. We love Argumedo."

⅜

Two months later, bored with nothing else to do but ride the wagon pulled by the billy goat, the children decided that they would talk Argumedo into repairing the old bicycle so that they could raffle it. Matías rigged the raffle and Juan won the bicycle back. Several weeks later, they raffled the bicycle again, this time selling only eight tickets: to Lupito, Herminia, Argumedo, Father Non, Sheriff Manuel, Don Napoleón, Don Bruno and Juan Garibay. This time Matías won the bicycle.

Father Non had planned to raffle Argumedo's bicycle again, but when he saw what the children had done, he decided that all raffles had lost their credibility. Father Non vowed never to raffle anything else if the children would do the same. Instead, he rode the bicycle through town wherever he went.

Sheriff Manuel finally gave in. He took the morning train to San Antonio one day and returned with Inez. They went straight home, where Inez took off her traveling clothes, rolled up her sleeves and prepared the best meal the sheriff had ever had—Father Jaillet's, Father Pedro's and Father Non's favorite recipes: roasted prickly pears swimming in vinegar and cactus oil, pan fried rabbit ears, garden salad on an armadillo shell, roasted armadillo flanks, mesquite beans boiled in lard, lard tortillas, large panochas. And for desert, a huge slice of prickly pear pie.

⨎

Doña Juanita, Herminia's mother, sent off to San Antonio for ten yards of lace and ten yards of white brocade. She and Mercedes, Lupito's mother, worked on Herminia's wedding dress for several weeks.

The wedding was on a Sunday morning, and the whole town was invited. No one could remember seeing Herminia as beautiful as she had looked walking down the aisle that morning. Don Bruno gave her away. María's children were behind her, carrying the train. María could not remember seeing all four of her children wearing shoes at the same time, not even at Gonzalo's funeral. Lupito smiled proudly throughout, as starched as he had ever been. Father Non spoke eloquently of the wonders of life: time, distance and fate. Afterwards, the crowd walked from the church to Doña Juanita's, and the celebration began, but not without the barbs from the two mothers-in-law. Doña Juanita was still piqued that her daughter had married a man with one testicle. Mercedes had hated to lose her beloved son, and she made it a point during the Dance of the Women—where only the women were allowed to dance—to tell Doña Juanita that if Herminia mistreated her precious son and did not starch his clothes entirely, she would reclaim him, salvage him, she said, like some foundering ship.

The only unhappy person was Argumedo. Seeing so much happiness, which had evaded him for so long, brought back his old memories. Genoveva Marín invited him to dance, but he refused. He could not be close to María, who was with the children serving punch. When the children found the time to come to talk to him, they found him distracted, immersed in another world of revolution, disgrace and lost causes. María glanced at him from behind the punch bowl and thought he looked unusually distressed. She thought that maybe he was preoccupied with his work.

Despite his thoughts, Argumedo admired María from afar. The one thing he wanted the most he could not have— the story of his life. So heavy a burden did he carry that night, seeing so much joy from the newlyweds, that he retired early to contemplate his fate.

He took a sheet of the same paper that Genoveva Marín's boarder had used before he took his life, and he began to write. But he could not put into words what he felt, and he knew he had failed once more. His pistols, like his thoughts, were empty. Had he had them, the Capsules of Oblivion the Sheriff had thrown away, he would have taken them by the handful. Had not Don Pedrito's dog accompanied him on his way home and slept with him, he would have found some way to take his own life.

Chapter Twenty-Seven

In the morning, Doña Juanita summoned Celestino from his milk route to tell him she needed half a barrel of bee's wax. After the milk delivery was over, Celestino, from his bee hives, collected half a barrel of bee's wax and delivered it to Herminia's mother.

After breakfast, the children ran to see Argumedo at work, but could not find him. They went by the post office to see Don Napoleón, but he had not seen Argumedo this morning either. Neither had Don Chema, the tailor. They stopped to ask the old codgers, but no one had seen him. Sheriff Manuel took them in the car around town, but nothing was seen of him. Sheriff Manuel left them at the courthouse. By chance, they came by the depot and found Lupito, perfectly starched and sitting at the telegrapher's chair. His dedication astounded the children. When he saw them, he showed his concern by biting his lower lip.

"Why aren't you with Herminia?" they asked.

"Children," he said, "I have bad news."

"Argumedo?" asked Cota. She sensed something was wrong with Argumedo.

It was Argumedo. "He left on the morning train," Lupito informed them. It was all he could do to keep from crying. "I hated to see him go. He was such a friend. A man."

The children began to cry, each one going to a separate part of the room in order to let go of his sorrow.

"Why?" Matías cried. "Why did he leave?"

Lupito said, "He told me he had tried, but that it was no use. He did not want to be in the way any more."

"In the way of what?" Juan asked him, rubbing the flow of tears from his eyes.

"Your mother's happiness," Lupito said.

"Oh, no," cried Frances. "We thought he loved our mother so much."

"He did," said Lupito. "That was why he left."

Cota said, angrily, "I will never be able to understand older people. Why couldn't he stay?"

"He felt it was the best thing to do," said Lupito. "He felt your mother would never marry as long as he was here. He felt that you needed a father more than anything else. He left for Mexico this morning. He went to see Juan Garibay this morning to turn the business back to him."

"Now to tell our mother," said Matías.

×

María was sitting at the table cleaning beans for the noon meal when they arrived. They slowly walked in, their eyes red from crying. María saw them and frowned. What had they been up to now?

"You children look like you have lost your best friend. Have all of you been crying? And if you have, what is all this crying about? Has Father Non died?"

The children shook their heads.

"Someone has died," María said. "I can tell from the way all of you look. Why has not Father Non rung the bell to announce the death?"

Finally Cota was able to blurt out the words. "Argumedo has gone!"

María was stunned. She did not know what to think. Had she heard right? Argumedo gone? But he would return.

"Gone to go get supplies for the shop," María said. "It

243

should not upset you so much."

Matías said, "No. He left for good. He went this morning and sold his shop to Mr. Garibay and took the money and left."

"He went to Mexico on the morning train," Frances said. María leaned back on her chair and placed her hand on her heart. She could feel her heart beating wildly. She had not known she would care so much. She could do nothing. The children began to cry once more. María tried with all her heart to comfort them. She hugged them, kissed them, but still they cried.

"Then," she said, "we have nothing else to do but to go see Father Non. Let him console us."

"What can he do?" asked Cota. She was back to being angry again.

"Father Non will just say words," Matías said.

Frances said, "Why can't we have any luck?"

María looked sternly at her and said, "Don't say that, Frances. We have all the luck in the world."

"No, we don't," said Cota. "We don't have anything."

Father Non had more than mere words to say. He explained to them the wonders of life.

He said, "We all have a duty to fulfill. There is a time to be born, and that fulfills the factor of time in this world. The world moves according to time and time cannot be changed. It cannot be hurried or slowed. It presses on to the inevitable end. You children must realize that there is an end to everything. Nothing lasts forever. Argumedo came for a purpose. His purpose fulfilled, he is now gone."

"Will he ever return?" asked Cota.

"Only God knows that," said Father Non. "If his mission is not completed, he will return. When? Who is to say? Whenever he finds out if his work here was completed. There is no use in crying over something that one cannot control. Even death. Distance then is something else. His departure has increased the distance between you. You feel the agony of separation through distance. He felt that to increase the distance between you and him would solve his problem and yours. Now comes fate. How one is to die. In one way distance eases the pain of death. That is God's intentional way of alleviating pain. Some day, Argumedo will die and you will not know. That is the value of distance. If he ever returns, then your closeness will lead you to more pain. Which is it to be?"

Matías said, "I would rather be close and feel the pain."

When Father Non asked the rest, they all agreed.

"I'm glad," he said. "That shows maturity in all of you. Now you know that all relationships cause pain through distance."

The whole town knew of Argumedo's leaving by the time the noon church bell sounded. María was walking back home from the rectory, holding Cota's and Frances' hands. Up front, Matías and Juan had felt the urge to run ahead of them, and they could be seen several blocks ahead. María felt so sorry for the children and for herself. What could she have done? Had she not encouraged Argumedo to stay? Maybe if she had been of a different character she would have been more forward. As she thought of her predicament, Pedro came over and walked with them for a while. He had heard about Argumedo. He gave some hint that he might still be interested in María. Cota said, no, as did Frances, even before María could rebuff him herself. After waiting a reasonable time for María's answer, he tipped his hat, turned around and went toward the rectory.

"I hate him, Mamá," said Cota, watching the man fade away.

Frances said, "I hate him too, Mamá. We all hate him. He's so mean. The only one we love is Argumedo."

"Don't judge people," María said. "Remember Father Non and what he said. He spoke so well. I hope you children understood what he was trying to tell you."

Cota said, "I don't understand half of what he says when he gets serious."

"I don't understand too much," said Frances.

Up ahead they could see Matías and Juan running back screaming, waving their arms. They were shouting something, but the words were lost in the distance.

María said, "What are they shouting about?"

"Don't pay attention to them," said Cota. "They are always trying to fool us."

"They seem serious," María said.

The closer Matías and Juan got, the clearer their words became. They were shouting "Argumedo! Argumedo! Argumedo!"

María and the children began to hurry to meet them.

"It's Argumedo!" Matías and Juan yelled. They were breathless. "He is here!"

"You must have seen a ghost," said María.

"It's not a ghost!" Juan shouted.

"You better not be lying," María said. "If you are, I don't know what I'm going to do to you, but it's not going to be pleasant."

"No! No! No!" the two boys kept insisting. "It's true. Argumedo is home. He's waiting for us."

Cota and Frances began to run to the house. Juan and Matías did not wait for their mother. María hurried along, not wanting to seem too anxious. What would Argumedo think if he saw her running? She had to maintain her composure. Maybe he had returned for something else, for Juan Garibay to pay him. Up front she could see the children running and hopping along, shouting, singing. She had never seen them this happy.

Benjamín Argumedo was sitting on the porch steps surrounded by the children hugging him when María arrived. He appeared scraggly, as if he had fallen among the brush and had cut his hands and arms. He looked at María and smiled.

"María," he said, "I have a story to tell you. You will find it hard to believe, but I swear it is true."

"You'll tell it to me with a cup of coffee," she said.

"What a pleasure that would be," he said.

)(

To a Widow with Children

"I did a foolish thing," Argumedo informed them, crossing his legs. "I was so desperate when I saw Lupito and Herminia married. I felt that I would never find the happiness they found. I left the wedding early, and I went to my room and contemplated my life. What a waste I felt it had been. Many things tried and nothing achieved. The revolution went bad for us. All we fought for was gone. My country is the same as always. And then Father Non's words came to me. The wonders of life. I had met my time. I was in the distance, the far-off distance that I craved. The only thing left was fate, and I could not stand it. I decided to leave without any farewells. To leave the way I came. Mysterious and out of the sky. In the morning, I left Genoveva a note, and I walked to Juan Garibay's farm to tell him what I intended to do. He didn't want me to leave. But I was insistent, and he said that in the end I might be better off. He promised to sell me the shop back should I ever want to return. He paid me off what little money I had invested, and I was on my way. I spoke to Lupito and took the train. As I was leaving town, I looked back and saw the little houses. I saw Celestino on his horse, delivering milk. I saw Don Antonio and Nepomucena walking to God knows where. And then Don Chema, the tailor; Don Porfirio, the druggist; the widow Juana going to church so early to cleanse her little sins; Don Lupe, the mayor, was struggling to get past the old codgers who had already descended to the middle of town. Sheriff Manuel and Inez, eating outside on the porch. Filipita, the telephone operator, walking to work with the headset covering her ears. I saw Don Bruno walking with Herminia to the courthouse to scan the tax rolls for money that isn't there. I was getting carried farther and farther away. The figurines of people became smaller and smaller. The town became smaller and smaller. And then I saw you at a great distance, so small as to be disappearing, standing at the porch, covering your beautiful eyes to shield them from the morning sun, looking for Celestino to come with the milk for the children. I realized then that the greatest of wonders is distance and that I could not live far from you and the children."

"What did you do?" asked Cota, who along with the rest of the children were sitting at the table with Argumedo and María.

"Why, I did what any man in love would do," replied Argumedo. "I jumped off the train."

The children went wild with laughter. They had never heard of anything quite so funny. No one had ever jumped from the train. It moved so slow that all one had to do was to walk off.

"And that is how you got scratched all over?" María said.

"You are right, María," said Argumedo.

"You could have walked off the train," said Matías.

"Yes, I know," Argumedo agreed, "but I wanted to dramatize the thing."

This brought on more laughter from the children.

"Benjamin Argumedo," said María, "you are so funny."

"I walked all the way through the brush," Argumedo said, "and this is the condition I arrived in."

"How far did you walk?" asked Frances.

"Ten miles, at least," said Argumedo.

"And," said Cota, trying to get something going, "you say love made you do it."

"I have to confess that it did," Argumedo said.

"Who do you love?" Cota asked.

"I love your mother," Argumedo finally said after so much time.

María blushed, got up and went into her room, leaving Argumedo with the children.

"Don't worry, Argumedo," said Cota, "she will marry you."

"She will?" Argumedo asked. The thrill in his voice could not be denied.

"Oh, yes, she will," said Matías and then Juan and Frances and Cota. "We will make sure she does."

Argumedo, emboldened with the support he had from the children, went to María's door and said, "María. I know that I am not good with words, but you heard me tell you that when I saw you slowly disappearing before my eyes, I

knew I could not live without you and the children. I am
here to live close to you. If you love me, show me some sign.
If you don't, I will be content just to be near you and the
children. I know I am not rich nor have I the means to support you and the children like I would like for you to live,
but all I am, I offer it to you and the children. Will you
marry me?"

The children said, "Yes, she will."

"I suppose," María said inside her room, "that if the
children want you for their father, that I would do them
harm by not accepting."

Argumedo felt he would burst with joy. "Then," he managed to ask with a dry mouth, "it is to be?"

"Yes," came the reply from behind the door.

The reply sent the children wild. They were running
around the table and then, in an act of sheer joy, they
jumped on top of the table and began dancing. María, hearing the commotion, walked out and scolded them.

"What will Benjamín Argumedo think?" she asked them.

"Please, leave them alone," said Argumedo. "They are
happy. But not as happy as I am." And having said it, Benjamín Argumedo felt so much pleasure, felt the weight of all
the unhappy years lift off his shoulders, that he gave the
longest yell María and the children had ever heard. When
the children began to shout also, María covered her ears
and laughed. Argumedo, in capturing the moment of
requited love, felt so much like renewing his life that he
hugged each of the children and carried them down to the
floor where they held hands and began to dance.

Off in the distance, Father Non's roosters heard the
noise and began to crow at the unusual hour. Father Non,
in the rectory, overheard the roosters, walked to the back
door and wondered what all the crowing was about. At the
same time, Don Antonio awoke from his nap and, thinking
something might have happened, decided to alert the town
by cranking the siren. Father Non, hearing the siren and
thinking it was noon, felt his stomach, asked it what it felt
like eating, and went into the kitchen. He glanced up to the

wall and saw the clock. It was not time to eat.

"The town has gone completely crazy this morning," he said.

Chapter Twenty-Eight

When they had exhausted themselves dancing, the children begged to make plans for the wedding. Cota and Frances wanted to do something special. They agreed to choose what María was to wear, and when María gave a hint that she might object, the daughter's pleaded their case to Argumedo. María could not convince Argumedo to allow her to pick her own wedding dress.

"Let Cota and Frances choose," said Argumedo. "After all, it is their mother getting married."

And Matías and Juan, not to be outdone, volunteered to help Father Non with planning the ceremony. In this, neither Argumedo nor María had a say so.

Argumedo had to leave to go see Juan Garibay to tell him he had returned and needed the keys to the barn. As he was leaving, he tipped his hat and María said to him, "I'm really so glad you returned. You know you were breaking my heart."

Argumedo let out a yell and walked off. The children and María were left behind laughing. Never had they seen a man so full of joy. It did their heart good that they could cause such a reaction in a person they all loved.

But before Argumedo's yells could reach the center of town, the old codgers sniffed a sense of the commotion and, being so acutely attuned to the town's goings-on, they looked at one another and smiled. Those were the yells of a man who had found love. Gumercindo nodded all the way around, and they came simultaneously to the conclusion right away that Argumedo had returned, that he had not been able to withstand the expansion of distance over a small amount of time, that his love for María had caused him to abandon the train and run back to ask for her hand in marriage. From the nature of the yells, they surmised that Argumedo had been successful, for these were the primitive yells of requited love and not the yells of the pain of rejection.

"There's going to be another wedding," said Gumercindo and everyone agreed.

"Be careful with a man in love," said one of the other ones. "They have been known to jump off trains."

"Cliffs," said another one, and again they had to agree.

So by the time the girls arrived at Doña Juanita's and the boys had arrived with Father Non, the word had been spread. Argumedo had returned, and María had consented to marry him.

The smile on Doña Juanita's face betrayed what she knew.

"Our mother is getting married to Argumedo," said Cota to Doña Juanita.

Doña Juanita kept on smiling. She said, "Yes, I know. The whole town knows. The codgers have spread the word around."

A disappointed Frances said, "We had wanted to tell you."

"No one can spread the news like the codgers," Doña Juanita reminded them.

"Those horrible, stinky old men," said Cota.

Doña Juanita said, "If you are looking for Herminia, she doesn't live here anymore. She lives with Lupito. Which means that I live by myself now. What a lonely life without Herminia."

"But Herminia should come to see you every day," said Cota. "If she isn't, we can tell her that she has to come see you every day."

"Oh, she comes every day," said Doña Juanita. "She comes to eat at noon and we talk. I have never seen her so happy. Now I can die knowing that someone is taking care of her. How sad for a mother not to be able to marry her daughter off. I had lost all hope. If only Lupito were intact, it would seal my joy."

"But Herminia is so beautiful," said Frances.

"And such a nice lady," said Cota.

Doña Juanita smiled again, this time the smile of contentment, and said, "No wonder Herminia loves you so much. You flatter her so."

"And we love her," said Cota.

Doña Juanita took steps toward the door. Lately she had been busy with rearranging the house. She said, "Well, go on and look for Herminia. I'm sure you didn't come all the way over here to see an old lady like me."

"But we did," said Cota. "We have a favor to ask."

Doña Juanita stopped and wondered what she could possible do for María's two daughters. "And what would you ask of me?" she asked.

"Herminia's wedding dress," Cota said quickly. "If it's not too much to ask. Could we borrow it for our mother's wedding?"

Doña Juanita began to giggle at the innocence of the two children. "I can't let you have the dress," she said. "I have imbedded the dress in bee's wax to preserve it for eternity."

"In wax?" asked Cota.

"In wax," said Doña Juanita.

"Why would you do a thing like that?" Frances asked.

Doña Juanita began a discourse on the preservation of wedding dresses—the use of smoke from green mesquite, the use of borax water, vinegar and salt, but the most reliable way was to imbed the dress in melted bee's wax and then allow it to dry in the coolness of the back porch. It would keep forever and never fade. The only danger was the first few days when the angered swarm of bees would try to take the wax back to their hives.

253

"And then, what do you want a white dress for?" she asked the girls. "Your mother cannot be married in a white dress."

"Why not?" asked Cota.

"Because your mother is not a virgin," she replied.

"Like the Virgin Mary?" Frances asked.

"Yes," Doña Juanita responded, "like the Virgin Mary." María's daughters wanted Doña Juanita to explain why their mother could not be married in a white dress.

"Because," Doña Juanita said, speaking in euphemisms, "your mother has known a man."

Frances said, stomping her foot, "Well, I don't understand. Herminia has known a lot of men and she married in a white dress."

"I beg your pardon," said the hurt Doña Juanita. "Herminia never knew a man, and as far as I can tell, she doesn't even know Lupito right now."

"Herminia doesn't know Lupito?" Cota asked her. "She knows Lupito and Don Bruno and Don Napoleón and Celestino—all the men in town. Everyone knows Celestino. He delivers the milk. And anyway, how can Herminia be married to Lupito and not know him?"

"Your mother has had children," said Doña Juanita somberly. "That's what I mean. Can I put it more plainly?"

Cota and Frances were silent for a while. Doña Juanita could see their little minds working.

"Now I know," said Cota.

"Know what?" asked Frances. "Didn't the Virgin Mary have Jesus?"

Cota would tell her later.

"So, what do we do?" Cota asked Doña Juanita.

Doña Juanita said, "I'll help with the dress, but it must not be white. You girls chose any color but white."

"And the material?" asked Frances.

"I have the material," Doña Juanita said. "I have a lot left over from Herminia's dress."

"And we don't have money," said Cota.

"I knew that," said Doña Juanita. "And I insist that you

and your brothers do not engage in any shenanigans in order to get money. For the sake of the town, I will do it for free. The only payment I will insist on is that you love Herminia as you have always loved her. When I'm gone, I want you to see after her."

Cota asked, "Where are you going, Doña Juanita?"

Doña Juanita had to laugh again. "When I die," she explained. "Make sure my daughter finds happiness. I want you to love her always."

"Oh, that's easy," said Frances.

"And you're not going to die," said Cota. "We made our mother promise she would never die and she said she wouldn't."

"Well," said Doña Juanita, "if you insist. I will not die. But will you promise to love Herminia?"

"Yes," said Frances.

"And now, for the color of María's wedding dress?" asked Doña Juanita. "Remember, any color other than white."

"Red," Cota replied.

"Can she have a little white on the collar?" asked Frances.

Doña Juanita shook her head.

"Then trimmed in blue," said Frances.

María would have preferred a different color, but when Cota and Frances told her, and she saw them so excited, she did not have the heart to ask for a change. When Argumedo found out what the colors for the wedding dress would be, he was so emotional that he sat down and cried. Those had been his mother's favorite colors and the colors he had chosen for the regimental flag.

Juan and Matías found Father Non sitting outside on the back porch. He had just gotten the word from the codgers about Argumedo and María.

He said, "He knew Argumedo left. I predicted that he would return. No man, as in love as he is, can stand the turmoil caused by distance. The only man I know who could stay away and not be concerned would be the man who has found love and lost it, or who is into the sameness of married love, like the priest and his church."

"Why don't you get married?" Matías asked him.

"I can't," Father Non replied. "Don't you see, the church will not allow it? The bishop would throw me out of the church."

"And you can never get married?" asked Juan.

Father Non said, "That's the way it is."

Matías said, "The bishop never comes to see us, so how would he know? You could marry the widow Juana. She's in church all the time anyway. And the people say she cooks better than Inez."

"That would never do," said Father Non. "And now tell me why you two are here? To what do I owe the pleasure of this visit from two of the town's leading men?"

"We want to help you with the wedding," said Matías.

"Well," said Father Non, thinking, "the only way would be for you and Juan to be altar boys during the ceremony."

"We would like that," said Juan.

"To help marry off our mother," said Matías.

But they needed to do more. So they gathered the iron filings from the grounds around the depot and put them in tobacco sacks until they had what they thought were enough for Argumedo to make two rings at the foundry.

Argumedo was pleased to be able to make the rings, but only under Matías' supervision and expertise. And they melted the filings and poured the separate forms for two rings, one María's size and one to fit Argumedo. When the rings had cooled, Matías took them out of the wooden blocks in which the forms were carved and he said, "These rings should be kept separate until the wedding."

Argumedo replied, "As you say, Matías. Who am I to argue with an alchemist?"

So Matías and Juan took the rings for safe-keeping, Matías with Argumedo's ring and Juan with his mother's. Every night they would rub them with lambs wool as they sat on the railroad tracks.

"Why do we do this?" Juan asked Matías.

"Because," Matías answered, "we love our mother and Argumedo."

The lantern lights burned long into the night for Doña Juanita as she and Herminia prepared María's dress. At his farm, Juan Garibay was showing his wife, Carolina, which of the sheep were to be sacrificed for the wedding.

Carolina, who hated mutton, asked, "And there is not to be any turkey?"

Juan Garibay showed his perplexity by taking off his hat and scratching his head once more, saying, "We cannot. We seem to have someone's turkey. One more than we ought to. I would not kill anyone of them until I was sure it belonged to me."

"We're starting to overrun the farm with chicks," Carolina complained mildly.

"I know," said Juan Garibay, tenderly, taking her by the hand and leading her away from the pasture.

In the distance they could see the children playing. Anna, the oldest, was chasing Petra and Antonio and Gabriel with a stick.

"I'll eat mutton," said Carolina.

Juan Garibay looked at her and said, "In the end you always do."

Don Antonio sounded the siren for the noon hour, followed by Father Non and his bell.

Chapter Twenty-Nine

*T*he Sunday of the wedding came. The early morning found Celestino's milk bottles jiggling their way through the little town. Relincho was unusually spry this morning. Celestino would pass by the church during the wedding, and he had not wanted for his horse to look spavined and old. So earlier that morning he had fed it arsenic along with its feed. In half an hour, Relincho was a new horse, alert, prancing, jostling around when Celestino put his halter and rigging on.

Celestino said to him, "You know there's a wedding going on, don't you? You know you always get arsenic when we have a wedding. Does you good. But not too much, old man. We don't want to hurt you. I need for the both of us to die on the same day, and I'm not ready to go yet."

Rebecca had come out to see who he was talking to. Celestino and Relincho moved off. Rebecca was in the process of fixing herself up for the wedding.

Don Bruno came out into the yard and saw the town as the sun began to rise and could not see another single thing to tax. He went inside where Panfina was fixing his breakfast. Sheriff Manuel was enjoying his first heavy meal of the day. Inez, early riser that she was, had set the food on the table and left him to eat by himself as she fixed her hair. Mr. Rodríguez, the school principal, and his wife, had spent a restful night under the covers of María's quilt and were getting ready. Don Lupe, the mayor, always agreeing, had seen his wife, Celia, go by the hallway dressed in white. He could not remember seeing her so radiant, as if it were she who was to be married. He became disoriented for a moment, thinking perhaps he was young and getting married again. Lupito and Herminia and Mercedes ate quietly, Mercedes not quite knowing how to treat her new daughter-in-law. Mercedes reminded them again of the love her husband had had for her. "I could not even go to the bathroom without him going along with me to guard the door," she said.

Herminia found the conversation slightly disgusting for the breakfast table, and she quit eating. Lupito complained to his mother, but she insisted in bringing up other love-demonstrating occasions: the time he ate raw prickly pears, thorns and all, to prove his love for her was digestible, the times he covered her flapping underwear on the clothes line with his sheets.

The two widows named Juana were already on their way to the church and they met at the park and went inside to get the best seats possible. Father Non had not even finished his second dream. He was in the middle of the month of rain, and he had died, and the children had revived him with the contraption that Dr. Benigno had ordered. He had lost all his hair and had grown a beard. He had shed his skin like a lizard. Frogs, instead of epistles, were coming out of his mouth.

Martina, across the street from María, awakened Francisco, but he complained of the weather and said he would not go. He had already anointed himself with mentholatum for the year and could not be endured in public. Martina took one smell of him and agreed. She said, "You stay here. I'll bring you a plate of food."

Don Porfirio, the druggist, had awakened to the taste of arsenic and he remembered he had taken some out of his large bottle and given it to Celestino. Somehow, handling the arsenic, he had absorbed it through his skin and he felt as good as Relincho. Diana, his wife, was up and dressing, and he surprised her by planting a big kiss on her cheek.

At seven, Father Non had arisen and gone in his night shirt to ring the first bell. Don Antonio, at the fire station, echoed the call by turning on the siren. Don Pedrito's dog, who had taken to sleeping with Argumedo, awoke and licked Argumedo's face. Argumedo had been dreaming of kissing María, but got this instead.

Don Napoleón, the postmaster, went by the depot and Lupito gave him the mail for the day. He walked to the post office, dropped his meager sack and went on home to pick up his wife. Juan Garibay had made arrangements for the slaughter of five sheep and one hog. Carolina had the children ready by the time Juan Garibay returned from the barn.

Genoveva Marín went to the back of the house to wake Argumedo and found him in an embrace with Don Pedrito's dog.

Don Chema, the tailor, made a gesture to his wife, Marilisa, and she took the iron off the stove and began to press his suit.

Everywhere in town all the activity centered on the wedding. Even the old codgers had begun to meet at the front of the drug store. Gumercindo was wearing his suit.

Cota and Frances had been ready since six o'clock. Now they sat quietly at the table, not moving for fear of wrinkling their clothes. Matías and Juan were in their room, dressed neatly, their hair plastered down and glistening with brilliantine. Matías made sure Juan had his mother's ring in his pocket. He felt for Argumedo's ring in his. They were ready. At seven, when they heard Father Non's first bell, Juan and Matías started for the church. At the second bell thirty minutes later, María and Cota and Frances stepped out onto the porch and saw the beauty of the morning sky, the bright orange sun not yet visible over Martina's house. María closed the door, and the three were on their way.

Juan and Matías found Argumedo and Juan Garibay, the best man, in the sacristy. They noticed Argumedo unusually pale and slightly incoherent. When they went to the front of the church, Juan and Matías saw the two widows Juana, sitting up front in the middle pew, each one trying to out-shout the other saying the Rosary.

At the sound of the third and last bell, the church was full. María and Cota and Frances arrived at the church. Matías and Juan emerged from the sacristy, followed by Father Non. Behind them came Argumedo and Juan Garibay. Father Non stood at the altar rail with Juan and Matías at his side. Argumedo and Juan Garibay stood at his left. The church became quiet as Father Non raised his hand and beckoned for María to come. From the rear of the church María began her slow walk toward the altar, with Cota and Frances leading her. Each carried a bouquet of wild flowers which they had picked on the way. On her neck María wore a necklace of corn which Matías and Juan had woven for her. No one could deny how beautiful María looked that morning. Argumedo, when he first saw her step into the church door, bathed in the orange sunlight, almost fainted at the sight of her beauty. He had to hold on to Juan Garibay. Slowly María made her way to the altar as the people nodded and smiled. Celestino and Relincho passed by and the crowd heard the buggy stop. Celestino had seen María through the door and had to come in to see her. He spotted Rebecca and went to stand by her.

Father Non began the ceremony. This time he spoke not only of the wonders of life but of its beauty. "And why not," he explained. "The beauty of life has been fulfilled in the pairing of these two. And now," he continued, "there will never be any distance between them. As to their fate, God only knows and that is a blessing." And with that thought he asked for the rings. Matías gave his to Argumedo and Juan gave his to his mother. As they repeated the words which Father Non recited, each placed the ring on the other's finger, and when the two hands met to exchange their vows, the pull of the magnets which Matías had melted into the rings forced them together, and neither María nor Argumedo could separate their hands from each other.

There was a stir from the old codgers. The rest of the crowd picked up the dilemma soon after. Father Non tried to keep a straight face, but when he saw Argumedo not able to separate his hand, he said, "How lucky you are, Benjamin. To be attached to such a beautiful woman."

)(

After the wedding, when Father Non went to his office, he opened the desk drawer to place his collar inside, and he noticed for the first time since the raffle that the box in which he kept his magnetic ring did not have the iron filings covering it. He opened the box and the ring was there, in perfect condition, except that now, when he put it on his finger, he was able to walk across the hall without his hand becoming attached to the metal umbrella stand.

The reception followed at Juan Garibay's farm. The crowd overflowed the barn into the pasture. Inside the barn, Inez had set up her stoves and ovens. While the crowd danced, she cooked the biggest meal anyone had ever seen. Even the mutton tasted fine to Carolina. Inez baked a panocha that measured twenty by thirty feet, baking sections of two by three feet at a time. Her specialty, fried jack rabbit ears, were devoured in no time. The dessert was her prickly pear pie. There was enough belching that the crowd created a cloud of gas which, with the help of the moonlight, helped illuminate the dance. Afterwards, the town knew just what Sheriff Manuel had endured and how tough his intestines were. The people concurred that someone of that constitution should be allowed to be the sheriff for life. María and Argumedo, their hands together, danced all night long. The children fell asleep early. They had had a long, exciting day. Tomorrow would be another day.

)(

In the morning, Father Non was awakened by the fighting going on between the old and the new rooster at the top of the hen house. Then, when the two had settled their territo-rial dispute, came the crow of the old, followed by that of the new rooster, a competing mixture of the harsh and the melodic that Father Non was having a hard time getting used to, the sounds reverberating through the town, waking up everyone.

Father Non got up, walked to the window and looked outside. He saw the two roosters butting heads, a small stack of feathers scattered around the feet of the two warriors. He picked up one of his shoes and threw it at them. "If only María's children would allow me to raffle those two as a pair," he lamented. But he knew that to start the raffles would bring renewed repercussions beyond his control. He found solace in the thought that someday the children would leave and he would be able to start the cycle once more. Father Jaillet and Father Pedro would be proud.